W9-CBY-845

STAR TREK
THE NEXT GENERATION®

BOOK TWO

THE NEXT GENERATION®

BOOK TWO

John Vornholt

POCKET BOOKS

New York   London   Toronto   Sydney   Singapore

POCKET BOOKS, a division of Simon & Schuster, Inc.
1230 Avenue of the Americas, New York, NY 10020

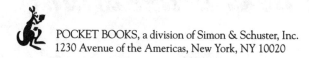

This book is published by Pocket Books, a division of Simon & Schuster, Inc., under exclusive license from Paramount Pictures.

ISBN: 0-7434-1181-1

First Pocket Books hardcover printing April 2001

10 9 8 7 6 5 4 3 2 1

POCKET and colophon are registered trademarks of Simon & Schuster, Inc.

Printed in the U.S.A.

For Erin, who has come to our rescue many times

one

Geordi La Forge had never before doubted the information his ocular implants imparted to his mind, but he could barely grasp the vivid spectrums and soaring electromagnetic pulses surging across the plains of Myrmidon. He staggered to remain on his feet in the fierce wind, which the phase-shifting did nothing to stop. The air smelled like tar, and his thumping heart told him this was not a sight that anyone should expect to see . . . and live.

Worriedly, Geordi laid hands upon the two interphase generators, each standing about two meters high, buttressed by struts and platforms. Only their phase-shifted field prevented the fifty thousand souls in the dry river bed from perishing in the holocaust.

Experienced at close range, the Genesis Wave was even more spectacular than he had been led to believe. Like a wildfire set loose in a parched forest, it ripped apart all molecules in its path and recombined them on the fly—only it moved with incredible speed. Instead of leaving spent ashes, the wave left a throbbing quagmire of new life, exploding into existence with barbarous fury. Just outside their field of protection, geysers spewed and mountains dissolved in the bubbling, churning morass. The horizon was undulating like a sine wave, and people and animals were mewling with fear all around him.

Without warning, the earth heaved under Geordi's feet, and the sand swiftly dissolved into a thick liquid. His first terrified reaction was that the Genesis Effect had reached them through the ground. But when the human didn't melt into a puddle, he figured it was liquefaction of the soil. Knowing the dissolving sand was a side effect didn't make it any less horrifying. Geordi felt as if he were slogging through molasses. He lunged for the generators and the gel packs, but the heavy equipment was also shifting and sinking into the muck. La Forge squirmed to his knees and dug a shoulder into a tilting strut to keep it level.

Now panic gripped scores of frightened Bolians in the riverbed, and many of their animals bolted into oblivion. Shrieking and wailing, the inhabitants lurched past him, hardly caring that they were all going to die if sand clogged the generators. La Forge grabbed an armful of gel packs and tried to keep them from sinking out of sight while he strained to hold the rack upright. When a distraught Bolian collided with him, knocking him into the sand, Geordi felt himself slipping downward. He rolled onto his stomach and swam over the moist sand to the generators, which he grabbed like a drowning man.

La Forge lifted his head and looked for his fallen comrades—Admiral Nechayev and Dolores Linton—but he could barely trust his vision. In every direction, there was nothing but turmoil. Despite the sensory overload, he tried to tell himself that only a few seconds had passed, and the worst of it would only last a few minutes. He would have to be patient and stay at his post with the generators, now half sunken into the sand. If the phase-shifting failed, nothing could keep them safe from the staggering forces reworking the planet.

As he hunkered down, Geordi tried to remember the strange events that had occurred just before the wave hit. Explosions had ripped through the riverbed, and they hadn't seemed accidental or part of the Genesis Effect. Geordi had seen concentrated flashes that had looked like beamed weapons to him. In the melee, Admiral Nechayev and Dolores Linton had both fallen. He had seen them on the ground, but he had stayed at his post, ignoring their plight.

Was it self-preservation, a sense of duty, or fear that kept me from helping them? he wondered. A howling gust of foul-smelling wind forced him to hunker down, and he tried not to be too hard on himself. He was in the middle of a world that was hemorrhaging and birthing at the same time, and the lives of a few carbon-based animals seemed to pale beside these momentous changes.

With a groan, the ground shuddered and then seemed to solidify—either that, or he and the equipment had sunk down to more solid rock. Maybe the effect was beginning to lessen, he thought with hope. Geordi looked up to see that some of the panicked inhabitants had stopped their mad flight, but many others had lost their minds entirely. In the distance, one Bolian dashed outside the protective field and dissolved like a swarm of bees breaking apart.

But most of the survivors realized that there was nowhere to run. They huddled in small groups, curled protectively over the wounded. He still couldn't see either Nechayev or Linton, but he mustered some hope that they would live long enough for him to get help.

Help? he thought derisively. *Where? How?* Even if they lived through this initial phase, Myrmidon's civilization had been reduced beyond rubble to nonexistence. The churning sludge bore new life writhing in its depths, but it bore no resemblance to the sacred planet which had existed here before. All of its people's efforts paled in comparison with the throes of Myrmidon in its destruction and rebirth. He didn't want to watch the carnage, feeling shame and helplessness, but he couldn't tear his gaze away.

We should have done better for these people than this! he thought miserably. *This isn't survival—it's insanity.*

After a few moments, he found himself appreciating the fractured kaleidoscope in the sky, but the more he saw, the sadder he
became. Although it looked as if much of the populace would survive, how could they live in this hellish place? It didn't seem possible that Myrmidon would ever revert to normal, although the spirit
of a proud people like the Bolians would account for a lot. They had
lived, but for what purpose?

La Forge fumbled in his belt for his tricorder, thinking that it
should be safe to move around soon. If the effect was beginning to
ebb, or at least enter its sustainable mode, he wanted to be ready.
With reluctance, he tore his attention away from the swirling sky
and writhing landscape to concentrate on his readings. The effect
was lessening, but it was still too complex for the tricorder to regis-
ter at all levels.

Although Project Genesis had been named for the first chapter
of the Bible, this version reminded him more of the last chapter,
Revelations—when the world was torn asunder in a great cata-
clysm . . . and the dead rose from their graves.

Captain Jean-Luc Picard rushed down the corridor leading to
Transporter Room One, where Beverly Crusher and the crew of the
Neptune were under arrest. At least he hoped they were under
arrest, because their actions and treachery had endangered the
entire operation on Myrmidon. The *Enterprise* had barely escaped
from the Genesis Wave, because they'd been forced to disable the
rogue ship. Even so, several installations on the ground had been
severely damaged, and there was no telling how many lives had
been lost because of the unexpected friendly fire.

The captain was hoping there would be a logical explanation,
but he couldn't imagine what that could possibly be. At first, he
feared the attack might have something to do with the Bolians'
predilection for suicide, but there were no Bolians among the skele-

ton crew on the *Neptune*. No matter how he looked at it, the *Neptune*'s actions made absolutely no sense, especially coming from the one person he trusted most—Beverly Crusher.

Taking a deep breath, Captain Picard charged into the transporter room, ready to confront just about anything. The first thing he saw was a phalanx of Starfleet security officers; their broad backs were toward him as they faced the transporter platform. Their weapons were lowered, and they didn't seem unduly concerned.

Upon seeing the captain, the security detail opened a path for him, and he caught a glimpse of a shimmering force field stretched across the transporter platform. Stepping closer, Picard saw Nurse Ogawa and a medical team poised for action just outside the force field. He still hadn't seen anyone from the *Neptune*, but Ogawa's worried eyes told him where they were. Piled haphazardly like a collection of discarded dolls, Crusher and seven others lay sprawled across the transporter platform.

"Are they dead?" he asked, trying to mask his alarm with a calm tone of voice.

"No, it's like they're in a coma . . . and not breathing well." Ogawa consulted her tricorder, and Picard took a closer look at the distressed crew members. Now he could see them squirming weakly, gasping for breath even as they remained in a deathlike trance.

He looked at Ogawa, who shook her head worriedly. "They're alive, but they're dying of asphyxiation. Their lungs seem to be paralyzed. Please, Captain, won't you allow us to help them?"

Worf wasn't aboard the *Enterprise* anymore, but Picard could hear the Klingon warning him about quarantine procedures. He also knew that Beverly Crusher—the woman who meant more to him than any other—was curled in a fetal position, looking like she was on the brink of death. He would just have to count on the biofilters in the transporters to do their job.

"Lower the force field," ordered the captain, "and get them to sickbay. Let's station security in sickbay until we get an explanation."

"I don't think they'll be any threat," replied Ogawa dryly. She rushed forward with the rest of the medteam, and they quickly applied oxygen and hypos to the sick prisoners. Within a few seconds, all of them were on portable ventilators.

The captain tapped his combadge. "Picard to Riker."

"Riker here," came the response.

"I need you on the bridge," said Picard, "while I monitor the situation in Transporter Room One. How are Counselor Troi and the Bolian girl?"

"Fine. I just dropped them off at sickbay. Deanna has a concussion, but she'll be okay. I'm on my way to the bridge."

"Thank you, Number One. Picard out."

When the antigrav gurneys and more medical personnel arrived, the captain just stood out of the way with the security officers until the patients were ready to be moved. As Ogawa guided Crusher's floating gurney toward the door, the captain caught up with her.

"How does it look?" he asked hoarsely, gazing at Beverly's face, which was obscured by a respirator.

"We've stabilized them," said Ogawa, "but she's barely able to breathe on her own. Until we do complete scans, we can't say what's wrong with them. The catatonic state looks bad, but we can deal with that. I don't like their labored breathing."

The nurse brushed past him and out the door, leaving Picard in her wake, helpless to do anything more for Beverly. The condition of the skeleton crew was frightening enough, but it raised a disturbing question: How could they have flown the ship and fired weapons in that physical condition? The *Neptune* had been a ghost ship when it arrived, and it had gone down in flames, still a ghost ship.

He tapped his combadge. "Picard to bridge."

"Yes, Captain," answered Commander Riker.

"What's our status?"

"We're on course to the rendezvous," answered the first officer, "and our ETA is in four hours. Starfleet is calling the Myrmidon operation a qualified success, although there's been no word from anyone on the planet. That won't be possible for at least half an hour."

"I'll be in sickbay," said Picard. "The *Neptune* crew came aboard in poor health—comatose, having trouble breathing."

"How's that possible?" asked Riker.

"I don't know, but I intend to find out. In fact, have Data review the logs of our final encounter with the *Neptune*. Tell him to look at everything—we might have missed something while it was happening."

"We'll get right on it," promised Riker. "Will they . . . recover?"

"We don't know enough about their condition." The captain watched glumly as the stricken officers were pushed out on gurneys. Since the Genesis Wave appeared, there were always new questions, but never any answers.

His legs churning through the gritty mire, Geordi La Forge threw himself onto the rack of equipment and pushed for all he was worth. Although the dry riverbed had stopped liquefying, it was still treacherous. The interphase generators lay half-buried in the grime at a dangerously tilted angle, and some of the gel packs were covered. He was afraid the delicate machines would give out at any moment.

With a glance at the horizon, La Forge could see that the Genesis Effect was lessening, or moving into another phase. Instead of undulating and mutating, the landscape was now blossoming with misshapen trees, thick hedges, and ruby-red flowers. Overgrown stands of gnarled trees sprouted like weeds across the horizon, probably fed by water in the liquefied soil.

The winds remained ferocious, whipping at the new flora like a hurricane, and the skies continued to ripple with unbridled power.

Geordi began to shiver as he glimpsed snow flurries at the edge of their protective field. The survivors were relatively calm now, huddling together, shivering and staring in amazement at the evolving landscape.

With a grunt, La Forge returned to the task of pushing the main generator into a more upright position. But now the sand had coagulated around the buried struts, and the going was tougher than ever. Geordi was weakened already from his efforts, and all he got for his strained muscles was more futility.

A figure suddenly fell in beside him, also pushing and grunting against the tilted generator. With a grinding noise, the platform actually moved, and Geordi peered at his mysterious helper, who was covered with grime.

"Dolores!" he shouted with relief.

"Don't look at me," she said jokingly. "I'm a sight."

With a dumb smile, he gazed at the muscular young geologist, thinking she looked great, even though there was blood on her forehead and scratches all over one side of her body.

"I have a mild concussion, which I deserve," she grumbled. "I figured there would be a little liquefaction in the riverbed, but this whole thing is . . . beyond what I envisioned."

"It sure is!" agreed Geordi, shouting into a gust of wind. "Where's Admiral Nechayev?"

Dolores gulped and glanced over her shoulder at the huddled masses. "She's out there somewhere, but she's hurt badly. They found her a Bolian doctor. I couldn't help her. What was the deal with all those explosions?"

La Forge squinted at the swirling khaki sky. "From where I stood, it looked like an attack—a strafing run with phasers. But I can't say for sure. I'm glad you're here, so you can watch the generators while I take some readings."

"How much time is left?" she asked worriedly. "I mean, before the worst of it is over?"

"I'll try to find out." La Forge opened his tricorder, thinking that it was impossible to guess how much time had passed. With a whole world evolving from primordial ooze right before their eyes, it seemed like eons. But it had probably been only a few minutes.

He checked his tricorder and saw that almost six minutes had passed, which was something of a relief. "We're well past the halfway point."

The engineer turned and surveyed the blooming forest, then he looked helplessly at his tricorder. "These readings don't tell me much—just a lot of numbers that don't make sense. If I didn't have to stay with the generators, I'd like to chuck a rock outside the phase-shifting field to see what happens to it."

"I can do that," replied the geologist with a smile. "You stay here and watch your boxes, and I'll go to the edge."

"Not too close," warned Geordi. "Take a tricorder and don't get any closer to the edge than ten meters. Will that get you close enough?"

Dolores sniffed with pride. "I'll have you know I was regional shot-put champion in college, and I competed in the Martian Olympics, where I finished second."

"It's still dangerous," said Geordi fretfully.

"It's only a rock," said the geologist. "That's funny for a rock hound like me. After the Great Flood, Noah sent a dove to see if it was safe. But we'll have to send a rock."

She stretched her grimy legs and surveyed the sticky riverbed. It was populated by frightened, dirty clumps of Bolians, who were as much in shock as any group of survivors could possibly be. With their vacant, hopeless expressions, they looked like the homeless refugees they were.

"It will probably take me a minute to get there," added Linton, scraping the mud from the sole of a boot. "We'll try combadges, but I don't think they'll work. Just keep me in sight, and I'll wave to you if it's safe." At his worried look, she smiled and tapped the pouch on her belt. "Don't worry, Geordi, I've got my tricorder."

Unexpectedly she kissed him full on the mouth—a kiss that was warm, urgent, and gritty from sand and sweat. Dolores pulled away, grinning, and she was one of the most dashing figures he had ever seen. "Keep dinner warm." she said playfully, "I'll be back."

Geordi nodded forcefully, unable to think of anything else to say. A moment later, Dolores dashed off, her strong legs churning through the mud, and he hurriedly pulled some field glasses from his toolbox. Placing the lenses to his implants, Geordi watched the strong hiker as she wound her way between the masses of people. Here and there, she offered words of encouragement to the survivors, and she also stopped to pick up and inspect several fist-sized rocks.

All too soon, Dolores's distinctive infrared image got muddled with the others, and he lost sight of her. After making a quick inspection of the generators, La Forge went back to watching the riverbed. Although all the land looked wet and new, it was easy to see where the safety net ended and chaos took over. Their circular field was the only land in view that wasn't erupting with freakish new life. In this muddy riverbed, the old life hung on with dogged tenacity.

Another check of the equipment showed a twenty percent drop in power since the last check, and La Forge surveyed the perimeter with added urgency. He finally spotted Linton, crouched at the edge of the sand, facing a huge geyser that spewed brackish water eighty meters into the air. He assumed she had to be getting wet from the spray and wind, but she stayed in place, braving the ungodly elements.

Through his field glasses, La Forge studied the crouched figure as intently as she studied her tricorder. Finally Dolores took a deep breath and squirmed forward on her knees. With a lunge, she hurled the rock straight toward the geyser, and he could finally comprehend her logic. Because the glistening soil around the geyser was the only smooth terrain in sight, except for the riverbed, the rock was still visible. If she had tossed it anywhere else, it would have vanished in the teeming underbrush.

Although he couldn't see the rock any longer, he was certain Dolores could. Several tense seconds passed, and Geordi forced his eyes away from the figure on the periphery to check the generators. The primary generator was now down thirty-seven percent, probably because of the damaged gel packs. It they were going to get a reprieve from this calamity, now would be a good time, Geordi thought.

He heard a cry of joy that pierced through the wind, and he looked up to see Dolores running toward him, waving her hands. "It worked!" she cried. "The rock didn't change! It's all over but the shouting."

"All over?" mumbled survivors doubtfully. It was clear that misshapen plants and squirming animal life were still growing at an accelerated pace, even if the crust of the planet had stopped its upheaval. It didn't look as if anything had changed, and La Forge was hesitant to turn off the generators.

A loud clicking noise sounded, and a humming noise faded out. Geordi hadn't even noticed the hum until it stopped, and he saw immediately that the primary interphase generator had died. Seconds later, the other generator stopped too, making his decision moot. Geordi tensed, waiting for the Genesis Effect to rip through him, turning his body to sludge. But nothing happened. They had won the battle, and their prize was a chaotic, primitive planet that bore no resemblance to the sophisticated, peaceful world they had known.

Overcoming his gloom, he ran toward Dolores, and they hugged each other with tearful relief. The moment of joy ended quickly, when he had to ask, "Where's Admiral Nechayev? Can you take me to her?"

Dolores nodded her head and grabbed his hand, leading the way. They wandered among the Bolians, who peppered them with questions. Geordi found himself repeating over and over, "It's safe to leave the riverbed, but be careful out there. Stay in a group."

"Is it always going to be this chilly and damp?" asked an elderly Bolian.

La Forge shrugged. "I don't know. We'll have to learn about Myrmidon all over again."

A few moments later, they reached a clutch of Bolians and Starfleet officers gathered around a prone figure. The smile erased itself from Geordi's face when he stepped close enough to get a look at the wounded admiral. Much of Nechayev's face and left side were badly burned, and she was unconscious, breathing with a labored rasping sound. Only a few tufts of her reddish gray hair were left on her charred skull.

A Bolian doctor worked steadily on the admiral, but all he had was a first-aid kit. It was clear from the frustrated expression on his face that he wasn't happy with her progress.

"How is she?" demanded La Forge.

The doctor frowned, producing a ripple of double chins under his dour blue face. "If I had a proper medical facility, maybe I could help her. But out here . . . I'm afraid she's dying."

"Doctor!" someone else called, yanking on his shoulder. "You've got to look at my wife! Please!"

The doctor shrugged and rose to his feet. "I'm sorry, but I've done all I can for the admiral. Now I've got to look at the others—"

"Go ahead," Dolores answered with sympathy. She knelt beside the fallen officer and picked up a bloody gauze from the sand.

"All I could do was give her something for the pain," the doctor added apologetically before he was dragged off.

With moist eyes, Dolores looked up at Geordi. "If she dies, you're pretty much in charge of this entire operation."

La Forge wanted to say reassuringly that Alynna Nechayev wasn't going to die, but her gaunt visage gazed up at him, belying those words. He watched helplessly as a light snow fell on the admiral's charred face and cranberry-hued uniform.

two

La Forge stared helplessly at the injured Admiral Nechayev, wanting to protect her from the downy snowfall. All around him in the dry riverbed on Myrmidon, survivors stirred from their traumas and tried to nurse the wounded and frightened. Geordi continued to stare at the admiral, wanting to dab at her burnt and scarred flesh, when he noticed something remarkable. Where the snow flakes fell on burnt skin, there was a foaming reaction. Nechayev was so deeply drugged that she didn't react, except to breathe a little more deeply.

"Wait here!" Geordi ordered, jumping to his feet. He dashed through the wet sand to the periphery of their protective field, about a hundred meters from the interphase generators. He could tell they had ceased operating, because the jungle of new growth was starting to encroach . . . rapidly. He skirted alongside the vines and bristling greenery, looking for a damp section where the soil was still evolving. Time was running out, because the flora, as bizarre as it was, had already started to stabilize in its new matrix.

He saw a seething hollow where it was still like a swamp, with fist-sized slugs writhing in the ooze. With a grimace, La Forge dug his hands into the primordial soup and came up with two teeming gobs of it, which he swiftly carried back through the crowds.

The refugees stumbled away from him, muttering and gasping, but Geordi delivered his precious cargo to the admiral's side and began smearing it over her burns like a medieval salve. Several Bolians fell back with cries of disgust, but Dolores leaned forward with curiosity.

"It's a good thing the doctor left before he saw this," she remarked. "I'm not sure he'd approve of whatever it is you're doing."

"It's a last resort," answered Geordi, "but still worth a try. This material is still mutagenically active at the moment. It's incredibly fertile, and it promotes new growth. So it ought to promote healing as well."

"Can we do without the leeches?" asked Dolores, wrinkling her pert nose. "Or whatever they are."

Geordi nodded and brushed off all of the squirming slugs, three of them. They should be worried about what these repulsive creatures were going to grow into, but one step at a time. Right now, he needed to save Admiral Nechayev any way he could.

"Geordi!" exclaimed Dolores. "Look!" She pointed down at the admiral's face, where the mutagenic salve was having a dramatic healing effect. Her burnt skin was regenerating with rapid cell growth, no doubt aided by the protomatter in the matrix. Whether there would be disastrous long-term side effects, Geordi didn't know, but the admiral took an untroubled breath and seemed to fall into a deep sleep.

"Now I think I'd better get the doctor," Dolores said, rising to her feet. "He might want to see this . . . for other patients."

"I'm afraid I got to the last genetically active soil," La Forge said sadly, glancing at his tricorder. "The mutagenic effects are wearing off. We got to her just in time."

"What else do we have to learn about this place?" asked Dolores

Linton, gazing at the overgrown jungle of snow flurries and mist which surrounded them. "This could be a whole career, just cataloguing what happened to this poor rock."

"You're not thinking about staying here?" asked Geordi in amazement.

She shrugged. "Sure, why not? It's got to be safe. Hasn't the worst already happened? Besides, aren't you curious about this planet? This is a whole new world, waiting to be explored."

The engineer shook his head wearily. "To tell you the truth, I would just like to get back to my ship. Preferably, in this lifetime."

Dolores gave him an impertinent smile. "You're only here because you were ticked off when Leah Brahms went looking for revenge."

La Forge scowled and turned away, unwilling to admit that she was right. "All right, so why are you here?" he demanded.

"Call me old-fashioned, but in an emergency, I would rather be on the ground than in a spaceship. Besides, you looked like you needed someone to look after you."

Geordi couldn't argue with that either, but they both might live to regret their rashness. He wondered whether Leah would regret her decision, too. It was hard to find much solace in revenge. He couldn't imagine how Leah and that crazy Klingon, Maltz, were going to track down and defeat the perpetrators of this war all by themselves. They were like Don Quixote and Sancho Panza, tilting at windmills.

He finally decided that each person had to face the end on his or her own terms. What exactly had he chosen to do by staying behind on Myrmidon? At the time, it had seemed like he was confronting the Genesis Wave head-on. Now it seemed like he was hiding from it.

"You know," Dolores said softly, "we're not leaving this planet unless someone figures out a way to come back and rescue us. It makes sense to plan what we're going to do, in case we stay. I know the Romulans said they would come back to get us, using cloaking devices, but will they? Everyone out there is going to be really busy with the Genesis Wave . . . maybe forever. But here it's come and gone."

"That's a very practical outlook," Geordi said, slumping wearily into the damp sand. "I guess I should stop worrying so much about myself. We're alive, and that's as much as we could expect."

"Besides," said Dolores, sweeping her hand toward the field of demoralized refugees, "we can't leave all of them."

"Did you ever think that it might not be over?" asked La Forge. "That this is only the beginning?"

"Of what?" she asked worriedly.

"Well, someone terraformed this planet for a reason. That means someone plans to come here and use it. Who? And when? Those are the next questions to ask."

Dolores nodded gravely and sat down in the sand beside him. She gripped his hand, and wordlessly their gazes drifted to Admiral Nechayev. The injured woman was sleeping peacefully, aided by the drugs of Starfleet and the massive forces that had ripped apart the planet, and were now healing it.

In the middle of an overgrown hollow that had once been a city, the blue-skinned barber gathered his courage and rose to his feet. Mot and his parents had been sitting near the door of the sanctuary when the conflagration struck, and he had seen most of it through the doorway. He still could not believe even half of what he had witnessed, but he had waited long enough inside this lone building, protected by the interphase generators.

None of the others would move, but they hadn't seen the ground stop quaking and the skies stop churning.

"Come," he told his aged mother and father, helping them to their feet. "It's time to go out and see our new world."

The jam-packed crowd of tens of thousands, plus children and animals, all hushed at once. Crouched in the darkness, they watched to see what this fool would accomplish when he stepped into the obscene terror outside the door.

Mot touched a door handle, and it disintegrated, leaving a fine silt on his fingertips. He pushed the creaking door open, and it fell off its hinges, landing in the thick underbrush with a muffled thud. Ferns and evergreenlike plants grew in abundance, unfurling long pistils and colorful red blooms. Misshapen, twisted trees towered above them, casting cold shadows, and the air reeked of ammonia.

The ground was crawling with wormy and fishy creatures, and Mot forced himself to walk forward. He held his parents tightly, one in each arm, but he had to stop when the brush got too thick and imposing. Mot sneezed as a gust of fog swept through the hollow, and he wished he had a crate of machetes.

"Is it . . . is it really safe?" asked his frightened mother.

Mot shrugged his beefy shoulders. "Safe or not, it's all we've got."

A few hearty survivors followed them out, but they recoiled from the foreboding plant life and squirming slugs. Mot turned and looked back at the golden dome of the sanctuary. It stood amid the chaotic jungle and wispy fog like an alien spaceship that had landed in the wilderness.

Commander Jagron lifted the fluted glass of Saurian brandy to his thin lips and took a sip. His patrician nose flared slightly as the smoky solvent cleansed his throat. The Romulan officer needed the drink after viewing the logs of the disaster at Myrmidon. Despite the happy face Starfleet wished to paint upon their haphazard operation, the planet had clearly been devastated by the force called Genesis.

This was supposed to be a victory celebration, hence the brandy. But no sane person could consider the debacle on Myrmidon to be a victory. Those inhabitants fortunate enough to survive were certainly not fortunate now. They had been reduced to pathetic, homeless refugees—a drain on the Federation.

None of the other commanders in the briefing room on the *Terix* offered an immediate comment either. They quietly sipped their drinks and considered the sobering facts. After it wiped out Earth and a large chunk of the Federation, the Genesis Wave was going to cut a swath through Romulan space. Many of their colonies would suffer the same fate as Myrmidon, Seran, Hakon, and the other planets that had already perished; and there was nothing that could be done to stop it.

"We are trying to save these fools, when we should wipe them out for their carelessness," muttered Commander Horek of the *Livex*. There were nods of agreement from the other three commanders of the task force.

Indignantly, Commander Damarkol added, "How do we tell our people about this? How do we prepare them for such a disaster?"

"Everyone at home must know by now," answered Tomalak grimly. It was upon his warbird they were conferring, and he was senior among them, thanks to his considerable experience with the Federation. "We're the only ones of our people who have seen it firsthand, but a hundred of our finest ships are on their way here."

"They come only to watch more worlds die," grumbled Damarkol, a frown on her leathery face. "Even so, Genesis is an impressive achievement . . . if they could only control it. Technology like that needs a firm hand and tighter security."

"There has been too much secrecy connected with Genesis already," declared Commander Jagron. "What we need is cooperation and more information about it."

Tomalak looked at his young colleague with a wry smile. "If you think you'll get the Genesis secret from the Federation, you're wrong. They lost that knowledge when they lost Dr. Carol Marcus. Even when they had it, they didn't know what they had."

"Are you still going back to Myrmidon to rescue Admiral Nechayev?" asked Jagron.

His host nodded. "Yes. Despite their bungling, the Federation are still the ones who are most likely to find a solution. The survivors on Myrmidon have really seen the wave firsthand, and may have learned something."

"May I offer the *D'Arvuk* to go in your place?" Commander Jagron suggested, taking a sip of his brandy.

The elder Romulan blinked with surprise. "Why, that is most kind of you, Commander, considering the risk. But it was my idea, and I feel indebted to carry it out. Sort of a favor for Captain Picard."

"Why do favors for humans?" asked Horek with a disdainful sniff. "They've been nothing but a curse to us, and this is just more of the same."

"Ah, but the galaxy would be a duller place without them," replied Tomalak. "To be truthful, I don't know if I'm going back to Myrmidon at all, because I haven't gotten an answer on my request. My science officers will have to be satisfied with the long-range scans before I endanger this ship."

"After that, will you rendezvous with the *Enterprise?*" asked Jagron.

"I suppose so. They'll be at the forefront of whatever action is next. I wonder why I haven't received an answer from High Command." Impatiently Commander Tomalak moved toward the burnished conference table and ran his hand over a companel. "Commander to bridge."

"Yes, my liege," a voice answered crisply. "Centurion Londerval at your command."

"Centurion, have we received any dispatches from High Command?"

"Yes, sir, a considerable number of them," came the answer. "Subspace traffic is very high, and the encryption we must use in Federation space is slowing down our processing time."

"I don't want excuses!" barked Tomalak. "Did we receive an answer about returning to Myrmidon?"

"Yes, Commander, but I didn't feel the orders were urgent, since they don't involve us."

Tomalak scowled. "What do you mean, the orders don't involve us?"

"High Command has ordered the *D'Arvuk* to Myrmidon to rescue Admiral Nechayev, and retrieve the interphase generators. We are to await orders."

The gray-haired commander gave a sidelong glance at his young peer, and Jagron shrugged his shoulders, feigning surprise. "They probably want to send the most expendable crew of the four of us."

"I'm sure it wasn't an accident," replied Tomalak pointedly. His dark eyes drilled into the eyes of the taller officer, who blithely looked away. Jagron knew this assignment was the doing of the Proconsul of the Senate, to give him a chance to steal the Genesis technology, if an opportunity presented itself.

"You'd better return to your ship and receive your orders," said Horak.

Jagron carefully set his fluted glass on the table and turned to his host. "May I ask for the criteria your science officers have been using? I'd like to know when it's safe to proceed."

"Of course," Tomalak answered cheerfully. "I'll forward all of our data to your ship. Give my regards to Captain Picard, will you? Tell him to watch his back."

"If he hasn't learned that already, he's not worthy of his reputation," Commander Jagron replied as he strode toward the door.

Feeling frustrated, Captain Picard stepped from the turbolift onto the bridge of the *Enterprise*. He had spent almost an hour in sickbay, where no one would tell him anything about Dr. Crusher and her ill-fated crew. Finally Dr. Haberlee, a resident on the ship for less than six months, had suggested that he leave, saying they would contact him when they had results from their tests. Beverly and the others were out of immediate danger, although their long-term prognosis was still in doubt.

Commander Riker rose from the captain's chair and bounded forward to meet him. "Captain, we looked at the logs of the Myrmidon operation, as you ordered, and we found something unusual."

The first officer led the way toward Data's station, where the android was hard at work, his fingers flying over the membrane keypads. "The *Neptune* didn't go down empty-handed," said Riker.

"What do you mean?" asked Picard.

Data looked up from his readouts. "I cannot account for how this happened, which is troubling. Although all eight members of the temporary crew are accounted for, the log clearly shows that *one* humanoid life-form perished with the ship when it struck the wave."

"Why didn't the transporter room locate this person?" Picard asked, frowning at the implications.

"He was shielded by the warp core containment field," answered Data. "The log only picked him up when the warp core failed."

"Hiding?" asked the captain. "Are we talking about a stowaway?"

"That would be the logical assumption," answered the android, "except that Commander Riker, Dr. Crusher, and I searched the *Neptune* and found no one on board."

"Could he have kept hidden from us?" asked Riker.

The android frowned slightly. "I personally searched the engine room, which is the only place on a ship of that size where he could have remained hidden. The facts would indicate that I was negligent in my duty."

"I doubt that," replied the captain. "Could somebody have beamed aboard the *Neptune* when the crew went over? Or even later?"

"That theory would also fit the facts, except there is no record of any other transporter activity during that time. And none of our crew members are missing." Data cocked his head thoughtfully. "We have had many passengers on board recently, and one of them could have stowed away on the *Enterprise*, waiting for this opportunity."

"That must be it," said Riker.

Data shook his head doubtfully. "To hide successfully on both ships and to conceal transporter use—that would require detailed knowledge of Starfleet procedures and spacecraft. We would be talking about a very sophisticated provocateur."

Captain Picard scowled, not liking any of these explanations, or the questions they raised. "Something happened over on that ship—in the space of a few hours—and we're going to find out what it is. We owe it to Dr. Crusher and the others. I put them into a dangerous situation, and I feel responsible."

Riker cleared his throat and said, "The admiral ordered you to staff that ship."

"Yes, but knowing its history, we should have been more careful."

"A lot was going on at the time—you can't blame yourself." The first officer's defensive posture softened to one of sympathy. "How are they doing?"

"They're comatose, breathing artificially, surrounded by an armed security detail. It seems absurd to keep them under guard, but we're sticking to procedures until I get an explanation." The captain paced toward the command chair and circled thoughtfully behind it.

"We haven't gotten any new orders," said Riker. "Do you want to maintain this position and keep waiting for the Romulans?"

"Yes, I want to assist them when they go to rescue Admiral Nechayev and Commander La Forge."

"If they are still alive," Data added bluntly.

"Yes," admitted Picard quietly. "At any rate, we need to have a firsthand report from Myrmidon."

His combadge beeped, and a deep voice said importantly, "Sick-bay to Captain Picard."

"Picard here."

"This is Dr. Haberlee. You'll be happy to know that we found the cause of the illness that's affecting Dr. Crusher and the others. It may explain their actions, too."

Picard glanced at Riker, who gave him a confident nod, as if to say that all would become clear in time. "I'm listening," said the captain.

The young doctor cleared his throat and went on, "We're almost certain that their illness is caused by some kind of fast-growing fungus that's infected their lungs and brains. We have similar fungi on Earth, like the aspergillus niger, which can live inside an old tomb or a cave for thousands of years. Histoplasmosis, valley fever—two more deadly diseases which come from fungi. This fungus is probably airborne, too, and it works fast once it hits the lungs."

Picard nodded thoughtfully. "I've read about aspergillus niger. It was thought to be the cause of King Tut's Curse, which claimed about twenty people when Tutankhamen's tomb was first opened."

"Exactly," Haberlee answered, sounding pleased that the captain understood. "It causes high fever and hallucinations. Maybe that's what killed the original crew of the *Neptune*."

"What happened to their bodies?" asked Riker.

"We're still looking into that, Commander," replied the doctor. "But now that we know what it is, we can proceed with treatment. I expect a full recovery."

"Thank you, Doctor, that's excellent news," said Picard. "I still want to talk to them as soon as possible. Now that you know what it is, maybe you can answer this question: Could those eight officers have been fit enough to fly that ship and mount an attack on the planet, just seconds before we beamed them aboard?"

After a long pause, Haberlee replied hesitantly, "I'm not sure. From what we saw, I'd have to say no, because they couldn't even stand up. But I believe they might have been weakened by the transporter beam, which threw their systems into shock. Mind you, they weren't doing well before, but they might have still been on their feet. A fungal infection can go very suddenly from the symptoms of a mild cold to a raging fever and hallucinations. It would have shut down their lungs, hearts, and brains if we hadn't caught it."

Picard nodded solemnly, trying to piece it all together. There were still gaps in their understanding, but at least two of the questions had been answered. "Are you sure that there's no danger to the crew?"

"Absolutely," answered Haberlee. "We've been keeping on alert both here and in the transporter room, scanning all the time. And we haven't found any airborne particles. The biofilter probably got any off their clothes and skin, but the fungus was too metastasized in their bodies."

Picard glanced at his strapping first officer, who looked as healthy as ever. "Commander Riker went over to that ship on the initial away team, and he didn't come down with this disease."

"There are reasons for that. Dr. Crusher and her crew got a much longer exposure than the first team, and they spent time in every part of the ship. Maybe Commander Riker didn't go where the fungus was active, or he was only there a few seconds. It's like all those people who died after entering King Tut's tomb—the first ones in got a stronger dose. Plus people's bodies react differently to a thing like this. It might lie dormant in one person for years, and another person could have immunity, thanks to their genetics. Just to be on the safe side, you should send the commander down here for a checkup."

At that, the smile faded from Will's clean-shaven face, and he frowned at the captain. "I'm on my way." Squaring his shoulders, the first officer marched toward the turbolift.

"Thank you, Dr. Haberlee," Picard said. "I appreciate your quick work on this."

"My pleasure, Captain. But I should ask—we aren't going to be getting a lot of injured refugees, are we? If sickbay gets flooded again, it will be difficult to give them the proper care."

"I think we can avoid that, but I can't promise anything. The fleet is falling back to the next inhabited planet in the path of the wave, but we're staying near Myrmidon. We might have to pick up casualties there."

"Commander Riker is here," the young doctor reported. "I'll keep you informed."

"Thank you. Picard out." The captain turned to Data on the ops console. "Have you had a chance to run long-range scans on Myrmidon?"

"I have, but I have not had time to analyze the data. The computer refused to identify Myrmidon as a recognized planet, so no comparisons were possible. It classified all plant and animal life as 'unknown,' and declared the atmosphere to be highly unstable. It is essentially a class-L planet with class-M characteristics along the equatorial belt. The computer predicted there would be a moderate likelihood of intelligent life on the planet."

"That's what it seems to me," muttered Picard grimly, "a *moderate* likelihood."

For several seconds, Captain Picard stood in the center of his bridge, gazing at the tranquil darkness of space on the main viewscreen. Only it wasn't tranquil at all. In that soothing darkness lurked a monster, devouring everything in its path and leaving behind strange hybrid planets. What was the method behind all of this madness? Despite those who had always wanted to turn it into a weapon, Genesis had never been about destruction. It was always about growth and regeneration.

Perhaps Carol Marcus and her team had been arrogant to think that their vision of a useful planet was the only vision. Even a lifeless rock or dust cloud deserved its unique existence without being destroyed in the name of progress. No matter how one looked at it, the Genesis Effect was about playing God, which was always a dangerous and selfish endeavor.

Who is playing God with us? he wondered.

When the comlink chimed, it stirred the captain from his reverie. "Riker to bridge," barked a voice, and Picard instantly recognized the urgency in Riker's tone.

"What is it, Number One?"

"One of Crusher's crew, Ensign Paruk'N, is missing."

"How is that possible?" asked the captain with concern.

"That's a good question, considering that the other seven are still unconscious. When I got here, Dr. Haberlee took me for a tour and showed me his patients. We got to the last bed, and it was empty, with blankets rolled up to look like a person."

"But the security detail—"

"Didn't see a thing. It is hectic down here, and we're hoping the video log will indicate something. Dr. Haberlee is mortified, but he needs to concentrate on his patients. I'll stay here awhile and try to sort it out."

"Good." The captain took a deep breath, fighting the temptation to rush to sickbay himself. What could he do that Riker, Haberlee, and half a dozen security officers couldn't? Faced with the Genesis Wave, they hardly needed this.

"Keep me informed," said the captain, although every time he learned something, he seemed to know less. "We'll try to find him from here. Picard out."

Studying his console, Data shook his head. "Ensign Paruk'N is not on board the *Enterprise*."

"Go to yellow alert," said the captain grimly.

three

Leah Brahms twisted and squirmed on the rock-hard slab upon which she was expected to sleep. The crew berths on the *HoS* were like big shelves carved into the bulkhead, and it was hard to believe that even Klingons could sleep on one. Nevertheless, three of her shipmates snored loudly in nearby berths.

As Brahms had learned, on a Klingon vessel the size of the *HoS*, even the captain didn't get a separate stateroom. She slept in the austere crew quarters along with the rest of them. This presented some privacy problems, as did the lack of other amenities on the *HoS*, but Leah was determined to fit in and earn her crew's respect. However, she had claimed an unused laboratory near the transporter room as her private lair; right now she was thinking about making a mattress from rags and hiding it down there.

As she lay on the hard berth, unable to sleep, Leah checked her chronometer. With a start, she realized that it was two hours past the time the Genesis Wave was due to hit Myrmidon. How had they fared? she wondered. Had the phase-shifting protected people on a large scale as effectively as it had protected her alone? If so, there were now millions of people who had the unique displeasure of having lived through the Genesis Wave. Leah took some grim satisfaction from knowing that she and Deanna Troi weren't the only ones anymore.

Will any of them be driven to revenge the way I am, she wondered? *Or am I the only one, besides Maltz, who wants an eye for an eye, a tooth for a tooth?*

There was no answer in the dreary bowels of the Klingon attack cruiser, only the chorus of snoring Klingons. Leah realized that she couldn't sleep, at least not here and not now. She rose to her feet and quickly pulled on her blue jumpsuit. She felt odd dressing differently from her crew, but she couldn't really see herself in all that stiff, garish body armor. She wasn't really a captain, except in Maltz's view, and it hardly felt as if they were part of any fleet at all. Leah felt as if she was a renegade, with allegiance to no one; her only possessions were her pain and anger.

Trying not to wake anyone, she stepped lightly from the sleeping quarters and found herself in the narrow corridor.

She chuckled at herself, her voice echoing gently in the corridor. To think that she could find and destroy the ones perpetrating the Genesis Wave, when a task force had failed, was ridiculous. But she shared a common belief with Maltz: This damnable evil had come straight after both of them, trying to crush them as it had crushed everything in their lives. But they had escaped. The enemy's plan was almost perfect, but not quite.

Nature hated perfection, so it had let them live to fight again, Leah decided. At the root, this was a battle between nature and a coldhearted, artificial substitute for nature. Where nature moved slowly to cut down on risks, Genesis rolled with abandon, destroying the good along with the bad. That the technology had originated with her species was mortifying, but also typical . . . of humans. But they would never have used Genesis in this fashion, even if they knew how. Who would?

As Brahms walked that lonely corridor, she decided that she had to make a profile of the kind of species who would have such desperate needs—and so little regard for life—that they would unleash the Genesis Wave.

Without really knowing where she was headed, Leah rounded a corner and plowed into a hulking Klingon coming from the other direction. She bounced off a barrel chest covered in thick sashes and chain mail, and he grabbed her arm brusquely to keep her on her feet.

"Captain," grumbled the Klingon, not hiding his mirth at her embarrassment. As he let go of her arm, Leah remembered that he was the weapons master, named Gradok. Judging by the number of scars on his rugged face and his noticeable limp, she wondered how good a weapons master he could be, but she didn't say that.

"Master Gradok," she replied, "just ending your shift?"

"No, I was checking the aft phaser arrays," he said, taking a step toward her. "And where might you be headed?"

"I'm familiarizing myself with the ship," answered Brahms, taking a step back. "I should be sleeping, but I . . . just wasn't tired."

The big Klingon smiled, showing gaps in his collection of teeth. "Our berths are not what you're used to in Starfleet, are they? You like a soft bed with a firm . . . mattress. But I could show you that a hard bunk is better. For many reasons."

When Gradok took another step toward her, Leah realized this could quickly get out of hand. She was alone with this muscular stranger in a deserted part of the ship, and *he* knew every access shaft and air lock. She could run from him, hit her combadge, and call Maltz for help; but that would make her a laughingstock. Once again, Brahms told herself to be as tough as Admiral Nechayev.

She punched him in the chest as hard as she could with the heel of her hand, knocking him back a step. "Keep your distance, Crewman! I'm not on the *HoS* for fun and games—I'm here to fulfill my Blood Oath."

Gradok blinked at her and nodded with surprise. Before he could get his momentum back, Leah spun on her heel and marched quickly toward the turbolift. This time, she was going straight to the bridge, and she wouldn't be taking any more long walks by herself in unfamiliar parts of the ship. She had always heard that being captain of a Klingon vessel was not for the fainthearted.

Brahms strode onto the bridge, where it was overly warm and smoky, but it was still beginning to feel like home. Maltz rose from the elevated command chair and motioned for her to take it, but she shook her head. Making a leisurely inspection of the manned stations—ops, tactical, and conn—Leah strolled to the most distant corner of the bridge. She motioned for the grizzled old Klingon to follow her.

When Maltz caught up with her, Leah was staring out a small triangular viewport, watching the stars streak past at warp speed. "What's the matter, Captain Brahms?" asked the lanky Klingon.

In a low voice, she answered, "Keep your voice down. One of the crew cornered me and tried to get romantic."

Maltz nearly thundered in disapproval, but with considerable effort, he controlled himself and whispered, "Who was it? I'll hang him by his heels over the warp core."

"That's why I'm not going to tell you," answered Leah. "I just wanted to know if I handled it correctly."

"What did you do?"

She told him more or less what she had done, and the old Klingon chuckled. "You handled it like a true daughter of Kahless, because you left him with his honor. And you put the emphasis on our Blood Oath and duty. That is where it should be."

"Then I won't have any more problems?" asked Leah.

Maltz scratched his white stubble and leaned against the bulkhead. "That's hard to say. Often a female captain on a Klingon vessel will choose a consort from among the crew. But no one would be so presumptuous as to volunteer. This crew member showed a lack of respect."

"Well, they're probably still trying to figure out *why* exactly I'm captain of this ship." Leah shrugged and gazed out the viewport. "I'm still trying to figure it out myself. But I know what we want to do—what we *have* to do."

"And that is why you are the captain," Maltz answered confidently. "I would not have volunteered to be your first officer if you hadn't shown that you could lead and act quickly in an emergency. That's all anyone expects from a captain."

"That's not all," answered Leah. "They expect a captain to act a certain way—especially a Klingon captain. I've been in charge of research stations with dozens of people under me, but that was different. This is life and death, and there can't be any hesitation when it comes to following my orders."

"I will enforce your will," declared the Klingon.

"But as we've seen, you aren't always there." Brahms paced for a moment, thinking that if she had learned anything in this prolonged nightmare, it was that she couldn't depend upon anyone but herself. "My husband, Mikel, was like my first officer, and he spent a lot of time shielding me from things. And now he's not around."

"Did he die bravely?" asked Maltz.

"He died with a look of terror and surprise, not knowing what hit him," answered the engineer. "I've never seen such stark terror."

"And that is why you are here," answered Maltz through clenched teeth. "Because a death like that *must* be avenged. Trust me, this is something our crew can understand. Maybe they're not the best or the brightest in the fleet, but they have seen enough of war to know when it's serious. I'll keep an eye on them, anyway."

She turned her pale-blue eyes on the old Klingon and smiled gratefully. "Thank you, Maltz."

His aged eyes twinkled for a second. "In the meantime, if you would like me to pose as your consort, that might work to keep them in line."

Leah smiled in spite of her dour mood, "Thanks for the offer, but I want to keep it strictly business with everybody. Why don't you let them know that my mate died only a few days ago . . . that I'm still in mourning."

"I will remind them." Maltz's eyes narrowed to bloodshot slits. "Take heart, Captain—there is no cure for grief like revenge. And we're going to get the ones responsible for this, starting with Carol Marcus."

Brahms nodded and turned back to the triangular port with its view of the blurred starscape beyond. She certainly hoped the old Klingon was right, because at the moment all she felt was rage and emptiness. Maltz had a focus for his anger—Marcus, the scientist who had invented Project Genesis, the one who had been kidnapped six months ago. But Leah wasn't sure who to be mad at. That's why she needed a profile of the intelligence behind this monstrous weapon.

She looked around and spotted an unused console, blinking in readiness. "I need to do some work. Can I use this terminal?"

"Use any terminal you like—you're the captain." Maltz snapped to attention. "Do you want to check the efficiency of engineering?"

"No," answered Leah, sitting down at the console. To her lack of surprise, the seat was very hard. "I want to get to know our enemy. What are they like?"

"Despicable! Cowardly! Murderous!" Maltz started to sputter and curse in Klingon, and Brahms cut him off with a wave.

"You're right, of course," she said. "But that's only *our* viewpoint. We hate them, but what do they think of *us?* Nothing. From their actions, they think we're like the worms you crush under your feet as you walk. They don't think we or any part of our planets are worth saving. The Dominion, the Borg, the Cardassians—they all wanted to plunder and steal what we've got. Not this enemy. They don't want a single thing that we have, not even a building to live in once they get here."

Maltz stroked his stubbled chin thoughtfully and said, "They're probably not humanoid."

"Yes," agreed Leah, entering a few shorthand notes on the membrane keypad. "What else do we know?"

"They couldn't do this thing by themselves," answered Maltz, pacing rapidly. "They had to kidnap Carol Marcus and obtain her cooperation."

"They could have been planning it for years. How do you think they found out about Project Genesis, when it was such a big secret?"

Maltz stopped pacing in order to scowl and shake his head. "That could be *my* fault. I can't remember how many strangers I have told about Genesis over a mug or two of ale. I'm a fool—and all of this could be *my* doing."

"It's too late now to blame yourself," said Brahms, working her console. "Although the details were a secret, other people knew about the Genesis Planet and what happened there. All of this tells us something about the enemy. They, or their agents, are able to move among us, collecting information. And they kidnapped Carol Marcus under heavy security."

"Who would cooperate with fiends like this?" growled Maltz.

"Maybe people like you, who didn't know they were cooperating," Leah answered. "You know how the changelings infiltrated the Klingon High Council and Starfleet just before the Dominion War."

"Yes!" said Maltz urgently. "Do you think the Dominion has returned?"

"No, they couldn't have mounted an operation like this so deep in Federation space, and I heard that a changeling from the Alpha Quadrant is running the Dominion now. But that brings up a good question: How did this enemy remain hidden in the middle of the Federation?"

Maltz frowned in thought, then grinned triumphantly. "They're not humanoid, and they don't live on a class-M planet."

"Bingo!" answered Leah, her fingers flying over the keypad. "So we look for a planet like the ones that are being created with the wave. Now we know what that is, class-L, bordering on M."

The Klingon leaned over her shoulder. "Your task force thought the wave originated near an asteroid field, called the Boneyard. That's where they disappeared."

"Okay, so let's avoid the Boneyard for now—we'll look for a planet near there that fits the bill. I know exactly where it is." Her fingers never stopped moving over her console, bringing up star charts. A few seconds later, she cried again, "Bingo!"

"What does this 'bingo' mean?" asked Maltz curiously.

"It means, 'victory.'" Leah looked happy for the first time in a week as she pointed at her screen. "It also means that we have a new destination—a planet called Lomar."

"Helm!" barked Maltz. "Prepare to change course!"

Carol Marcus awoke from her troubled dream and sat up in bed, sweating and feverish. Her white-blond hair was plastered to her square-jawed Nordic face, and her blue eyes stared straight ahead. The dream—about the death of David and the awful destruction of the Genesis Planet—was the first vivid dream she'd had in months. In fact, it had been years since she'd had such a memorable dream. What did that dream mean, after so many months of tranquil bliss? She loved her life—living here on her peaceful island, going to work in the lab with David and Jim. David wasn't really dead—she saw him every day.

Still, the old woman shivered, although it had never been cold in her bedroom before. The temperature had always been just right. Carol pulled her blankets around her slight frame and lay back on her bed, trying not to be troubled by the dream, which had dredged up repressed memories. Although frightening, the dream had also been exhilarating, like an unexpectedly scary adventure. It was the first memory she'd had since returning to her work . . . that Klingons had murdered David over ninety years ago.

This place and my new life shouldn't exist, she told herself with awestruck realization. The joy at being reunited with David and Jim Kirk had made her overlook two troubling facts: Both of them were dead.

Carol sneezed violently, and followed it with a ragged cough. It felt like she was coming down with a cold, which might explain her fuzzy brain and grim disposition. She looked around her bedroom, a faithful reproduction of the simple, sunny room she had on Pacifica. The breeze blew through an open window, rustling the white linen curtains. In the back of her mind, the scientist had always known she couldn't be near the planet Pacifica and her Regula I space station at the same time. They were light-years apart and in different time periods—two more facts she had conveniently overlooked.

Her body feeling achy and weak, the old woman forced herself out of bed and to her feet. After casting off her blankets, she shivered as she dressed herself in her usual white scrubs and lab coat. Then she crossed to the door and grabbed the door knob, giving it a turn. Only it wouldn't turn—it was locked.

"What the—!" the old woman exclaimed. She didn't even know this door could lock! And why would it lock from the outside, turning her bedroom into a cell? That made no sense at all!

She tapped the combadge pinned to her lab coat. "Marcus to Marcus. Come in, David."

When there was no reply, she tried, "Marcus to Kirk. Jim, are you there?"

"Yes, of course I'm here," came the familiar voice with its boyish enthusiasm. "What do you need, sweetheart?"

"I need to get out of my bedroom!" she snapped, her voice sounding hoarse and raw. "I'm locked in!"

"I know," answered Jim Kirk, sounding terribly upset and sympathetic. "You don't feel too well today, do you?"

"Well, no," she admitted. "But what's that got to do with me being locked in my bedroom?"

"You're sick. You have an infection, and you've been quarantined. None of us can come into contact with you. Doctor's orders."

"What doctor? I don't remember seeing any doctor." Carol began to pace the confines of her room, growing agitated. She made a dash toward her open window, only to be propelled backward onto her bed by a force field.

"Relax, Carol," Kirk said soothingly. "He examined you while you were asleep and left some medicine for you. Just take it with the food we're transporting into your quarters, and you'll be good as new."

Carol leaped to her feet and sputtered with indignation. "That . . . that's absurd! I want to see my doctor on Pacifica. His name is—"

"No one can see you," said Jim slowly, as if talking to a child. "You're very contagious, and none of the rest of us need to be sick at the moment, not when there's so much work to do. In fact, this is going to be our last conversation for a while. Just take your medicine, eat well, and rest. Soon life will be back to normal. I promise, my love. Good-bye."

"What! Come back! How can you do this to me!" shouted Marcus, dissolving into a coughing fit. She finally had to sit back on the bed, but she continued to cry hoarsely, "Jim! David! Somebody talk to me!"

With frustration and anger, she plucked the combadge from her chest and hurled it across the room, where it skittered into a corner.

Taking a wheezing breath, Carol tried to remain upright, but all the agitation had weakened her, leaving her suddenly feeling all of her 135 years. With a tinkling sound, an elegant serving tray appeared on the nightstand beside her bed. On it was a bowl of her favorite soup, split pea, a large glass of orange juice, and a standard Starfleet hypospray.

With a snarl, Marcus gave the tray an uppercut and sent it spinning; the soup flew across the room and decorated a wall, and the hypospray clattered to the floor. Although a bout of coughing followed this outburst, the moment of insubordination felt good.

An instant later, another tray with the same contents appeared on her nightstand, and Carol wept into her trembling hands. Now she was moving from an unpleasant dream into a brutal and disturbing nightmare. Those people out there *weren't* David and Jim. Her son and his father were dead and had been dead for decades. Whoever—whatever they were—she had told them everything! They knew more about Genesis than *she* did. Worst of all, she had helped them to perfect a beamed delivery system which could span light-years.

"What was I thinking?" she rasped through her ragged tears. "I was their reference manual . . . their source material. This isn't paradise, it's *hell!*"

What everyone had feared would happen for ninety years had finally happened. An unfriendly force had seized her and had plumbed her mind for knowledge of Genesis. Her own guilt and loneliness had only made it easier for them to fool her. Anger welled within the old woman, making her more feverish and nauseated than the unknown disease. What they had done to her was bad enough, but God only knew what they had done to billions of innocent souls!

"It's my fault!" she told herself, weeping. "All my fault!"

Choking back furious sobs, Carol rummaged through the drawer of her nightstand until she found a small pair of cuticle scissors. Her first instinct was to ram the scissors into an artery and take her own worthless life. But that was the cowardly way out. She was sick and disillusioned, but she was no longer confused. The enemy was out there, somewhere beyond that door, and she had to survive long enough to defeat them. Whatever else she had done with her life— whatever opportunities she had squandered or seized—nothing mattered as much as this one moment of clarity.

"It's *not* my fault!" she bellowed hoarsely. "It's them! *Them!*"

Marcus knew that she had to grip reality and hang onto it like a life vest. Chills overwhelmed her, and so did a wracking cough—but the sickness was *good*. Somehow the illness had freed her mind . . . had given her another chance. She would take their medicine, eat their food, and get stronger, while waiting for a chance to get revenge on them. Whoever, or whatever, they were.

With firm resolve, Carol reached toward the tray on her nightstand and seized the hypospray. She lifted the device to her neck, but she paused before administering it. *What if it's the food and medicine that are keeping me under their spell?* she wondered. But that didn't make sense, because she had first seen "David" at her secure compound on Pacifica.

Then she had another worrisome thought: *These beings have exerted extraordinary control over me, and that only stopped because of my illness. What if I get well, and I'm not strong enough to resist their mind control?*

I have to remember how much I hate them, came the answer. *I have to remember that David and Jim are dead.*

As a little girl, Marcus had seen her mother use a trick to remember things . . . important things. She put down the hypospray and grabbed the scissors, and she cut a small slit in the hem of her nightgown. Very carefully, Marcus drew a long pink thread from the slit and wrapped it around her left finger. Using her right hand and her teeth, she tied the thread tightly, but not too tightly. Her captors would have no clue what it meant if they saw it, but she would know.

When I see that thread on my finger, I will remember that my captors are evil . . . and that David and Jim are dead.

Feeling faint, Carol picked up the hypospray, and she used her last scrap of strength to administer the injection to her neck. Within moments, a grogginess overcame her, and the tightness in her lungs and throat seemed to ease a little. The old woman forced herself to drink half a glass of juice, then she slumped onto her bed.

Even though she was obeying their orders, she had to get well in order to resist them.

I will remember, she told herself. Carol Marcus gathered the blankets around her frail form and closed her eyes.

I will remember what they did to me.

four

The blue-skinned child smiled as she groomed a human doll's hair, under the watchful eye of Deanna Troi. Although Dezeer had no hair of her own, she seemed to know exactly what to do with it. They were in the counselor's office, having been released from sickbay just before the crew from the *Neptune* were brought in. Troi was anxious to find out what had happened to Beverly and the others, but she also knew that she had to stay away and let the sickbay team do their job. Besides, she had head injuries from which to recover, and she was still feeling groggy, her empathic skills reduced.

She also had a new charge in her life—Dezeer—and she was going to make sure that nothing else happened to the child. Deanna couldn't remember anything about her rescue from Myrmidon, but she knew that Dezeer had saved her life when she led Will Riker to her unconscious body just seconds before the Genesis Wave hit the planet. The counselor considered the young Bolian to be a good-luck charm, and vice-versa. After all, Troi's combadge, pinned on Dezeer by her dying mother, had been the child's own salvation. But how

many other children had not been so lucky? Despite their monumental efforts, the death toll had to be in the thousands, maybe millions. They wouldn't know for sure until the Romulans went back,
and that might be a grim and pointless journey.

She gave Dezeer a wan smile as she watched her play, although
the child's preternatural calm continued to disturb her. Dezeer was
about the size of a human eight-year-old, but Troi had quickly discovered that she had the mental development of a five-year-old.
She might be an exceptionally large child, even for a Bolian, or she
might be suffering from some sort of disability. The girl had spoken
very little since losing her parents to suicide and nearly losing her
own life on Myrmidon. It had only been a couple of hours, and Troi
wasn't going to push her. She had left her alone for short periods,
but she wasn't going to let Dezeer be shipped off at the first port
with the other evacuees. She considered the child to be her personal responsibility.

Her combadge chirped, and a familar voice said, "Picard to Troi."

"Troi here," she answered, rising from the couch and walking out
of earshot of the child. Anything she said in these trying days was
liable to be disturbing.

"Dr. Haberlee says that Beverly and the others are out of danger,"
began the captain. "In fact, he says he can wake her up and let us
question her."

"Is that wise?" asked Troi with concern. "She's been very ill."

"If it wasn't for our missing crewman, Ensign Paruk'N, I wouldn't
be taking these measures. But we have to find out what happened
over there . . . and what might happen here."

"Yes, sir," answered Troi, knowing he was right. "When are they
going to awaken her?"

"As soon as possible. I'm on my way to sickbay now."

"Yes, sir." Deanna lowered her voice and said, "I have to leave
my patient with a Bolian family, then I'll meet you there."

"Thank you, Counselor. Picard out."

With a sigh at the unpleasantness facing her, Deanna turned back to her young patient. Mustering a smile, she strode toward the girl and leaned over to look at her doll. "I think Miss Barbara is ready for her party. Are you ready to meet some more people?"

The blue-skinned girl shrugged and continued working on the doll. "It doesn't matter . . . my mommy's here."

Troi frowned, her smile fading. "Your mommy is on board the *Enterprise?*"

"I've seen her." Dezeer picked up the doll and carefully put it in a duffel bag Troi had given her, as if she didn't have a care in the world.

Deanna hated dashing the child's illusions, but accepting reality was part of getting well. "Dezeer, your mother isn't on board the *Enterprise*. We picked up very few passengers on Myrmidon."

The blue-skinned being looked with pity at Troi, as if *she* were the one who was delusional. She put her fingers to her lips and made a hissing sound—the traditional sign for a secret. Then the child bounded off her seat and headed out the door, forcing Troi to rush to catch up with her.

At least, thought the counselor, this delusion was giving the child some peace. Dezeer remained calm, if quiet, when Troi dropped her off at the quarters of the Hutamps, a Bolian couple whose own children were grown and living elsewhere. Dezeer didn't say anything to them, but she complied with their wishes. Most important, Deanna was able to leave the child there and head to sickbay, as per the captain's orders. Still she felt guilty about deserting her charge even temporarily.

When Troi reached sickbay, she found Captain Picard, Dr. Haberlee, and Nurse Ogawa conferring in the anteroom. Through the windows, she could see the sick crew members from the *Neptune*, and the security guards hovering over their beds.

"Hello, Counselor," said Picard. "I'm just getting up-to-date on their condition. You were saying, Doctor?"

The young man cleared his throat and looked very serious. "Dr. Crusher is quite weak, but the fungal infection is in remission. Her lungs are clear, and she can breathe on her own. But she's not leaving that bed for a while. The others are in the same condition, a little behind or ahead of her."

"When would she wake up on her own?" asked Troi.

"That's hard to say—in a day, maybe in an hour," replied the doctor. "Since the fungus has infected her brain, we're leery about this comatose state. We would probably bring her out of it, anyway."

Ogawa nodded in agreement. "Yes, it's the right thing to do. I'm sure Dr. Crusher would want to take the risk."

"What risk?" asked Picard, his eyes narrowing.

Dr. Haberlee cocked his head and looked apologetic. "Although we've done lots of scans and don't see any major damage, some things may have escaped us. The fungus entered through the bloodstream, and possibly the nostrils and ears, and we don't know exactly what it's done to her. It could be safer to wait until all trace of the fungus is out of her system, but that could be a few more days."

"There are only four days until the Genesis Wave reaches Earth," said Picard grimly. "The Romulans will arrive any moment to conduct a rescue mission to Myrmidon, and we're their only support. We have to function at peak efficiency, and we can't do that with this illness hanging over our heads. We need answers. Proceed, Doctor."

"Yes, sir," answered Haberlee hoarsely. The young doctor nodded to Ogawa, his beseeching eyes asking the veteran nurse to take over the procedure.

Ogawa led the way toward the row of examination tables in central triage, where all seven patients lay unconscious. An empty bed at the end of the row, plus the presence of a half dozen security guards, reminded Deanna that Beverly's crew was in serious trouble as well as being seriously ill.

Troi thought about all the millions of people—even billions—

whose lives and homes were being destroyed as they talked. Yet their attention was riveted upon these seven people, and the eighth who had mysteriously disappeared within the bowels of the *Enterprise*. It was just one more horror in a chain of horrors, which showed no sign of letting up.

Shaking off her fretful reverie, Deanna turned her attention to Ogawa. The efficient medical worker disconnected nourishment tubes while an orderly applied restraints to Beverly's pale limbs. Her good friend looked as wan and ill as she had ever seen anyone, and Troi had to gulp back her conflicted emotions. Part of her wanted to beg the captain to let Beverly heal before she had to be interrogated, but the other part knew that time was their most immediate enemy.

Ogawa took some tricorder readings, checking them with the overhead display. When she was satisfied with the status of her patient, she lifted a hypospray and carefully loaded it with a fresh vial. "Synaptic stimulant ready," she told Haberlee.

The young doctor nodded, looking grateful for having Ogawa at his side. "Go ahead."

The nurse pressed the instrument to Crusher's neck. After delivering the injection, she immediately passed the hypospray to an orderly and took up her tricorder. The security officers pressed forward, as did Deanna, and the captain motioned them back. "Give them some room to work," he said calmly.

Troi returned her attention to the troubled face of Beverly Crusher. Beverly's furrowed brow looked troubled, and she puckered her mouth as if she were tasting something sour. Deanna started forward, disturbed by these involuntary muscle contractions.

"She's not in pain," explained Ogawa to the observers. "This is a typical reaction. Look, her limbs are moving, too."

They all glanced down to see her arms struggling weakly against the restraints, and she moaned softly as if coming out of a dream. "If she falls into normal sleep," Dr. Haberlee said, "I won't use another stimulant to wake her up. Even in a semiconscious state, she may be able to answer your questions."

"Mmmm," said Beverly, her tongue darting over her lips, her eyelids fluttering. "Need to stop them . . . the attack . . . target their bases." Her voice was a croak, barely audible, but her instinctive struggle against her bindings grew more intense.

Captain Picard leaned over the doctor and gently brushed the hair from her right temple. "Beverly, what do you see down there? Why are you firing at the planet of Myrmidon?"

"The Dominion," she answered hoarsely. "We've seen them. Starfleet told us . . . to watch . . ." Crusher shook her head and seemed to run out of energy as she slumped back onto the table. Deanna Troi let out a nervous breath, hoping she was okay. She wanted Beverly to be allowed to rest, but she doubted if that would be the case.

"Vital signs unchanged except for brain activity," said Ogawa, monitoring the readouts carefully.

Without warning, Crusher's eyes popped open, and she stared wide-eyed at her companions, seeming to recognize them for the first time. "Wesley? Is Wesley okay?"

"Your son?" asked Deanna uncertainly. "Wesley's not here, but you're safe, Beverly. You're back on the *Enterprise*."

Crusher screwed her eyes shut and wept quietly. "But he was on the ship with us. I *saw* him." She struggled involuntarily against the straps on her wrists.

"Can't we take her restraints off?" asked Captain Picard.

"Certainly." Dr. Haberlee loosened the restraints, and Beverly finally relaxed, letting her body sink into the bedding.

"Wesley?" she asked again. "Is he okay?"

"I'm sure that Wesley is just fine," said the captain soothingly. "He's . . . not here now, though."

Crusher nodded, and her eyes closed as she seemed to drift off to sleep. "Yes, he's gone . . . I can tell he's gone."

After a moment, Nurse Ogawa reported, "She's asleep."

"I don't think Wesley would have told her to attack her own shipmates," said Troi. "For whatever reason."

"I don't believe Wesley was ever on that ship," answered Picard. "It must have been part of her hallucinations—along with the Dominion and everything else she mentioned. Has she talked about him lately?"

Troi nodded. "We talked about him just a few days ago, as we often do. She misses him a lot, and the strain of their separation—without any word at all—is beginning to show. But I didn't think it was serious. In fact, it's normal."

"Not anymore," muttered the captain. "The question is, what if these aren't delusions?"

"If her crew thought the Dominion was down there, wouldn't they have contacted us?" asked Troi.

"Perhaps they were all having delusions . . . some kind of mass hysteria," answered Dr. Haberlee. "Maybe they didn't know *we* were here."

Silence followed, as everyone in the room considered the possibilities, all of them troubling. The captain's combadge sounded, and a familiar voice broke in, "Riker to Picard."

"Yes, Number One."

"We've been contacted by the Romulans, who should arrive in about fifteen minutes."

"Give my regards to Captain Tomalak," answered Picard absently, his attention still on Beverly Crusher.

"It's not the *Terix* but the *D'Arvuk* that's coming," answered Riker. "We'll be dealing with Commander Jagron. He was the young one, as I recall."

Now the captain frowned and looked away from the sleeping woman. "Yes, that's right. I hope nothing has happened to Tomalak."

"This is a dangerous mission," conceded Riker. "They sent their youngest—let's hope he's their best."

"Alert me when they're in transporter range," said the captain, his gaze returning to Beverly. "I'd like to be left alone until then. Picard out."

Dr. Haberlee looked as if he had been thinking hard during their conversation. "I'd like to run more tests before I bring any more of them around. I don't think you're going to get much more information than you've already gotten."

"Do you think she has further brain damage?" asked the captain.

"I don't think so." Haberlee turned to Ogawa, who was busy checking her tricorder. "Did you catch anything, Nurse?"

"We have a lot of data to analyze," the sickbay veteran answered, "but I don't see anything offhand. It's natural for her to be disoriented. In truth, she's doing as well as can be expected, and I hope to have her up and eating very soon."

"I hope so," said the captain. "If any of them should wake up and want to talk about what happened, make a log of it, and notify me as soon as possible."

"Yes, sir," answered Dr. Haberlee, still massaging his sore neck. "Just to be on the safe side, we'll get started on making a vaccine for the fungus."

"Make it so," ordered Picard.

"I'll stay for a bit." Troi gave her captain a look of confidence she didn't entirely feel.

"What do *you* sense?" he asked, looking pointedly at his half-Betazoid counselor.

The question shouldn't have surprised her, but Deanna appeared stunned for a moment as she considered her answer. The truth was, she didn't have an answer. It was as if her empathic skills were clouded.

"I haven't sensed anything yet," she said with puzzlement. "Maybe my senses are overloaded . . . with all the death, uprooted families, and misery."

"Don't forget your head injury," Dr. Haberlee added . "You probably are a bit foggy. You really ought to take the spare bed on the end."

"No, thank you," answered Troi. She shivered, thinking that she *did* sense an emotion, one which had been prevalent lately: fear. Only she wasn't sure if the fear emanated more from those around her—or herself.

"Keep me posted." Captain Picard lowered his head and strode toward the door. From the stiff angle of his shoulders, Deanna could tell he was tense, and she could think of no way to console him. At this point, giving him the merest word of encouragement seemed like offering false hope.

Captain Picard stood in Beverly Crusher's quarters, scrutinizing the tasteful surroundings. In her choice of furnishings, Beverly revealed a romanticism that she didn't show in her everyday demeanor. There was the delicate oil lantern on the antique desk and the embroidered pillows on the settee, arranged just so. He noticed gifts he had given her, a Regulan horned beetle encased in amber and a collection of nested dolls from Ogus II. It was the kind of room that showed its owner to be meticulous yet sentimental and playful—a person like Beverly Crusher.

Normally he wouldn't have taken the liberty of letting himself inside a crew member's private quarters, even one he had visited many times; but this was an exceptional case. Beverly was facing a court-martial, demotion, or worse for her actions, unless they could come up with a justifiable explanation. Picard wasn't sure what he could possibly find in her quarters to exonerate her, but he was determined to spend a few minutes looking.

The captain paused at her vanity to view three holographic photos he had seen many times before. One featured Jack Crusher on a fishing trip, grinning and holding up a freshly caught trout. Beverly's husband had been his best friend, and Jack's death was still a painful wound after twenty years.

As a third wheel to the Crushers, Picard had spent so many years hiding his feelings for Beverly that he still couldn't quite bring himself to admit them. If she had only met him before she met Jack, how different their lives might have been.

The second photo was of Wesley, looking impossibly young and fresh-faced. Of course, there were no recent photos of him, and he had to be a man by now, with the glow of innocence gone. Picard shook his head, thinking that Beverly must have been in agony for years now, wondering if her only child was safe. They hadn't been callous about Wesley's absence, but they hadn't given her much solace either.

The third photo showed Beverly snuggling on a couch with Jack, while cuddling Wesley in her lap. The boy was little more than a toddler. Beverly looked achingly beautiful and deliriously happy in the photo, which only produced a deeper pang in the captain's heart. There was much to be said for devoting one's life to serving others, but delirious happiness wasn't usually the result. With planet after planet falling to the Genesis Wave—and Earth in the direct path—all of their sacrifices felt oddly hollow. Instead of a family to protect, he had the *Enterprise*. The ship was important, but somehow it didn't seem as important as the happy grin on Beverly's face in that photo.

Would anything ever make her that happy again?

"Captain?" said a voice. Startled, Picard whirled around, almost expecting to see one of the ghosts from the photos, but instead he saw Data, standing in the doorway. The android looked curiously at him, having never quite understood the tendency of humans to daydream.

"Yes, Data," said Picard. "Is something wrong?"

"No, sir," answered Data. "You asked to be left alone until the Romulans arrived, and they have arrived."

"Yes, of course," said the captain apologetically. "What is our status?"

"Commander Jagron is transporting over to meet with you, and Commander Riker suggested I accompany you to the transporter room." The android glanced around the tasteful stateroom. "Have you discovered any cause for Dr. Crusher's actions?"

"Perhaps." Picard looked wistfully at the photo of Beverly, Jack, and Wesley in happier days. Tugging on his tunic, the captain shook off his nostalgia and said, "Shall we go?"

"Yes, sir."

Walking in silence, the captain followed his second officer to Transporter Room Two, where Chief Rhofistan remained on duty.

"Hello, Captain," the dour Andorian said. "Coordinates for Commander Jagron have been laid in."

Picard nodded. "Energize."

Two swirling columns materialized on the transporter platform and swiftly coalesced into two slim Romulans, the young commander Picard had met earlier and a statuesque female. With grace typical of their race, the visitors stepped down from the platform to greet their hosts.

"Captain Picard," said Jagron with a stiff bow. "I am pleased to meet you again."

"You, too, Commander. This is my second officer, Data."

Jagron raised a curious eyebrow. "Yes, the android—how interesting. This is Lieutenant Petroliv, my intelligence officer."

Petroliv smiled charmingly at Picard. "I'll need to go to your bridge and check your sensor readings, to see if they correspond with ours. We don't want to return to Myrmidon prematurely."

"No, we don't," agreed Picard. "Commander Data can take you to the bridge."

The android gave the attractive Romulan a cockeyed smile, while Picard turned his attention to the young commander. "I hope that your presence here doesn't mean that some problem has befallen Commander Tomalak and the *Terix*," said Picard.

Jagron looked mildly annoyed, but he answered, "Both were fine when I last saw them. Commander Tomalak is a hero to us, something like yourself, and his presence was needed closer to home."

"I can understand that," answered Picard. "We are having our own problems—with a fungal disease that's infected several members of our crew."

Petroliv looked alarmed. "Is it under control?"

"It's confined to sickbay, but I'd like to keep contact between our crews to a minimum. There's no reason to share crew, is there?"

"That depends," answered Jagron. "I had hoped that you would join us for this expedition. We don't know what to expect, so we should have an observer from the Federation on board . . . someone who can make decisions on the Federation's behalf. For example, suppose we could save only a few hundred survivors? Who should they be?"

With a thoughtful nod, the captain considered the request, seeing the logic in it. If Admiral Nechayev and the others were dead, Starfleet would want his confirmation. He preferred to stay close to Beverly, but he was almost too close. Even if she and her crew recovered fully, he might never find out what possessed them to act as they had, except for the vague effects of a fungus.

"I'll return with you to Myrmidon," promised Captain Picard. "When do we go?"

"As soon as we get the sensor readings and have time to study them," the hawk-faced Romulan answered.

Captain Picard had a sudden inspiration, and he motioned to the android at his side. "I'd like to bring Data with me. He's very useful in places that may be dangerous for biological beings."

Jagron's eyes narrowed as if he didn't like the idea, but he still bowed and said, "If you wish. I shall return to my ship, while Lieutenant Petroliv consults your sensor readings on the bridge."

"Thank you, Commander," said the captain sincerely. "Your help in this dire situation is more than we could possibly expect."

"More than you deserve," the Romulan replied with equal sincerity.

five

Geordi La Forge sat on a large red boulder—at least it looked and felt like a boulder—and watched Dolores Linton weave a crude net from vines she had collected. There was no shortage of raw material on Myrmidon, but it was all extremely raw: gruesome mires, overgrown thickets, mammoth trees covered in grayish moss, slimy pools, and pulsing geysers. They were only about two hundred meters from their base at the riverbed, but it seemed as if they were two hundred kilometers from another living soul. A foul mist, which wreaked of ammonia and sulfur, hung over the dense forest, and Geordi shivered from the chill, even in his expedition jacket.

Dolores, meanwhile, was in her element in this forest primeval. Most of the survivors were sitting around in a stupor back at the riverbed, unable to grasp the horrible metamorphosis of their world. But in the last few hours, Dolores had gathered driftwood and debris from the unaffected part of the riverbed, explored the woods, and hacked her way through a mass of vines with an improvised knife. Now she was patiently weaving her vine cuttings into a net, for what purpose Geordi had yet to fathom.

"Will you ever tell me what you're going to do with that?" he asked. "You're not making a tree house, are you?"

"I'll show you in just a minute," she answered playfully. "Are you ever going to get off that rock?"

Geordi shook his head. "No. I feel safe up here—and unsafe when I'm walking around down there."

"The ground is okay, if you look out for sinkholes and quick-sand." As Dolores talked, her strong fingers continued to ply the thick strands. Something which looked like a large newt slithered up to her boot, and she shook it off without even glancing away from her work.

Geordi shivered again and looked around at their gloomy surroundings. The tall trees, which were shrouded in hanging moss, blocked out all but a minimal amount of sunlight. Nevertheless, the misshapen thorn bushes and treacherous vines continued to sprout like weeds without direct sunlight. Despite the incredible growth, the new planet was eerily quiet; Geordi could hear the vines scraping together as Dolores worked them with her hands.

He was reminded of the aftermath of a hurricane, an avalanche, or some other great disasters he had seen on away missions. Only in those cases, there were usually a few birds left to chitter and chirp in the rubble. On Myrmidon, there was no rubble, and no birds left to disrupt the silence.

He looked up to see the geologist tying a fist-sized rock to one corner of the net, but he knew better than to ask her why. Her fore-arm muscles bulged as she pulled the knots tight. He did feel guilty for not pitching in more, but he couldn't shake off his gloom. Leah had been right—this wasn't the kind of place anyone would want to live. To rebuild, the Bolians would have to be awfully determined. The worst had happened, but there was no sign of any relief. They could be in survival mode for years to come.

His thoughts returned to Leah, the real root of his misery. She was gone again from his life—just like that—and he hadn't even put up a fight to keep her. Instead, he had guaranteed they would remain apart by sticking himself on Myrmidon. All for spite.

"There!" exclaimed Dolores, jarring him out of his gloomy reverie. He looked up to see her tugging on the center of her net, testing its strength. There were now rocks tied to two corners of the net; stretched out, it was about three meters by two meters.

"That ought to work," she said with satisfaction.

"Are you going to tell me what you're doing?" asked Geordi.

"Oh, you're going to get a close look, because you're going to help me."

"I am?" he replied in a scratchy voice.

She nodded sweetly and batted her eyelashes. Grumbling, Geordi climbed down from the safety of his red rock and stepped gingerly over the mushy ground to her side.

"There's a good one," said Dolores, striding to the slippery edge of a brackish pool. Scum floated on top of the black water, and life-forms teemed under it, producing ominous ripples on the surface.

Geordi grimaced in disgust, then his implants widened with alarm. "Wait a minute! You aren't thinking about using that net in *there*. I'm an engineer, not a fisherman."

"That's too bad, because at the moment, we've got an opening for a fisherman but none for a warp-core engineer." Although Dolores said it in a kidding tone, there was the backbone of truth in her words.

With a sigh, Geordi picked up one corner of the net. "Okay, what do I do?"

"Just a second." Dolores drew her improvised knife and chopped a path all around the teeming pool. "There, now we have room to maneuver."

She had left loops of vine on the upper corners of the net, to be used as handles, and she handed one of them to Geordi. "Just drag it along your side of the bank, and I'll go along my side. We'll see what we end up with."

Geordi moved slowly, aping her movements as much as he could. As soon as he got close to the edge of the pool, he sank into mud up to his ankles. Dolores did too, but she somehow kept moving, doing a sort of shuffle through the muck. They finally got close enough to the pond to lower the weighted end of the net into the murky water, which smelled like a combination of tar and dead fish. The rocks dragged the net down quickly.

"Go slowly," ordered Dolores.

Geordi nodded, and once again, he mimicked her as he carefully dragged the net along the bank. About halfway across the small pool, the net got heavy and hard to pull, while the water churned with unseen life. Dolores grabbed her handle with both hands and told him, "Keep pulling, we're almost done!"

Slipping and sliding, getting covered with stuff that looked and smelled like sewage, Geordi tried to match her stride. He was only a few paces behind her when they finally got to the end of the pond. Dolores immediately began pulling her catch out of the water, and he strained with all his might to get his end out. As they pulled, a gruesome collection of flopping, wriggling creatures spilled onto the bank, and La Forge nearly gagged at the sight of them. There were tentacled white slugs, squirming lampreylike fish with toothy suckers, and things which looked like newts and tadpoles. Some of them were a half meter long, and a few were misshapen and half-formed, as if they were unsuccessful mutations.

His mind off his work, Geordi slipped in the mud, and his feet flew out from under him, landing in the squirming mass of life. He yelled as the creatures latched onto his legs and curled around his ankles.

Within seconds, Geordi felt strong hands reach under his armpits, dragging him from the wriggling morass. He gripped Dolores desperately, and she made a quick decision. "Get your boots and pants off!" she ordered.

La Forge didn't wait to be told twice, because many of the gruesome creatures still clung to his legs. With Dolores's help, he finally squirmed out of his pants, and she held the infested clothing at arm's length. With powerful strides, she walked back to his red boulder and beat the pants on the rock until the life-forms went flying. With her bare hands, she carefully wiped off the crushed tentacles and teeth.

Geordi felt light-headed and probably would have fainted, except that he was freezing to death. His bare knees knocked together as he tried unsuccessfully to cover his thighs with his jacket.

"Nice legs," said Dolores with a smile. She tossed him his pants.

Even though he was cold, Geordi hesitated before putting on the filthy pants. Instead he looked at the mass of life writhing in the mud, grimaced, and asked, "Please don't tell me you're going to eat those."

"Well, I'm going to cook them first," she answered. "That's why I gathered firewood. But I might try them raw, too. Who knows? Someday these things may be considered a great delicacy."

Geordi laughed out loud at the absurdity of it all. "I wonder what kind of wine goes best with them."

Dolores started giggling, too. Geordi figured the sight of a freezing man in the wilderness with no pants, cackling insanely, *was* funny.

After their laughter died down, La Forge caught Dolores admiring his legs again, he quickly pulled his pants back on, trying to ignore the glaze of slime all over them.

She gave him a smile and looked off into the woods. "I have a feeling that food won't be a problem, but it's going to get damp and cold at night. We can heat rocks with our phasers for warmth, but that's only temporary. We need to think about permanent shelter. We might have to phaser down a few of these big trees and hollow them out."

The engineer grabbed his boots and walked gingerly to the red boulder, where he found a dry spot to sit. He sighed and gazed up at the moss-covered trees. "I knew we might have to stay here for a while—without help—but I never thought about what it would be like. There won't be any quick rescue, because every ship in the Federation is occupied."

Nodding her head, Dolores sat down beside him. "This is really Genesis all right—it's like Adam and Eve."

"Except this isn't exactly paradise," replied Geordi as he poured rancid water from one of his boots.

She looked frankly at him with wide brown eyes. "It could be."

Geordi didn't feel very romantic, but anyone who had just saved his life deserved a kiss. Their mud-splattered faces came close together, and their lips met in a tentative kiss that probed for some kind of meaning in this madness. Finally Geordi gave in and let himself be swept away by her passion and vitality.

When their lips finally parted, he gulped and said hoarsely, "Yes, let's think about getting some shelter."

"What can we use?" Dolores rose to her feet and surveyed the dark canopy hanging over their heads. "There is a ton of that moss . . . mistletoe, or whatever it is. I wonder if we could press it into building blocks."

With his superior hearing, La Forge caught voices in the forest—angry voices, coming closer. "There's somebody headed our way," he said, jumping to his feet.

Dolores grinned. "It's a good thing you got your pants back on."

"Commander La Forge!" came a shout. "Where are you?"

"Over here!" he called. They kept shouting at one another until a search party of about a dozen people staggered into view. Geordi recognized the Bolian doctor and one or two others who were local dignitaries.

"Has something happened?" he yelled. "Is the admiral okay?"

"She's recovering," answered the doctor, panting heavily as he made his way toward them. "We just had to talk to you. What are you doing way out here?"

"Take a look!" said Dolores, pointing proudly at her pile of wriggling food.

"Oh, my!" the doctor exclaimed, with a grimace of disgust. Several members of his entourage looked away, their blue faces turning a mottled shade of purple.

"This is what I have to talk to you about," the doctor grumbled. "We can't stay out here, living like animals. We want to go to the neighboring village of Quonloa."

"Uh, there's no village left," replied Geordi.

"We know that," said the doctor testily. "But they put the interphase generators inside the sanctuary, so the sanctuary is still standing. At least they have a roof over their heads."

"But there's likely to be sixty thousand people crammed inside one of those places," Dolores countered. "We can *build* shelters, if we just fell a few of these big trees and collect some moss—"

"You do that, and you eat these disgusting animals, if you want. We're not going to." There were grumbles of agreement to the doctor's words, and he went on, "A lot of us feel that things must have gone better at the sanctuary . . . in the village."

"Things went fine in the riverbed," said La Forge defensively.

"You call losing ninety-three people doing fine?" snapped the doctor. "We've got nothing in this place—it's a hopeless wilderness."

"The whole planet is like this, or worse," Dolores said.

"We're going to the village!" shouted a woman in the crowd. "You can't stop us!"

"I won't stop you," Geordi said, with resignation. "I'd advise against it, because we don't know what's between here and there. I don't think you're going to find a lot of shelter."

"Anything has got to be better than this," the doctor muttered, to more shouts of agreement. "Do you want to come with us?"

"We can't," La Forge answered, "because this is where Starfleet is coming to look for us."

The woman cackled derisively. "Do you think Starfleet is coming back for you? They're too busy trying to save Earth and everywhere else. We're on our own."

"More reason to stick together," Dolores said, softly.

"Which way is the village?" demanded the doctor, cutting to the point of their visit.

Geordi took his tricorder from his belt and consulted it. "Almost due east from here, about twelve kilometers. If you backtrack to the riverbed, you'll have to go a bit northeast."

"Can we have that tricorder?" the doctor insisted.

"No, I need it." La Forge rose to his tiptoes on the red boulder, peering east and looking for a landmark that could guide them.

"Do you see that big geyser out there?" Geordi asked, pointing to a plume of steam rising over the treetops. "That's due east from here. Once you get there, I'd say you're close."

The doctor scowled. "All right. You won't change your minds?"

"No, but if you meet up with anyone, try to use the combadges, or send a runner back to tell us. Let's try to keep in contact."

"All right," agreed the doctor, his belligerence softening. "I know you told us this would happen, but . . . seeing the destruction . . . it's mind-boggling."

"I know," said Geordi. "I'm sorry. Good luck to you."

Chatting among themselves, the party turned and trudged back through the jungle the way they had come. Geordi and Dolores sadly watched them go.

"Now it really does seem like Adam and Eve," said Dolores. "Only this must be after they got kicked out of paradise."

The engineer nodded solemnly, feeling as if he should have done more to hold them together. But what could he offer them, besides slugs to eat? If Admiral Nechayev were well, maybe she could inspire them to stick together. But probably not. They were determined to see for themselves what was beyond the horizon, even if logic said it was the same foreboding wilderness as this.

"We'd better get back," said Geordi. "Let's fill up the net with as many of these slugs as we can carry."

Dolores mustered a wan smile. "We need to find a better name for them if we're going to convince people to eat them."

"Why don't we call them 'hot-fudge sundaes'?" asked Geordi.

"Works for me," Dolores said, with a laugh. "Before we leave, I want to check the depth of this pond."

She lowered one of the rocks to the bottom of the pond, noting how far the net extended into the water. Geordi watched absently as she took the measurement, and he noted how the water had gotten clearer now that most of the life-forms had been removed, allowing the sediment to settle. The water acted like a prism to distort the portion of the vines that were underwater.

Water bends light waves, he thought to himself. *Waves can be bent.* He suddenly remembered the testing back on the *Enterprise* before they had deployed the interphase generators on Myrmidon. He could never get the protomatter beam lined up with the target, because the protective force field kept bending it. He finally had to turn the force field off to complete the test.

He muttered aloud, "If the protomatter beam can be bent, maybe the Genesis Wave can be bent and redirected. If it passes through a convexo-concave lens, it can even be narrowed!"

"Pardon me?" asked Dolores.

He jumped up, grabbed the geologist, and kissed her excitedly on the mouth. "I think I know how to stop it!"

"What?" she asked, still in a daze from the kiss.

"I know how to stop the wave!" he exclaimed. "We've got to get back to the ship!"

"Geordi—"

He pounded his palms on his forehead. "I can't believe I didn't see this before! But there was so much going on, and we were committed to the phase-shifting. I've got to see if the subspace radio works!"

He jumped off the rock and landed in knee-high mud. After a few seconds of lurching helplessly in the muck, Dolores had to reach down to pull him back to safety. "Nobody rushes on this planet, Geordi. Just slow down, take your time."

"No, we haven't got any time!" he shouted. "I've got to get back. Right now!"

She gave him a wistful smile. "So much for paradise."

six

Will Riker scowled and considered doing something he hated to do—argue with Captain Picard. He had long ago given up the notion of fulfilling one of a first officer's primary duties, that of keeping the captain on the ship and out of danger. But even Riker had limits. Since they were in the privacy of Picard's ready room, the commander plowed ahead.

"Captain, I've got to disagree with your decision," he began, rising to his full height and looking down at the smaller man. "Even if you ignore the danger, which I can't, our command staff is already decimated with La Forge gone and Crusher out of commission. With you and Data gone, we'll really be shorthanded on the bridge."

"You'll have to press Troi into service for your relief," the captain said evenly as he stepped behind his desk. "I'm sorry about this, but I don't expect Data and I will be gone for very long."

"There's a good chance you'll never come back," the first officer said, with exasperation. "Do you remember what the residue of that wave did to our torpedo module?"

The captain sat down and studied his computer terminal. "We

weren't in a cloaked ship with phase-shifting. I'll admit, there's danger, but Commander Jagron is right when he says that someone from the Federation should go along. I'm a logical choice, and so is Data. I'll note your objections in my log, Commander, but this discussion is over."

Riker heaved a sigh and put the brakes on a half dozen other good arguments. That was the prerogative of being the captain—*you* decided when the discussion was over, and who won. Besides, he wasn't sure he could even bring up the point that bothered him most—he was worried about Deanna taking over the bridge. She had gone through hell both on Myrmidon and Persephone V, getting a head injury in the bargain. If the situation weren't desperate, she would be recovering in sickbay.

These words passed through his mind, but he said instead, "If you'll excuse me, sir, I think I'd better take a dinner break before you go. I'll alert Troi to come to the bridge."

"Very well, Number One." The captain looked up and gave his first officer a sympathetic smile. "You know, I've appreciated the freedom I've had to leave the ship—a luxury many captains in Starfleet don't have. It's all because of you, knowing the ship is in such excellent hands."

Riker's scowl lightened a bit. "Fleet scuttlebutt has it that you're going to take over the whole evacuation if Admiral Nechayev doesn't make it. Is that true?"

Now it was Picard's turn to scowl. "I'm afraid so. That's why I'm personally going to bring her back. Get some dinner and as much rest as you can, Number One. That's an order."

"Yes, sir." The tall first officer strode from the ready room onto the bridge. "Data," he said as he passed by the android's station, "do you have any idea when you and the captain will be leaving?"

Data checked his screen. "The Romulans have indicated that they wish to leave at nineteen-hundred hours, providing they are satisfied with the latest sensor readings."

"Then I have about forty minutes for a meal break," said the first officer. "You have the bridge. I'll send Troi up here in case you leave sooner than that."

"Yes, sir."

As he strode toward the turbolift, the commander tapped his combadge. "Riker to Troi."

"Troi here," said the counselor. "Did I forget a date for dinner?"

"No," Riker answered with a smile as he stepped into the turbolift. "Computer, deck eight."

After the doors snapped shut, he went on, "The captain and Data are leaving the ship to return with the Romulans to Myrmidon. I'm not thrilled with this decision, but—"

"You were overruled."

Riker sighed. "Let's just say, you are now my only relief on the bridge. I'm taking a dinner break, so report there as soon as possible."

"Yes, sir. There's not much going on here in sickbay, anyway."

"How is Beverly?"

"Sleeping peacefully," answered Troi. "They say she's getting better, but I don't see any change in her condition. None of the others have regained consciousness, but they're talking about bringing them around."

"That investigation is going to have to be put on the back burner for a while," the first officer grumbled. The turbolift came to a gentle stop, the doors opened, and he stepped briskly into the corridor.

"I would like to spend some more time with Dezeer," said Troi.

"After the captain and Data leave, I'll take over for you." Riker passed a crewman who was stopped in the corridor, studying a map of the ship on the public display. The ensign glanced at the commander, giving him a blank look, then he turned back to the display. If Riker hadn't already been involved in a conversation, he would have offered to help the man, but he kept walking.

"I'll let the Hutamps know they have to keep Dezeer for a little while longer," said Troi.

"I hope they're getting along." Riker stopped at the doorway to his quarters and placed his hand on the wall panel, which instantly read his palm print and opened the door. "I'd better let you go," he said. "Just alert me when the captain and Data are ready to leave."

"Eat something healthy. Troi out."

With that admonition in mind, he headed toward the replicator, walking past his trombone, music stand, and old record player. Riker rubbed his eyes for a moment, deciding what to order. "Computer, give me a large bowl of Chinese stir-fried vegetables over brown rice, easy on the soy sauce."

A steaming bowl of food appeared in the receptacle, and he took it and placed it on his dining table. Then he returned to the replicator and added, "Green tea, iced."

After that, all he needed were chopsticks, a napkin, and some reading material. For that, he picked up a padd containing a report on the just-completed repairs to the forward torpedo module. He ordered up some Benny Goodman instrumentals for background music and sat down to his dinner.

Riker was about halfway through his reading and his Chinese food when his door chimed. He quickly wiped his mouth and gulped down a mouthful of food before he replied, "Come in."

The door slid open, and a shapely figure entered. It took him a moment to focus his eyes and realize it was Deanna. He leaped to his feet, a smile on his face. "What are you doing here?"

"I contacted the bridge, and they're not leaving right away." She walked toward the table, sniffing the air. "Mmmm, that smells wonderful." But it wasn't the food she was looking at with hungry eyes, it was *him*.

She lifted her hand to stroke his clean-shaven jaw, as she gazed longingly into his eyes. "Oh, Imzadi, you mean so much to me. Why can't we ever fit in some time for ourselves? Why can't we get away and forget about everything else?"

"I'd whisk you right away," he replied in a husky voice, "if Earth and half the Federation weren't about to disappear."

"Well, just a minute or two won't make any difference," she whispered, her lips drawing closer to his.

He suddenly noticed something odd about her forehead—the bruise from her injury was gone. Before he could think any more about that, her lips clamped onto his. Her kiss, which was always wonderful, tasted extraordinarily delicious.

Riker was so engulfed by her kiss that he surrendered completely, and he didn't even know when he lost consciousness and slumped to the deck. He never realized that the creature he had kissed was not even remotely humanoid. With a shudder, the being pulled hundreds of loosely hanging strands of moss into the semblance of two legs, two arms, and a torso. It was a rough approximation, but that was all the parasite needed to be ambulatory in its waking state. A cloud of fungus, so small as to be invisible to the naked eye, floated around the amorphous gray figure.

A branchlike tendril reached down and plucked Riker's combadge from his fallen body, absorbing the small device into its wispy recesses. Then the cryptogamic creature shambled to the door and exited into the corridor.

On a makeshift cot in the moist sand of the riverbed, Alynna Nechayev lay sleeping. At times the admiral would moan or twitch, but she was still under the influence of the drugs the Bolian doctor had given her. She wouldn't wake up for hours. Geordi La Forge stood over the admiral, marveling at the signs of recovery. Not only wasn't there any scarring or discoloration, but the healed skin looked fresh and young. She would probably have to have cosmetic surgery to age the new skin to match her unburned skin. He just hoped there were no side effects from his desperate application of the soil while it was still mutating. Even if there was, he had done what he had to do to save her life.

La Forge wanted to wake the admiral up and tell her about his plan to stop the Genesis Wave, but she was in no position to help. None of them were. They were totally dependent upon the Romulans.

At his insistence, he and Dolores had rushed back to the riverbed only to find that they didn't even have enough juice left in the gel packs to power their portable subspace radio. All they had were their combadges, which didn't work because of the electromagnetic interference. No communications worked, except for screaming really loudly, which was what Geordi felt like doing.

"There they go," said Dolores Linton sadly.

La Forge looked up to see a mass exodus of Bolians trudging out of the riverbed, dragging their meager belongings and their bawling children and animals with them. It seemed that no one was going to stay with the three Starfleet officers, who had saved their lives. At least the survivors were headed east toward the geyser he had pointed out, Geordi noted with satisfaction.

The unruly mob got bogged down immediately when they hit the underbrush, bumping up against the advance party, who were supposed to be clearing a path with clubs and tools. Children were crying, animals were baying and struggling against their ropes, and some of the adults were complaining loudly. La Forge fought the urge to run over and help them get organized. When the Romulans came back to get them, he realized, none of these people would be able to leave. Perhaps it was just as well that they were showing their independence and determination, because they would need it.

Still he wondered how the people in Quonloa would react when fifty thousand more people showed up on their one and only doorstep.

"At the pace they're going," he observed, "it will take them days to get there."

"I don't feel right about letting them go out there alone," muttered Dolores. "I think I'm going to go with them."

"What?" Geordi asked with alarm. "You can't go with them. When the rescue party comes looking for us, they won't know how to find you! If our combadges aren't working, we will have no way to contact you. Yours will be just one of millions of life-signs!"

The attractive geologist gave him a shrug. "You're doing what you have to do by running back to the *Enterprise*. What if those people hit quicksand or sinkholes? They don't know what to look for, but I'm beginning to understand the geography of this place. Basically, they need a scout, and I'm the best one for the job."

Geordi's shoulders slumped, and he tried to think of some way to dissuade her. But he could see from the determination in her eyes that she wanted to be useful, and they did need her.

"If you don't get back in time, I'll try to convince them to look for you," he said. "But I can't promise anything."

Dolores gave him an affectionate smile and gently touched his cheek. "You save the Federation, Geordi, that's your job. I just want to save this group and take a look around this crazy planet."

She lowered her eyes and kicked at the sand. "If I don't get back in time, and you can't find me, do what you have to do. Don't worry about me—I'll survive."

"But—"

She stared at him with her dazzling dark eyes. "Geordi, you try to be happy, because that's one area where you don't try hard enough. If that means chasing after Leah Brahms, then chase after her. But when you find her, make sure you tell her how you *feel*."

Geordi opened his mouth to protest—to say that he didn't feel anything special for Leah anymore—but both of them would know that was a lie. Instead he grabbed Dolores. Her brawny arms wrapped around his back and came close to crushing him, while her body melted against his.

When their lips finally parted, she grinned at him and said, "*That* will get me back here quicker than a bunch of Romulans showing up. Take care, Geordi."

He didn't really trust himself to say anything, so he watched in silence as Dolores joined the throng making its way through the misty woods. He heard her voice ringing above the others, telling them to watch out for quicksand and sinkholes. They probably didn't realize it, but their luck had just taken a dramatic turn for the better.

What about my *luck?* Geordi thought glumly. Without that beautiful geologist, would his life take a turn for the worse?

"Picard to bridge," said the captain as he stepped upon the transporter platform. Data joined him, bearing two satchels full of their belongings and copious records about the Genesis Wave and the location of the shelters on Myrmidon.

"Troi here," came a crisp response.

"Hello, Commander," said the captain, mildly surprised. "Riker not there yet?"

"He sent word that he's on his way," she replied. "Said in his message he fell asleep."

"I'm sorry we had to wake him. I just want to make sure there were no further messages from the *D'Arvuk.*"

"No, sir, they're expecting you, and they hope to leave immediately."

"Very well. Maintain your position and wait for us." Picard would have preferred to have the *Enterprise* tracking them on sensors, but there was no chance of doing that while they were under cloak. "Picard out."

The captain had a moment of doubt, when he wondered whether he should leave the ship under such clouded conditions. He could only hope that the journey would be as swift as he envisioned, and as productive; but in reality, they had no idea what they would find on Myrmidon.

"Coordinates are laid in," reported the transporter operator, probably wondering why the captain was delaying.

Picard nodded and said, "Energize when ready."

"Yes, sir."

A moment later, the human and the android disappeared in two sparkling pillars of displaced molecules and refracted light.

"Stay close together!" shouted Dolores Linton to the ragtag band, which was strung out behind her for what looked like a half kilometer. To her right, a murky waterfall plummeted downward with a roar. Its origins were lost in the mist above the towering treetops, and it plunged into a jagged basin and promptly disappeared. The ground underfoot had the consistency of gelatin and smelled like reptiles pickled in formaldehyde.

"Stick to the path—no stragglers!" Although she kept yelling, Dolores doubted whether many of her charges could even hear her, and soon they wouldn't be able to see her either. It was getting dark in the cold, gloomy forest. The geologist couldn't tell if the gloominess was due to nightfall or the massive trees overhead. Here the hanging moss was so thick that it was like a shroud, and she was worried about stragglers falling behind and getting lost.

At least, thought Dolores, the underbrush was more sparse where the moss grew in abundance, and that made clearing the path easier. She had given up the idea of scouting ahead, because there was no chain of command. She had no one to pass information to, no one willing to make the unruly mob work together. With her tricorder, she was the only one who had a compass. In this power vacuum, Dolores was forced to do everything—from guiding the path-cutters to haranguing the stragglers to keep up. She had shown the advance party what the sinkholes and quicksand looked like, and so far they had avoided serious mishap.

"Tighten up there!" she bellowed, wondering how long her voice would hold out.

As she surveyed the horde spread out behind her, Dolores was reminded of crowds leaving sports stadiums in her native Ohio. By the downcast faces, lowered heads, and muttered complaints, it looked like a crowd that had seen the home team lose the game. They were stunned, wondering how in the universe this could have happened to them. The endless canopy of misshapen trees, dripping with moss, did nothing to cheer their souls, and the waterfall sounded like the roar of the victorious team.

We'll have to stop for the night, she thought gloomily. Most of them still had enough freeze-dried rations and water not to starve, but it was already damp and getting colder. Now Dolores wished she had forced them all—somehow—into making shelter instead of undertaking this mad trek.

A voice ahead of her shrieked, and the geologist whirled on her heel and peered into the gloom. She reached for her tool belt, grabbed a flashlight, and shined a beam into the shadows. At first, she thought it was snowing heavily, because puffs of darkness were falling from above. With a start, Dolores realized it wasn't snow but the moss that was falling; a second later, a wispy tendril brushed along her hair and face, and she suppressed a scream.

She looked up, squinting. For some ungodly reason, the trees were shedding layer after layer of the thick moss, and it floated downward like a gossamer net. Dolores quickly drew her knife and calmly sliced through the stuff as it cascaded down, but others around her screamed and tried to flee.

"Stay calm!" she shouted. "You can cut right through it!"

All of a sudden, Geordi La Forge appeared in front of her, staring into her eyes as if he had never seen a human being in his entire life. His ocular implants glowed like two orbs of ectoplasm, and his arms reached out for her. From his gaping mouth came the homey smell of her mother's rhubarb pie baking in the oven.

"Geordi!" she muttered, overcome by a combination of confu- sion and relief. "What are you doing here?"

"I love you," he answered, sounding the wrong inflections, as if he were speaking for the first time in his life. He wrapped his arms around her, only they weren't entirely arms, because part of his limbs felt like a prickly thorn bush.

Instinctively, Dolores brought her knife upward in a slashing motion, ripping through Geordi's gut. The being in front of her turned into clumps of moss, which fell apart like a poorly built scarecrow. Instantly, another Geordi La Forge rose up from the forest floor, leering at her with a demented smile.

Now Dolores screamed. Gasping for breath, she tried to run, but more of the gray shroud engulfed her as it floated downward. She stumbled and fell over others who were underfoot, and the weeds and slush became a quagmire of terrified Bolians. With horror, she stared at a woman who was smiling and cooing while she fondled a pile of the smothering moss.

Dolores struggled to get to her feet, but it seemed as if every breath she took only made her weaker. She slashed ineffectually with her knife at the clinging tendrils, but they engulfed her like a downy comforter. As the seconds crawled past, Dolores forgot why she was struggling, when sleep would be so welcome.

"We're only going to rest for a few minutes," she said to no one in particular. Darkness descended over her mind and the misty forest at the same time, as blankets of moss continued to float down.

seven

"Myrmidon," said Commander Jagron, motioning to the elaborate viewscreen on the bridge of the Romulan warbird *D'Arvuk*. "The dark areas are swamps; the lights you see are not cities, but volcanoes."

Captain Picard gazed at an olive-colored planet peeking through a haze of ominous gray clouds. The ugly globe looked as if it had been splattered with gobs of ochre, which meant it had swamps the size of oceans. Glowing embers of light sprinkled the primitive landscape, and there was a ring of volcanoes around the equator. The poles looked like frozen whitecaps shrouded in clouds. Jean-Luc Picard had seen a lot of planets in his life, but few more foreboding than this one.

"Are there any life-signs?" he asked.

The Romulan commander turned to the officer standing at the science station, and he pursed his lips. "The magnetic poles have yet to stabilize, and electromagnetic interference is making identification difficult. But there are many life-signs—the planet is teaming with life."

Data stepped closer to the science station and gave the display a look. The Romulan officer promptly angled his back, cutting off the android's view of his screen.

"Thank you, Commander Jagron," Picard said with sincerity. "You've fulfilled your promise and have gotten us back here without incident. I'm extremely impressed by your technology."

The cadaverous Romulan continued to stare at the dusky planet on the viewscreen. "And I'm impressed by your technology."

"Unless I am mistaken," said Data, "you cannot operate transporters while cloaked. How will we effect rescue?"

"You are mistaken," said Jagron with a smile. "We can't operate *normal* transporters, but we have a special transporter setting that is synchronized with our interphase generators. We can only transport one person at a time, over short distances, but we can get you to the surface and back."

"Is the planetary atmosphere stable?" the android asked.

"As a matter of fact, it is," answered Jagron. "That's an interesting feature of the Genesis Wave matrix—the planet returns to normal quicker than the surrounding space. If we had a low enough orbit, we might be able to launch a shuttlecraft."

"You've learned a lot about the Genesis Wave," said Picard, impressed.

"I'm a quick study." Jagron turned to a phalanx of six guards wearing skull-hugging metal helmets. "With your permission, I'd like to bring this security detail with us to the planet's surface."

Picard blinked in surprise at the tall Romulan. "You're coming down there with us?"

"Yes," answered Jagron. "My government wishes to know what's down there, too."

Data cocked his head. "Since combadges may not work, and we can only send one person at a time, I suggest that I go first. Then you can transport me back to deliver a report."

The commander put his hands behind his back and considered

the request. "Very well. But we won't be able to identify anyone on the planet, so we'll have to set up a blind transporter pad. Anyone who steps onto the pad will be beamed back automatically."

"That solution represents security problems," observed Data.

Jagron smiled and motioned to his six brawny centurions. "That's why they're going."

"We'll need warm clothing," said Captain Picard.

"It's all in our main transporter station. Shall we go?" With a regal wave of his hand, Commander Jagron led the procession off the bridge of the Romulan warbird.

Geordi La Forge shivered, even though he was sitting a meter away from a pile of hot, glowing rocks. Admiral Nechayev slept peacefully beside him, covered with both of their emergency blankets. La Forge picked up his phaser and shot a beam at the rocks in his pile, heating them back up to white-hot. But it made very little difference in the way he felt, and he finally decided that it was the oppressive darkness that was making him shiver.

Their lanterns didn't penetrate far into the gloom, and they only had a circle of light about twenty meters across. Beyond this fragile pool of light, the darkness wrapped around them like the feathered wings of a great vulture. Cloying fog drifted across the riverbed, carrying odors that brought back memories of the misshapen creatures dwelling in the mires. Although Geordi could have sworn the forest was quiet during the day, at night it was a cacophony of dripping, slurping sounds.

Their banishment to this place was an odd reward, he thought, for the people who had saved the population, if not the planet. For the sake of irony, though, it made sense. Leah Brahms had warned him repeatedly that no one could live on Myrmidon after the Genesis Wave, and now he was forced to prove her wrong. Or right.

Will I ever see Leah again? he wondered. With a start, he realized that she wasn't as important to him now as she had been yesterday. He had found her, held her in his arms, and made sure she was alive. In doing so, he had finally seen the woman with her shields down. Who knew her marriage was a sham? Who knew she had to struggle for happiness and balance in her life, like everyone else? No longer was Leah Brahms the ideal lover, companion, and brilliant physicist all in one beautiful package. She was just as prone to bad luck and bad decisions as the rest of them.

She was just a human being.

Dolores Linton, on the other hand, *was* a superior human being. That much he now realized. Of course, she also had a wanderlust, a craving for adventure, and an unfortunate aversion to spaceships. She wasn't the answer to all his prayers, but he sure longed to have those strong arms wrapped around him right now.

With a sigh, Geordi stared off into the velvety darkness, in the direction where Dolores and fifty thousand survivors had trudged off hours ago. He kept expecting them to return, saying they had been to the village, and it wasn't any better than the riverbed. Unfortunately, that fantasy wasn't going to happen, because they probably wouldn't reach Quonloa until tomorrow, even with Dolores as their guide. He doubted whether any of them would want to make the return trip right away.

So he listened to the night. La Forge wasn't sure when the random sounds emanating from the blackness shifted into a pattern—a kind of rhythm. But they did. As he listened, Geordi began to think he heard marching . . . or, rather, the shuffling of feet. A great many feet. He lifted his lantern and waved it at the darkness, but it was like trying to light all of space with a flare gun.

That's when he saw *them.* La Forge grinned and leaped to his feet. They had returned! Wave after wave of humanoid shapes came plodding through the forest, shuffling their feet. It was hard to make them out clearly, and he wondered if his ocular implants were malfunctioning somehow. *That's all I'd need,* he thought ruefully, *to have my vision go on me.*

"Over here!" he called, waving his lantern as if they couldn't see the only light in the forest. Wordlessly, the strange shapes kept marching toward him, the lantern light glinting off their bald, blue heads. As they drew closer, he saw one in the lead who wasn't a Bolian—it was a shapely female with tresses of auburn hair falling to her shoulders.

"Dolores!" he called, happiness and relief mixing with worry. "You've come back. . . . Is everything all right?"

She moved into the light, dragging her feet as if she was very tired. The others slowed down and finally stopped altogether, just outside the circle of light. It didn't matter, because Geordi's attention was riveted on the beautiful geologist.

He rushed forward to meet her and gripped her in his arms, while she gave him a tender hug back. She nestled her head on his shoulder. It didn't matter that they were surrounded by thousands of people in the middle of a bizarre wilderness.

Geordi lifted her chin to kiss her, and she purred, "I love you."

Without warning, a phaser beam streaked from the darkness. Dolores exploded, chunks of her flying in every direction, and a scream froze in Geordi's throat. His initial horror was replaced by utter disbelief, because her blasted corpse looked like a piñata full of shredded newspapers and confetti, fluttering down.

"What the—?" he gasped, whirling in the direction of the shot. To his astonishment, he saw Data standing there with a calm expression and a drawn phaser. The android turned and leveled the weapon at the crowd of Bolians who were creeping forward from the darkness. To Geordi's astonishment, they stopped and stood perfectly still, and their chemical composition seemed to change before his implants. Standing as still as hedgerows, now they looked more vegetable than animal.

"I am sorry to have startled you," said Data. "You were under attack, were you not?"

Geordi hurriedly wiped his mouth and spit. "Yes, I guess I was. But I thought it was Dolores Linton!"

The android cocked his head. "You have been without a girl-friend for too long."

"No, seriously, I thought it was a human being!" insisted Geordi. "It was a shape-shifter, or I was hypnotized . . . or something."

"Its shape never shifted," Data said with certainty. "Its mass changed after I shot it, but it remained some sort of animated vegetable matter."

Data picked up a sprig of the mistletoelike plant from the ground. "I will analyze this, but right now, we must leave. I see that Admiral Nechayev is injured."

"Yes," said Geordi, leaning protectively over the admiral. "She almost died, but she's—"

"Put down that phaser immediately," ordered a voice that sounded exactly like Captain Picard.

The captain was suddenly standing in front of Geordi, and just as suddenly, Data blasted the apparition to pieces. "You are in grave danger," he said. "You must transport up immediately."

With a rustling sound, the horde of Bolians stepped toward him, and La Forge blinked, trying to clear his vision and his mind. Something grabbed him by the back of his neck and lifted him off his feet. It wasn't until Geordi opened his eyes that he saw it was Data, holding him like a bag of garbage.

"You are leaving now," said the android, striding toward a glowing disk in the distance. Several of the Bolians shambled into his path, but he pulverized them with his phaser. A few others he clubbed into piles of rubbish.

"But I can't leave!" insisted Geordi. "The admiral needs help . . . and Dolores Linton is out there somewhere! They're all in danger!"

"I know," said the android, never slowing a step or pausing in his slaughter of the creatures, which looked like Bolians. "We can only transport one at a time, and you will go first. Tell the captain that Admiral Nechayev will follow you, and I will come last. I believe both of you will need medical attention."

"But—" There was no further discussion, as Data placed him on a glowing disk set into the ground, surrounded by gel packs. The engineer was instantly transported to an unfamiliar room, and he staggered from a transporter chamber to be caught by a brawny Romulan. The guard wrinkled his nose at the human's frightful appearance and smell, then dropped him to the deck.

"The admiral is coming next," La Forge managed to blurt out. "She's unconscious."

"Step aside," ordered Captain Picard, muscling his way through the helmeted and regally bedecked centurions. "Good to see you, Mr. La Forge."

"Thank you, sir." Geordi breathed, just as a slight figure wrapped in blankets appeared on the transporter platform. She tumbled into the captain's arms.

Picard cradled the admiral and laid her on the deck, then looked up at his Romulan hosts. "She needs medical attention."

A Romulan commander stepped forward, tapping an insignia that joined two of his opulent belts. "Commander Jagron to the Medical Center. Send a medteam to the main transporter station. Situation: urgent."

"Thank you," said Picard, his eyes steely cold. He turned to look at Geordi. "Are you all right?"

The engineer nodded weakly. "Physically, I'm okay. I'm shaken up . . . over something that just happened."

"And Data?"

"Yes, he should be coming soon. But he's immune to them."

"Them?" Picard asked warily.

La Forge nodded slowly, still unable to believe what he had seen. "There are creatures on the planet—they can hypnotize you into thinking they're people. One of them looked like *you*, Captain. It's some kind of plant that can move around, like Piersol's Traveler. I'm afraid for everyone left down there."

The captain nodded gravely and looked down at the fragile figure of Admiral Nechayev, still sleeping peacefully on the deck. Geordi could tell from the captain's puzzled expression that he had noticed the smoothness of her healed skin.

"What happened to the admiral?" he asked.

Before Geordi could fashion an answer, there came a flash, and Data appeared in the Romulan transporter. The android stepped down, holstering his phaser. "I suggest you turn off the automatic transporter pad."

"At once," Jagron answered, nodding at the operator.

"Are you well, Geordi?" asked Data.

"I'm okay," answered the engineer. "Thanks for saving me. But there are so many others down there! *You* saw those creatures . . . they looked like Dolores Linton and Captain Picard! How could they do that . . . how did they *know?*"

"They may be telepathic, capable of reading your mind." The android turned to Captain Picard. "I have a theory about what happened to Dr. Crusher and her crew."

"Go ahead," the captain answered gravely. La Forge saw Commander Jagron lean into the conversation, to make sure he didn't miss a word.

"I took some tricorder readings before I left," Data began, "and the creatures exude the same fungus that infected Dr. Crusher and the crew of the *Neptune*. I believe this fungus rapidly infects the brain, producing the hypnotic effect that Commander La Forge has described. It produces delusions, too. In fact, it may produce whatever mental state the creatures desire. They may be parasitic in nature, using this euphoric effect to control the host organism."

"Dolores!" Geordi exclaimed, jumping to his feet. "Captain, we've got to go back down there."

Before Picard could reply, a Romulan medical team barged into the transporter station. They looked to their commander for orders, and he motioned to Nechayev. The admiral was soon taken from the captain's care and loaded onto a gurney.

"Are we going to have to quarantine my ship?" asked the commander, sounding quite calm about the possibility.

Captain Picard looked frankly at his counterpart. "We're just starting to learn the truth about our enemy. My ship is already infected, and this may explain what happened to a missing crewman of ours."

"What happened to Dr. Crusher?" asked La Forge, trying to get control over his emotions. It was suddenly clear that they couldn't send rescue parties back to the planet, unless they had an army of inorganic androids, like Data.

Briefly, the captain explained about the *Neptune* and its unexpected attack on the planet. Commander Jagron's eyes narrowed, and his jaw worked furiously as he listened.

"Ah, so that's what happened to Admiral Nechayev," said La Forge. "She was a casualty from that attack." He explained what he had done to keep her alive during those first terrible minutes after the Genesis Wave had swept across Myrmidon.

"How did they get there?" asked Commander Jagron. "These parasites."

Data answered, "I believe they were created as part of the Genesis matrix. They were programmed to be grown on the planet, along with an environment to serve them. It is a rather cost-efficient way of colonizing."

"Procreation and colonization in one easy step," said Picard, his lips thinning in anger. "Our enemy has achieved the ultimate use of Genesis, but they can't plan for everything. The Bolians weren't supposed to be there after the wave swept through, so now they have to deal with them."

La Forge let out a troubled sigh. "Since our shelters were successful, there must be millions of people stranded on Myrmidon with those things. We have to save them!"

The engineer snapped his fingers and staggered to his feet. "What about environmental suits? Unless we breathe this fungus, we won't be infected, right? Can't we go down there in suits and be safe?"

Data shook his head. "I would not risk it. It is my theory that the fungus enhances the effect of their telepathic abilities, so an environmental suit would not offer full protection. Furthermore we have no idea how numerous they are—they could number into the billions and have a telepathic group mind. The *D'Arvuk* has a limited number of crew and the ability to transport only one person at a time. Searching and clearing huge tracts of forests of an ambulatory plant is an undertaking that would require years, even with unlimited resources."

"But we can't just leave them down there!" countered Geordi. He began to pace, remembering why he had wanted to be rescued so badly. "Captain, I've got something else to tell you."

"Go on."

La Forge gulped and spoke the words that would probably end this rescue mission and doom Dolores and the others to their fate. "I think I know how to stop the Genesis Wave."

The Sanctuary of the First Mother looked like a golden pillow dropped into an overgrown weed patch. A lone blue-skinned figure could be seen walking around its perimeter, chopping back the greedy underbrush just enough to get past. He wielded a kind of Bolian scythe called a *purka*, which made short work of all but the thickest branches. Even though he was working hard to keep the path clear, Mot still shivered and had to pull his jacket more tightly around his shoulders. It would be dark very soon, he thought with trepidation.

Solely because of his casual connection to Starfleet, the barber had become the de facto leader of this dispirited throng of forty-five thousand souls. He was setting an example by taking the night's first patrol around their perimeter, although the worst threats seemed to be hunger and depression. He was afraid that many of his fellow Bolians would resort to suicide if they grew too despondent.

Some of the animals were stuck outside with him, tethered and crying forlornly. A few of the younger and hardier survivors had ventured off on their own, trying to find someplace better. Mot didn't know about that, but he was sure they could find a place less crowded. It was even more chaotic inside the sanctuary, with the Mother who was ostensibly in charge more worried about protecting the Crown than her congregation. In fact, she had run off into the forest to hide the relic. At least, thought Mot, he had used his status to get his parents private quarters in a closet off the attic. He couldn't do much else for them.

With his scythe, he hacked at the thickets and vines, releasing sticky sap that smelled like black hair dye. "Damn this stuff," Mot cursed, panting heavily. "It's worse than cutting a Tellarite's beard!"

He began to get discouraged when he found himself battling the same brush he had cut back only an hour ago. The rampant growth was determined to claim the sanctuary, and he had no doubt that it would, given time. Already moss-laden trees towered over the dome, and vines were crawling up its golden inlay.

"Where's Starfleet?" he wondered aloud. The unfortunate and obvious answer was that they were probably setting up more shelters on other endangered planets. Those poor souls had no idea what was in store for them. If they knew . . . the suicide count would be in the billions. His mind wandering, Mot wasn't paying attention, and his sleeve got caught in a mass of thorns. He cursed loudly as he tried to extricate himself, but the vines seemed to have eyes as they pricked his limbs and snared his clothing.

"Just relax, Son," said a soothing voice.

Mot looked up to see his roly-poly mother, smiling benignly at him. "Mama! What are you doing out here?" He tried to restore some dignity to his pose, but that was difficult while caught in a thicket.

She moved toward him, shuffling slowly, as anyone would in this godforsaken place. Smiling fondly, the elder Bolian reached up and tweaked his cheek. "Oh, you're so funny, my little Teeko Bean."

He blushed, his blue skin turning purple. "You haven't called me that in years."

"Give us a little kiss," she cooed, standing on her tiptoes and puckering her dark-blue lips.

This moment of tenderness seemed to be wildly inappropriate under the circumstances, but how could he refuse his mother? Everyone was going a little crazy out here, including him and his parents. Besides, the shivers had finally left him, and Mot felt oddly warm in his mother's presence.

"That's a good boy," she said, pulling his face closer to hers. His mother smelled like powder scented with lollo blossoms, a scent he always associated with her. Mot took a deep, heady breath, and he was soon lost in her comforting embrace.

eight

"Mr. Mot!" called a voice, barely breaking into the barber's consciousness. "I apologize for this."

The first phaser beam struck the Bolian in the back, and he dropped to the ground like a big blue avalanche. Data stepped closer, adjusting the setting on his phaser pistol, and the moss creature flinched just before he blasted it into confetti with his second shot. As he holstered his weapon, gray tendrils floated down from the dark sky like feathers.

The android glanced around the ragged path that surrounded the dome, but he saw no more of the shambling plants, or any survivors. A quick tricorder reading assured him that most of the survivors were safely ensconced inside the domed sanctuary, although there were some animals at risk by the front door. Data picked up the big Bolian and slung him over his shoulder as if he were an old coat, then he took several tremendous leaps along the path and arrived at the front entrance.

As Data had feared, moss creatures were draped all over the domestic animals. Some animals were standing, some were lying on the ground, snoring, but all seemed to be in bliss. The android set Mot on the ground, propped him up against the building, then drew his phaser. With pinpoint accuracy, he drilled the parasites until there was barely enough left of them to brush off with his hand.

By that time, he heard a groaning sound, and Data turned to see the Bolian coming to his senses. "Mr. Mot," he said, kneeling beside his shipmate, "I am sorry I had to stun you, but I have discovered that a mild stun works as a sort of reset for humanoids. When they regain consciousness, the hypnotic effect of the fungus has been alleviated."

"What?" asked Mot, blinking puzzledly at the android. "What fungus?"

"That was not an acquaintance you were kissing—it was a creature native to this new planet. A very dangerous creature." Data took a padd from a bag on his waist and handed the electronic device to the startled barber. "I do not have time to explain, but all the information we have is there. Barricade yourselves inside this building and do not allow anyone to enter, no matter *who* you think they are."

"But . . . but we've got people out there!" Mot pointed helplessly into the gloom.

Calmly, Data placed his phaser pistol in the Bolian's outstretched hand, then he handed him a bundle of three more phasers. "If you are in doubt, shoot them with a mild stun. A true humanoid will fall unconscious for a short period but will not be harmed. If the stun has no effect, increase the phaser setting. These parasites are the enemy, probably the ones responsible for the Genesis Wave. Do you understand?"

His mouth hanging open, Mot nodded. "Right . . . parasites are the enemy."

Data rose to his feet and concluded, "Excuse me, I have many shelters to visit and only one shuttlecraft for transportation. Take heart, Mr. Mot, because you have not been deserted."

The android tapped his combadge and disappeared in the shimmering halo of a transporter beam. Mot looked warily at the foggy woods, the sleeping animals, and the sprigs of moss scattered on the ground. Clutching the padd and the phaser, he lumbered to his feet and dashed inside.

First officer Maltz eyed the star chart on the battle display, which was centrally located on the bridge of the *HoS*. The three-dimensional hologram showed an undistinguished stretch of space with no class-M planets and vast pockets of asteroids and dust. In distant epochs, those celestial graveyards had been stars or giant planets, thought Leah Brahms. It was an old part of space, and it looked it—used and worn out.

"Magnification by four," ordered Maltz, and a young officer at the tactical station hurriedly made the adjustment from his console. Leah was surprised by how little the Klingons used the ship's computer. It was as capable as those in Starfleet, but it seemed to be an adjunct to hands-on operation. Almost every system on the ship could be operated manually, including hand-pumped hydraulics to keep life-support going on the bridge. No wonder Klingon ships were notoriously tough to bring down.

A fist encased in a studded gauntlet jabbed into the middle of the display. "There it is," growled Maltz, "Lomar, class-L. According to our records, the last time it was explored by anybody of note was two hundred years ago. We have it lumped in with a million other planets nobody wants."

Leah frowned at the chart hovering in the air. "It doesn't look very promising, does it? But it's not far away from the Boneyard. Only two light-years."

"It's not too late to change course and go to the Boneyard," the crusty Klingon said. "We wouldn't lose much time."

Leah realized that once she made a decision, she had to stick with it, unless she was proven dead wrong. She couldn't give this crew even the slightest opportunity to question her orders. However, they did deserve an explanation.

"I've been thinking about the whole issue of the wave's origin," she began. "I wonder if we haven't been operating from a misconception. This doesn't have to be a continuous wave beamed from a fixed point, as we've assumed. It could have been launched with one massive burst. Then it would be like a tidal wave. It passes through and leaves behind refuse and wreckage, but life resumes."

"Some cowardly form of life," grumbled Maltz.

"Yes, they're cowards," agreed Brahms, "so they've probably covered their tracks by now. I doubt if there's anything left to find in the Boneyard, and that's why we don't see anything on our sensors."

Maltz's rheumy eyes narrowed. "Then what happened to the task force Starfleet sent there?"

"I don't know, but I do know one thing—*I'm* not going to blunder into danger like they did." Leah Brahms leaned over the chart and studied the unfamiliar legends in an alphabet she was just starting to understand. "We need to gather information before we go there. What's the closest inhabited planet or outpost? Maybe somebody nearby knows something about Lomar."

"Here," said Maltz, running his hand across a membrane keypad and shifting the view to a neighboring solar system. "There's not much, except for this dilithium mining colony, Protus. It's on the biggest asteroid in the sector—a planetoid. Freighters from Protus used to stop at Hakon, and I know there are freelance miners and prospectors there. Perhaps some of them have taken side trips to Lomar."

"We need more information than what's in this database," Brahms said with frustration. "I'm not comfortable with just showing up at this planet."

Maltz scratched his stubbled white beard and narrowed his eyes at her. "Captain, you know that every minute we delay, the more of your worlds and people die."

"I'm aware of that," Leah Brahms answered, her blue eyes grow-ing as cold as comets. Once again, she tried to muster the resolve and confidence of Admiral Nechayev. "If we fail, their deaths will be in vain. I can't be sure that anyone else will have a chance to stop them, so it's up to us. You have your coordinates, Mr. Maltz."

"Yes, sir." The old Klingon turned toward the row of consoles behind him. "Helm, prepare to change course."

"Change course now," ordered Commander Riker, sitting imperi-ously in the command chair at the center of the *Enterprise* bridge.

"Yes, sir," answered the officer on the conn, a female Antosian. "Course laid in for Lomar."

Deanna Troi lay huddled in a corner of the bridge near the door to the captain's ready room, shivering, and feeling violently ill. For over an hour, ever since Will Riker had strode confidently onto the bridge, she had been sick and bewildered. It was as if she had an instant allergic reaction to him . . . her Imzadi! But it was worse than that—it was as if neither her mind nor her body could func-tion in his presence.

Deanna realized that she had been feeling mentally fogged ever since her concussion . . . especially after the *Neptune* crew were brought aboard. When Troi pried open her eyes, she could barely focus on Riker anymore—he looked blurry and indistinct.

Despite the heaves in her stomach and wracking cramps, she tried to remain still, so they wouldn't know she was awake. Not that she posed much of a threat to this person who had calmly taken over the ship. Just looking at him gave her a severe headache. Her reaction was the complete opposite of the rest of the bridge crew however; they were prepared to follow him anywhere.

He had shut down the ship's internal and outside communica-tions, locked all doors and turbolifts, secured everyone and every-thing where they were, and had done so with enormous efficiency. Why Will had to do this was a puzzlement, because he was already acting captain of the *Enterprise*. In fact, she doubted if anyone in the crew knew anything was wrong. There were variations of red alert, where the bridge crew assumed command of every system and locked everything down. They were just dutifully following orders . . . orders that made no sense to Troi. Maybe she had misunderstood, but why should they go to a planet named Lomar?

The others kept talking, but she could barely hear them for all the pain and fuzziness that filled her head. Still she knew she had to do something. Just beyond the door to the ready room, which had been sealed along with the others, was an access panel to a Jefferies tube. Those crawl shafts would be the only means of getting around the ship until normal operations were resumed. But getting there, opening the panel, and crawling out seemed impossible to Deanna, who could barely lift her head off the deck.

Thinking and analysis seemed to clear her head a bit, and she decided that most of the damage being inflicted upon her was mental, not physical. His effect on the others was complete control, but she had the opposite reaction—revulsion, physical and mental. If they were in control of their minds, she reasoned, wouldn't they question having a senior officer cowering in the corner? But they didn't even seem to notice her.

While the bridge crew was busy making the course change, which seemed to take them longer than usual, Troi tried to quell the roiling in her gut. *I'm in control*, she told herself. She wanted to strike back mentally, but she didn't want to alert him. He was occupied for the moment, and it had been a long time since any of the rest had paid much attention to her.

Mustering all her strength and resolve, Troi rose to a crouch and leaped toward the access panel, grabbing the handles and ripping it open as she skidded past.

Riker leaped to his feet and pointed at her. "Tactical, stop that woman! Use your phaser."

Troi crawled into the opening just as the officer drew his weapon and fired. The phaser beam struck the top of the hatch, bombarding her with flaming sparks of molten metal, but she pulled herself through and dropped feetfirst into the tube. As she bounded down the ladder, Troi heard shouts and commotion above her, but her pursuers weren't fast enough to catch her. She reached the next level, kicked the access panel open, and tumbled into a corridor.

To her relief, the farther away from the bridge she got, the faster both her head and her nausea cleared. Troi was feeling hungover but almost herself when she rounded a corner in the passageway and ran into two shipmates. They were security officers, and she recognized them immediately. "Help me!" she pleaded. "They've taken over the ship. It's not Commander Riker up there . . . something is wrong. But we can retake the ship—"

A hulking security guard glowered at her and took a step forward. "That's what the commander said . . . a mutineer."

"Apprehend her," his comrade answered, drawing his phaser.

Without thinking, Deanna put a palm strike right in the chest of the closest officer and sent him sprawling into the one with the phaser. She dashed down the hallway and squeezed around the corner just as a red beam streaked past. Stretching flat-out, Troi dove headfirst toward the open access panel and gripped the opening with her fingertips as she slid past. Hearing footsteps behind her, Deanna ducked into the Jefferies tube just as her pursuers rounded the corner and squeezed off another beam.

Now she dropped faster than ever through the bowels of the ship, not stopping until another phaser beam streaked past her from overhead, barely missing. Without knowing where she was, Deanna jumped into an adjoining passageway, heading horizontally through the ship. *How far does his control reach?* she wondered in a panic. *Where can I go to find help?*

The more her mind cleared, the more absurd the whole thing seemed. Why was Will Riker commandeering the ship, when he had control of it, anyway? The answer was that he wanted to do something so out of character that the crew would resist his orders. Deserting the captain and Data to go to Lomar—wherever that was—certainly qualified.

At the moment, she couldn't face the more serious question— whether that really was Will Riker on the bridge. The answer might mean that her beloved was dead, or seriously injured, or he'd been possessed by some alien intelligence. Still, Troi knew she had to discover the truth, and the place to start would be Will's quarters. He had been normal when he left the bridge to go to dinner, and he'd been poison to her after his return.

Panting heavily, Deanna removed her combadge so they couldn't find her with the ship's computer. Then she stopped to listen—to see if anyone was following her. No one could scramble up and down these ladders without making noise, although she didn't hear any. Of course, even without her badge, they could use tricorders to find her, but they couldn't get around any quicker than she could, unless they reactivated the turbolifts. The worrisome thing was that she had no idea how many crew members had fallen under Riker's spell. Was she the only one who had an odd kind of immunity?

While stopped, Troi looked around to get her bearings. She finally found a plaque on the wall of the tube that identified it as serving deck nine. That was a small piece of luck; Riker's quarters were not completely out of reach from this part of the ship. She plowed onward until she found a tube leading up, then she began to climb.

Troi figured that she could get to Riker's door, but how could she get it open? She would need a phaser to disable the circuitry, and then something to pry the door open. Her arms and legs aching, she climbed until she reached the access panel on deck eight. She lunged for it, just as it popped open in her face.

Deanna instantly collapsed against the ladder, expecting a phaser beam to streak out of the opening, but instead a tentative voice called, "Hello? Who's down there?"

It might be a trick, thought Troi, but they had her in point-blank range, and there was no need for them to use tricks. She waited breathlessly until two blue antennae bobbed over the edge of the opening. Finally a long, blue head followed the antennae, and the saturnine face of Rhofistan, the transporter operator, peered curiously at her. "Counselor Troi?"

"Yes," she said, letting out her breath. "Are you . . . are you aware that the ship is headed to Lomar?"

"Lomar?" asked the Andorian. "Where's that? And why is everything locked down?"

"Help me out," she said with relief. "The ship's been taken over . . . by an intruder, I think."

"That would explain much," said the Andorian, lowering a long arm to her.

After pulling her out, the two of them stood in the corridor, looking around, trying to catch their breath. Troi noticed the phaser on his belt.

"Good, you're armed," she said, "and we need that."

"We must fight other members of the crew?" he asked in alarm.

"No, we have to get into a door."

"I'd like to get into a transporter room and several other places," said the Andorian, "but there are only crew quarters on this deck. Nothing vital."

Deanna frowned and brushed back a dark lock of hair. "That's probably why there are no guards down here yet. He's got command of everyone on the bridge, but not the whole ship."

"Who has control?"

"Come with me," ordered Troi. She led the way down the corridor, scanning the bulkheads for any tools or weapons they could use. Spotting an emergency panel, she opened it and grabbed a first-aid kit, a tricorder, and a small tool box full of spanners and wrenches.

A moment later, Troi paused in front of a turbolift, which didn't open at her approach. "We can't get in there," Rhofistan said glumly.

"I know." Troi continued to study the support frame surrounding the door. The long, slim pieces of metal looked awfully strong to her.

"May I have your phaser for a moment?" she asked, placing her other articles on the deck.

"Certainly, Commander." His blue fingers drew the weapon and handed it to Troi.

"Stand back." With pinpoint bursts, she sheared off two metal slats about two meters long from the door frame. Rhofistan gathered them up as they clattered to the deck.

"Come on, we're almost there." Troi handed the phaser back to the Andorian, picked up the other articles, and charged down the corridor. When they reached Riker's door, she flicked on the tricorder and checked for life-signs. To the relief of her thumping heart, she found one weak life-sign inside.

Deanna pointed to the control box to the left of the door. "Do you think you could disable that?"

"Yes, sir." The Andorian drew his phaser, checked the setting, and swiftly demolished the control box in a shower of sparks. A Klaxon sounded, and Troi looked around, knowing this forced entry wouldn't go unnoticed on the bridge.

Troi grabbed one of her metal rods and used it like a crowbar on the door. Grunting and groaning, she didn't make much progress until Rhofistan grabbed the other slat and slammed it into the door jamb. The big Andorian was about twice as strong as a human—almost as strong as a Vulcan—and he quickly opened a slit of several centimeters. As the siren continued to howl overhead, both of them gripped the door with their fingertips and pulled in opposite directions. With a cracking sound, the door finally broke loose and slid freely.

"Will!" cried Deanna, rushing into the room with the first-aid kit in hand. She found Riker sprawled on the deck, barely breathing, his skin clammy and hot as if a fever were raging. Her first instinct was to call sickbay for help, but then she realized that wasn't an option in the absence of her combadge. Not that calling sickbay would help in any case, at least until the imposter was exposed. As Rhofistan took up position at the door, phaser drawn, Deanna opened the first-aid kit and pulled out a hypo full of lectrazine, an all-purpose stabilizer.

"Hang on, Imzadi," she whispered. "I knew that wasn't you up there."

She administered the hypospray to his neck and held her breath, waiting for a reaction. Will looked as sick as Beverly and her crew, but she was hoping that she had caught him before he slipped into an actual coma.

Without warning, a phaser beam streaked down the length of the corridor, and Rhofistan returned fire. As more phaser beams criss-crossed the air, the Andorian was forced to duck into the stateroom. "They're coming!" he warned.

Deanna grabbed Will's shoulders and lowered her ear to his chest, but all she heard was his ragged breathing. "Come on, Will, wake up! Get better!"

Rhofistan shrieked, staggering back from the door with a nasty phaser burn on his thigh. Troi fumbled in the first-aid kit for any-thing that could bring Will around, but she heard the pounding of boots coming closer. She thought about picking up the phaser, which had fallen to the deck along with the Andorian, but she couldn't win a shoot-out with security officers. Instead she lifted Will's head and cradled it in her arms.

"Don't move!" shouted a voice, and Troi looked up to see gold tunics crowding the broken doorway, and phaser rifles aimed directly at her.

nine

For a moment, confusion reigned in the confines of Will Riker's quarters, as a security detail confronted what they thought was a band of mutineers. Deanna Troi could tell from their startled expressions that they didn't expect one of the renegades to look exactly like the acting captain they had left on the bridge.

Troi stared at the man she had punched in the chest a few minutes earlier, and he muscled his way past the others. He glowered at her, while his phaser barrel stayed pointed at her chest. "I . . . I don't know what's going on here," he murmured, "but you're going to the brig."

"*This* is Commander Riker!" Troi insisted desperately. "He's ill. We have to get him to sickbay. Believe me, I *know* Will Riker, and that's an impostor on the bridge!"

The officer's face showed a flash of doubt, but he finally stiffened his spine and waved to his comrades. "Arrest them all, and get them to the—"

"Johnson, don't be a horse's ass," croaked a voice. Deanna felt a rumbling in her breast, and she realized with joy that it was Will, talking and awake. She hugged him even tighter.

"I told you in your last review," Riker continued, his voice gaining strength, "that you react without thinking. You're a good man, but you want to get control of that temper of yours. There's always time in any situation to *think*."

Johnson looked really confused, and he backed out of the room, shaking his head. "I don't know . . . I don't feel well either."

"Help me sit up," Will whispered, smiling weakly at Deanna. She rose to her knees and pushed him forward, noting that his skin still felt clammy.

Riker gazed from one officer to another—they numbered four now that Johnson had run off—and they gripped their phasers nervously. "We're in no shape to hurt you," said the commander, "so you can lower your weapons and talk to us."

Hesitantly, glancing at one another, the officers lowered their phasers. The commander nodded and went on, "We're even, because I don't know what's going on here either. But I know one thing—when Ensign Paruk'N disappeared, we realized there might be an intruder onboard. We discussed that, remember?"

They nodded at one another, looking more accepting of the idea. Riker coughed and took a raspy breath, but he plunged on. "We also know I'm sick . . . and that you may be next. It's probably the fungus . . . the same thing that got the *Neptune*."

Troi hugged him protectively and said, "You have to go to sickbay. You got a strong dose of it."

He frowned worriedly at her. "You didn't come in when I was eating dinner . . . and kiss me? Did you?"

Deanna looked up at the dinner dishes left on the table and shook her head.

"I didn't think so," Riker answered, his body shivering. "I *know* where I got it."

"We can get him to sickbay through the Jefferies tubes," said a Deltan officer, reaching an arm down to Riker. He sounded convinced that it was Riker.

"Chief Rhofistan, too." Troi motioned to the wounded Andorian, who nodded appreciatively.

The four guards helped the first officer and the transporter operator to their feet and guided them into the corridor. Deanna retrieved Rhofistan's phaser from the deck and tucked it into her belt.

"Are you coming with us?" called the Delta officer as they helped Riker lower himself into the Jefferies tube.

Troi waited until her beloved was out of earshot, and she answered, "No, I've got to go back to the bridge."

"We could go—"

"No, you can't come with me," she insisted, gripping the phaser in her belt. "I'm the only one who can face him."

"The *Enterprise* is not there," said Commander Jagron, pointing accusingly at the elaborate viewscreen on the bridge of the *D'Arvuk*.

"What?" Captain Picard asked, taking a step toward the display and staring at it. He had heard Jagron give the correct coordinates for the barren stretch of space where they had left the *Enterprise*. He had personally given his crew orders to wait for their return. What had happened?

"Maybe it's the infection," suggested La Forge, standing at his side. "You said the *Neptune* also did unpredictable things."

"Yes." The captain frowned thoughtfully, then added, "Or perhaps they were called away by Starfleet."

Jagron sneered. "What is more important than this mission—to see if your shelters even work? Besides, the *Enterprise* is under quarantine, like us."

"All right, they're gone," said Geordi. "Can't we go back to Myrmidon and try to search for more survivors?"

"Before we do anything," answered Picard evenly, "we have to broadcast a subspace message, explaining your theory. All the parties have to know there's a chance that the Genesis Wave can be bent or narrowed by force fields. Do you have those notes I asked you to compile?"

"Yes, sir." La Forge took an isolinear chip out of his pocket. "I think we could use tractor beams on a massive scale to form a kind of convexo-concave lens."

"Let's get the word out." Picard looked expectantly at Commander Jagron, who scowled and led the engineer to a communications console.

Where would they go? the captain wondered to himself as he stared at the empty region of space. *If our enemy has captured the* Enterprise, *wouldn't they use it to help their cause?*

He walked to the console and looked over Geordi's shoulder. When the transmission was almost complete, he added, "Two more things: Let Starfleet know that Admiral Nechayev is alive, and put everyone on alert for the *Enterprise*. If they see it, they are to use caution and allow no person-to-person contact. Anyone who sees the *Enterprise* should contact the *D'Arvuk* immediately."

"Do you really think it will be that easy?" asked Jagron.

"No," answered Picard, working his jaw as furiously as La Forge worked the communications panel.

Using her mind like a homing device, Deanna Troi crawled through the Jefferies tube under the bridge, trying to find the false Riker. From the pain and nausea that overwhelmed her, she determined that he was sitting in the command chair, right where she had last seen him. He was pumping out telepathic energy like a generator. No wonder he had to sit and remain still. For her part, she tried to remain calm and keep a clear head while she waited in the cramped crawlspace. That meant fighting down bile churning up from her stomach, but Troi managed to maintain her position.

One of her patients was a member of the maintenance crew for the bridge, and he had described how odd it was to be working in the access space under the bridge, and to have your hand in the center of the captain's chair or the ops console. She could envision that now, and she had no trouble finding the circular compartment under the command chair.

Still Troi had to wait, fighting the revulsion, until she decided that her foe wasn't going to move or react to her presence, if he even knew she was there. They were on course to wherever, and they didn't seem to be worried about anything. That was all Deanna needed to know. She wanted to open the compartment, crank her phaser to overload, and stick it in a strut inside the command chair. The resulting explosion would put this creature out of commission. Permanently.

But tempting as the plan was, it wasn't an option, at least not one she could live with. So with a quick yet careful shot with her phaser she began to saw her way through the deck itself. If she could just talk to this being for a moment perhaps they could reach some sort of— Alarms went off, and the lighting in the passageway changed to red-alert status.

Guess he's not in the mood for a chat, she thought, as she continued drilling the deck with her phaser. Ducking back into the Jefferies tube, Troi narrowly avoided a collision with Captain Picard's chair as it fell through the fresh hole in the bridge's floor. Phaser reset to full stun, she popped up through the hole and fired before the imposter or crew could react.

What followed seemed to surprise the rest of the bridge crew almost as much as it surprised Troi herself.

Nothing happened at all.

Riker had been looking over the shoulder of the science officer when Troi aimed at his side. He didn't even seem to notice, much less react, when the beam first struck him. Finally, when he realized that his crew was staring at him dumbfounded, he began to draw his own phaser.

"Didn't I tell you to take care of her?" he said, apparently irritated, but at no one in particular. Troi's head pounded and she felt faint. She reset her phaser.

"Stop." Her voice sounded to her own ears like it was emerging from the end of a long tunnel. "Please don't make me kill you." The imposter continued to raise his weapon.

Whoever you are and whatever you want, I'm sorry I have to do this, she thought as she watched the form of the man she loved disintegrate under her fire.

When the acrid smoke surrounding the panel behind Riker cleared, Troi looked around at the bridge from an angle she had never expected to see. Scattered everywhere were sprigs of gray vegetation—like mistletoe—along with the pieces of the chair and deck. The bridge crew gaped at the wreckage and the bizarre remains of their commander. One of them bent over and dropped to his knees, vomiting. Deanna knew how he felt, although her own nausea was fading.

She dragged herself out of the jagged hole. "That was not Commander Riker. The real Riker is in sickbay by now."

She crossed to the ops station, trying to sound confident and collected. "Computer, turn off red alert!" she ordered. The noise instantly stopped, and the lighting returned to normal.

Deanna breathed a loud sigh of relief. "Let's get communications going, and all systems back to normal. Conn, bring us to full stop."

When they just stared at her, the counselor resorted to her most sympathetic tone. "It's all right, none of you are to blame. The ship is infected by . . . something. We'll get things squared away in no time." She hoped that would be true.

Pacing the bridge, Troi stopped at the conn and noted that they were still on course to a planet she had never heard of. "Do any of you know why we're headed to Lomar?"

Still stunned, the young officers looked at one another and shook their heads. It was as if they had collective amnesia and couldn't remember being under the sway of a clump of moss, which was now scattered around the deck.

"Okay," she said, "at least put out a distress signal, and do it now."

That order was simple enough that the tactical officer, the same one who had fired at her earlier, managed to tap his board. "Distress signal going out on all channels."

"Full stop," reported the conn.

"Unlocking transporters, doors, and main hatches," the officer on ops said.

Troi nodded slowly and smiled. "Thank you. Get a repair team up here, too." She looked around at their stunned expressions and added, "And call relief for yourselves. I think all of you could stand a visit to sickbay."

While the crew numbly obeyed orders, Deanna's gaze traveled to the viewscreen and its panorama of star clusters and distant nebulas. Somewhere out there was a vile enemy, dangerous beyond belief, which wasn't above using biological warfare in its most horrible permutations.

"Tactical," she ordered, "bring up everything we know about our last destination . . . Lomar."

"Admiral, good to see you!" Captain Picard said heartily, mustering more cheer than he felt. He strode up to Nechayev's bed in the tasteful medical center aboard the Romulan warbird. La Forge was a step behind him, but the engineer couldn't muster a smile. Dozens of worlds stood at the verge of destruction, and La Forge remained concerned about the two women caught up in the tragedy. Picard supposed that was the hallmark of a true crisis, when one's priorities shifted in unforeseen directions.

"Captain Picard," Nechayev said, squirming in her bed. "Why am I cooped up here? I feel perfectly fine!"

The captain sighed. "You nearly died on Myrmidon."

"From what?" she demanded. "If I'm still here, that means the interphase generators worked as planned. Either that, or La Forge here is a ghost. Hello, Commander."

"Hello, Admiral," the engineer said with a respectful nod. "The interphase generators *did* work, and I'm not a ghost. Don't you remember the attack just before the wave hit?"

"No, tell me about it."

Nechayev scowled thoughtfully as La Forge and Picard related the story about the *Neptune*'s treachery. Coupled with the discovery of the fungus, at least they had a probable explanation for what had happened to the task force. It would also explain the sudden disappearance of the *Enterprise*.

"That's not all," said La Forge. "When the dust cleared, we weren't alone on Myrmidon." When he described his experience with the moss creature who impersonated Dolores Linton, the admiral cringed.

Picard went on, "Since Data is immune to the effects of the fungus—and the creatures who spawn it—we left him behind, to warn the survivors."

"Why did you have to leave Myrmidon so suddenly?" asked Nechayev.

La Forge lowered his head modestly. "We have a theory on how to stop the Genesis Wave."

After hearing the details, Admiral Nechayev tried to jump out of bed. "I'm alive, and we've got lots to do. Let me tell the captain we need a shuttlecraft."

Picard steadied her arm, although he wished she would return to bed. From nowhere appeared a gray-haired Romulan doctor, who sneered at his patient. "You will lie quietly until I release you from that bed, or I'll put you in the brig. Perhaps this is a good time to show you a mirror."

From behind his back, the doctor produced an ornate looking

glass, which he thrust into Nechayev's hands. The startled woman took the mirror and slumped back onto the bed. She stared at her reflection, marveling that one side of her face was perfectly smooth, like a teenager's cheek, while the other half showed the wrinkles, folds, and spots she had so richly earned.

"Somebody did a great . . . half a job," she muttered.

"That would be me," Geordi answered sheepishly. "You were dying, and I used the mutagenic soil while it was still active . . . applied it directly to your burns. I reasoned they would help you heal, and they did."

"Am I infected with this fungus, too?" she asked.

"No," answered the doctor. "As far as I can tell, you're not. You seem to be very healthy . . . for an elderly human."

She blinked at the Romulan, but Picard could see her tense anger fading to a warm glow. "Thank you for helping me, Doctor. By all accounts, I should be dead twice over, but I'm not. So I'm not going to complain. However, if I'm healthy now, I presume I will be allowed to leave your care."

"I suppose," he said. "But you should be under observation, in case there are unexpected consequences of your unorthodox treatment."

"Believe me, when I get back, I'll be under observation," said the admiral, looking again at her two-sided reflection in the mirror. "Let me get back and help save both of our worlds. I've faced the Genesis Wave head-on, and it's a part of me now. I won't have to explain its power—I'll just point to my face. I'll also prove that we can stand up to it and *win*."

"Go on," muttered the doctor. "I don't think you will ever be a satisfactory patient."

Nechayev leaped to her feet and wrapped the sheet around her slight form. "I need a new uniform. Where's your replicator?"

The doctor scowled. "Do you think we can just replicate Stafleet admiral uniforms? That we have them in our data bank?"

"Please," said Admiral Nechayev, her eyes narrowing. "Time is precious."

The Romulan doctor grunted his disapproval and stood ramrod straight. "I will see what I can do."

When he marched out of the room, Picard tapped his combadge. "Captain Picard to Commander Jagron."

"Jagron here," came the disdainful voice. "How is the admiral?"

"She's well, and your doctor is going to release her. She'd like a shuttlecraft—to get back to the front and put La Forge's plan into effect."

"She'll have to leave immediately," answered the commander. "Because we have a new destination."

"Where is that?" Picard frowned, dreading to hear that they had been ordered to Romulan space or some other hot spot.

"The *Enterprise*," answered Jagron. "We've received her distress signal, and we're the closest ones to her. They're halfway to the origin point."

La Forge lowered his head, a crestfallen look on his face. Both of them knew they weren't going to return to Myrmidon any time soon. Picard wanted to tell him to trust Data, but Myrmidon was a bewitched and unpredictable place. He feared that the *Enterprise* was also compromised.

"We shall depart as soon as the admiral is off the ship. Jagron out."

Picard turned to Admiral Nechayev, still huddled in her sheets, and asked, "Admiral, can you get some help to Myrmidon?"

"Yes, Captain, I will," she promised.

"Fire!" barked Mot. Nobody did, and the barber shouted again, "Fire phasers! They're not our people—they're not people at all. Fire!"

Still his small cadre of soldiers nervously gripped their weapons and stared at the advancing horde of Bolians, shuffling toward the front door of the sanctuary. They looked like people they knew—relatives, lovers, children, old friends. It was extremely eerie, because reason told them that these people were not on Myrmidon. Or if they were, they were far away with no means to get here. Still the onslaught of friends and relatives, shambling out of the forest, was enough to paralyze anyone.

Mot shook off his malaise and grabbed a weapon from a startled youth. He raked the front line with phaser fire, and nothing whatsoever happened. "That's on stun," he said. "See, they're not *us*. We can't let them get too close."

The big Bolian cranked up the setting and his courage, and his next volley of beams cut the advancing party into shreds. His cohorts were horrified, and there were angry shouts all around him; more than one phaser was pointed at Mot.

"Look at them!" he shouted. "Look at the dead ones!"

There weren't any dead ones, they discovered to their shock, just leaves and sprigs caught in the underbrush. Some of the creatures in the back took on the identities of the ones who had disappeared, and they kept shuffling forward.

Mot stuck the phaser back into the boy's hands and growled, "Fire!"

He did, and soon all of them were wantonly firing phasers. The primeval woods lit up with blazing streaks, felling trees and foes alike. Clumps of moss came tumbling out of the sky, and smoke swirled everywhere. It was like shooting up a row of hedges that kept advancing in unison. The hulking shapes no longer tried to disguise themselves—they just looked amorphous and menacing.

The intrepid band kept firing, but there was no relief and no end. The faceless shamblers kept pouring out of the dense woods, their ranks never diminishing. They were crowding into the clearing. "Fall back!" Mot shouted, discouraged. "Into the sanctuary!"

With tears in his eyes, he hustled his frightened squad into the nebulous safety of the golden dome, and bolted the door behind him. Mot cried because of all that had been lost—an innocence as well as a civilization and a home. The might of Starfleet and the resources of the Federation had always protected them before, even from the Borg and the Dominion. But Starfleet crumbled in the face of this heinous weapon and the demons who sprang from the slime.

ten

"Welcome back," said the smiling face of Beverly Crusher as Captain Picard stepped off the transporter platform onto the deck of the *Enterprise*. The captain beamed at his companion and gripped her by the shoulders. That was when he noticed the hypospray in her hand.

"Oh, this is an official greeting," he said with disappointment.

Beverly grinned and lifted the hypospray. "This is my first official duty since getting well, and I requested it. Believe me, you'll be glad you got this inoculation against the fungus." The doctor administered the hypo with her usual efficiency.

Picard nodded with appreciation. "Good work on the vaccine."

"I had nothing to do with it, except for being one of the guinea pigs," she admitted. "It was all Dr. Haberlee. He's still a little nervous but he held sickbay together. We don't need the security detail anymore."

"It sounds like we needed them on the bridge," muttered Picard.

Another sparkling column appeared on the transporter platform, and Geordi La Forge stepped down. The engineer still looked gloomier than usual. "Sorry it took so long," he said. "The Romulans are still cloaked and are only sending one at a time."

"Taking precautions, are they?" Crusher asked, moving toward La Forge with a loaded hypospray. "They needn't worry—we've got a vaccine now."

"We won't get sick?" asked Geordi with relief.

"You'll be okay with the fungus, but you're still susceptible to their telepathic abilities. It was Troi who finally got rid of the moss creature who infected our ship . . . and the *Neptune.*"

Crusher looked pained and apologetic at the memory. "On the *Neptune*, it pretended to be Wesley. I thought he had come back to help us. Here, it pretended to be Commander Riker, and it nearly killed him."

"How did Troi stop it?" asked the captain, moving toward the door.

Beverly frowned for a moment. "Uh, you'll see as soon as you get to the bridge. We're lucky that Troi got an allergic reaction to it, not the euphoria . . . the willingness to believe that affected the rest of us."

"Why is it some people get violently ill," asked Picard, "while others can resist for days, or never become sick?"

"The creatures are cryptogamic parasites," she answered. "They don't want to kill you—not right away—they prefer to keep you alive to do their bidding. When they're done with you, they can give you a fatal dose of the fungus that will kill you within hours. The toxics and chemicals in that fungus are quite an evil brew. We think the fungus might even be a symbiotic plant growing within the moss—it's a complex creature."

Picard nodded grimly as he stepped into the corridor. "Make sure you get the formula for the vaccine to Starfleet Medical. We have to send it to every ship and port in the Federation."

"We have," she answered wearily. "But immunizing everyone is a massive undertaking . . . along with everything else that's happening."

Picard straightened his tunic, trying not to be overwhelmed by everything that needed to be done, at once. They were only one ship, and he was done playing defense—he wanted to go on the offensive. "How is Riker doing?"

"Still recovering. He should be out of sickbay in a day or so." Crusher headed off in the opposite direction. "If you'll excuse me, we've got to inoculate everyone on board."

"Beverly," said Picard with compassion, "I'm sorry that Wesley didn't come back."

"Me, too." The doctor nodded sadly, then lifted her chin and charged off down the corridor.

Picard and La Forge took the turbolift to the bridge, and the captain found out what Beverly meant when she said he would know what had happened to the intruder. There was a giant, scorched hole in the deck where his command chair used to be.

"Hmmm," said La Forge, "interesting decorating decision. Very bold."

Counselor Troi lowered her head, looking chagrined. "I'm sorry, Captain. The repair crew is replicating what they need to fix it. I had to use the Jefferies tube to acess the bridge so I could confront that . . . being."

"Quick thinking, Commander," said Picard with an appreciative nod. "I don't think I'll be doing much sitting, anyway. Where was the intruder taking the ship?"

"To a planet called Lomar," Troi answered, bringing up a chart on the main viewscreen. "It's old and mostly barren, but it bears a resemblance to the worlds created by the Genesis Wave. Captain, do you know . . . what those creatures are like?"

"Yes, Myrmidon was infested with them. Terraforming is only a part of what they're doing—they're using the Genesis Wave to colonize and procreate."

Troi grimaced. "We've got to stop them."

"We will." The captain's stern expression softened a bit. "Now that I'm back, Commander, why don't you take a break. Go check on my first officer."

"Thank you, sir!" With a relieved smile on her face, Deanna hurried to the turbolift.

The captain strode behind the ops station. "Ensign, find out how close the Boneyard is to a planet named Lomar."

"Yes, sir," she answered, working her board furiously. "They're close, about a light-year away from each other. The Boneyard is closer to our present position."

Picard nodded, making a decision. "Tactical, alert Starfleet and the *D'Arvuk* that we're headed to the Boneyard. Following that, we'll be going to a planet named Lomar."

From the tactical station, a young Deltan announced, "Captain, Starfleet has recalled all ships to Earth . . . for the final evacuation."

"There won't be an evacuation," vowed Picard. "We've got a plan to divert the wave. Contact Starfleet and tell them that we're on a mission approved by Admiral Nechayev. She'll back us up."

"Yes, sir." The young ensign worked his board for a few moments, then he reported, "Messages sent. The *D'Arvuk* is replying . . . they request permission to accompany us."

"Tell them we don't expect to come back until the enemy has been defeated." The captain's lips thinned.

The young officers on the bridge exchanged nervous glances, then quickly turned back to their consoles. The Deltan sent Picard's message, and a few seconds later, he reported, "That is acceptable to the Romulans."

"Thank them for their courage, and send them the coordinates for the Boneyard." Picard paced the deck, carefully avoiding the gaping hole. "Conn, set course for the Boneyard, maximum warp."

Carol Marcus shook herself awake and stretched her arms luxuriously in the coolness of her bed, a lilac scent priming her senses.

With her illness fading, she could smell again, and she noticed the fresh vase of flowers on her nightstand. For what seemed like the first time in days, her body wasn't consumed by wracking coughs and pain, and her mind was clear. Everything seemed normal—except for the pink string tied around her finger, slightly pinching it. At first, Carol couldn't remember why she had tied that string there, then it all came rushing back to her.

They're not human, she told herself. *David and Jim are dead. Those creatures out there are not my loved ones.*

Carol primped her flat and dirty white hair, thinking that she felt strong enough to take a shower. They would be coming to see her again, now that she was almost recovered from the fever. Although the old woman despised her captors, she found herself looking forward to their contact once again. She then shuddered with self-disgust at that desire. If she hadn't been so lonely, she wouldn't have been such a prime candidate for their deception.

But she had to admit they did a good job impersonating David Marcus and Jim Kirk. Of course, they certainly had plenty of raw material to work with, all of it dredged from her own mind. She longed to see them again, even though she knew they were inposters. Quite excellent imposters.

If they can read my mind, she thought suddenly, *won't they know that I'm onto them?*

I'll have to act, too, she realized. *My surface thoughts can't betray me. I'll have to play this game of pretend, too.*

Some forty years ago, she'd had a yoga expert for a bodyguard, and she had trained extensively with him. She would have to use all of her powers of meditation and concentration to fool them, but she could do it. She would *have* to do it. Her life—and countless other lives—depended on it. It was important for her to present a facade of normality.

The old woman sat and practiced her yoga for a long time—how long, she didn't know. Finally she was satisfied that she could face them without her thoughts giving her away. Now that she was mentally prepared, it was time to make herself physically presentable. She rose to her feet and walked toward the bathroom.

Although the door and windows to her bedroom were locked as tightly as a vault, she still had access to her bathroom. Like everything else, it was a replica of the one in her home on Pacifica. Now Carol could see that the sunshine beaming through the skylight overhead was artificial, not the hot island sun. This house had many conveniences, she thought ruefully, such as being close to Regula I, a space station that had blown up ninety years ago.

Where had they been when she was on vacation at her family home on Earth? *Probably right here,* came the answer. *Wherever here is.*

She turned on the shower and climbed inside. At least the warm water felt real, as did the smooth, tiled walls of the stall. She decided that her bedroom and bathroom had to be real buildings, albeit replicas. They had remained solid all through her illness, even after her captors had backed off.

Of course these walls are real, she thought disgruntledly. *They have to function as a prison cell.* As Carol washed, she was very careful not to disturb the string tied around her finger. Getting out of the shower, the old woman toweled off and put on a fresh jumpsuit from the closet. She felt a bit weak and hungry, but otherwise fine.

As if somebody had read her mind, a transporter beam flashed, and a tray of food appeared on her vanity table.

"Thank you," she said cheerfully as she crossed to the table and grabbed a slice of toast. She lifted the cover off a bowl and smelled the contents. "Ah, oatmeal with cinnamon. My favorite!"

"You feel better?" asked a disembodied voice, which sounded vaguely like Jim Kirk.

She told herself it was Kirk. "Yes, Jim, I feel much better. My compliments to the doctor who took care of me. He did a great job."

"Yes, he did," agreed the voice. "Your vital signs look excellent."

"How does the project go?"

The fake Kirk hesitated before he responded, and Carol tried to keep a cheerful disposition while she waited and ate.

"Not so well," said the voice. "There have been some complications with the initial wave. We'd like to do another discharge."

And wipe out how many more planets? Carol thought briefly. She purged that thought from her mind and concentrated on how delicious the food tasted, even if it came from a replicator.

"Whatever you say," she answered with her mouth full. "I'm always ready to go to my lab."

"There's just one thing," said this Jim Kirk, who suddenly didn't sound as confident as before. "You'll see us, but we still can't come into close contact with you. It's not safe."

How interesting, thought Marcus. *For whom isn't it safe?* she wanted to ask. Instead she concentrated on a problematic equation for the Genesis matrix, so they would think she was working.

"No kisses or fooling around for a few days," he added.

Carol tried not to let her stomach disgorge all the food she had just gulped down, and she forced a laugh. "I just want to see some people—I'm tired of being cooped up in here."

"Of course, my darling," he answered, sounding chipper again. "Sorry, but it was necessary. You were very sick. And we wouldn't want a relapse, would we?"

"No, you took good care of me," answered Carol, injecting a note of truth into the conversation. There was a hint of apology in Kirk's words, as if they were responsible for getting her sick . . . by accident.

"Anyway, too much kissing isn't good for anyone," she said offhandedly.

Suddenly her bedroom door clicked, then it creaked open a few centimeters. Carol polished off another couple of bites, wiped her mouth with her napkin, then rose to her feet. She walked briskly out the door, anxious to see what was out there with sober eyes.

The first thing she noticed was the darkness and the outdoor breeze, damp and sulfurous smelling. She had never noticed that smell before. Her island might be out there—or a facsimile of it— but all she could really see were a few dark shapes outlined by a canopy of stars. It looked like every star in the universe was out; she had never seen such a vivid night sky before. On the other hand, she seemed to be on a world bereft of life or light.

"We're going to be staying on Regula I from now on," said a cocky voice. She turned to see the fake Kirk standing about twenty meters away. A pang of love drove deep into her heart, and she was overwhelmed by all her old feelings for the dashing young officer. For a moment, she was certain that she had to be mistaken. Surely, Jim was real!

Then Carol looked at the thread around her finger, and her memory returned. The Kirk in front of her grew a bit indistinct to her eyes, and she instantly turned her mind to neutral thoughts.

"Is David on the station?" she asked.

"Yes."

"Then it's all right with me if we stay there." She smiled wistfully. "I've spent plenty of nights there, I can tell you."

"That's good," said Kirk with relief.

"What went wrong with the project?" Marcus asked innocently. "The last I heard, it was going better than the simulations."

"So it was." He turned away from her and looked at the brilliant starscape, his face covered in shadows. "The transformation was incomplete on some of the targets. There was interference—a kind of phase-shifting. But we've isolated it, and we need your help to make the carrier wave immune to it. We thought we would try again, in a different trajectory."

"I'd like to see your scans, the raw data," replied Marcus, feigning concern.

"Patience, my darling, we have time to fix it." The fake Kirk opened an old-fashioned communicator and spoke with his familiar clipped tones. "Kirk to Marcus. Beam us up, David."

Carol Marcus tried to maintain a benign smile on her face as her molecules were rearranged and then whisked off to a place that hadn't existed for ninety years.

Data stood in a dismal forest, surrounded by towering trees, the sunlight obscured by layers of thick, hanging moss. The android checked his tricorder, then gazed at the trees. Very deliberately, he took a stride forward. At once, clouds of moss came fluttering out of the treetops, bombarding him with fluffy gray tufts. In a few seconds, the moss draped over him like an old ragged overcoat, but it slipped off at his slightest touch.

"Interesting," Data said aloud, recording his voice on his tricorder. "Apparently they are alerted to the presence of prey by vibrations." Even more clumps of moss fluttered down, and he watched them fall like filthy snow. "They are also alerted by sound. Even though I can attract the moss creatures, they do not recognize me as a host animal."

Stepping lightly, Data walked a bit farther into the woods, coming upon a black, soupy swamp. There he found several moss creatures being dragged through the mire on the backs of ugly amphibians. The slimy white animals were about two meters long and looked like giant newts.

Data followed them for a bit, plodding through the muck and recording his log: "I have also observed the moss creatures feeding upon mobile amphibians. These would seem to be their preferred host species, as they were programmed into the Genesis matrix to be abundant."

Suddenly, his tricorder beeped, alerting the android to a preset condition. He stopped, standing chest-high in filth, and checked the readouts. To his surprise, he was picking up a huge group of humanoids—tens of thousands of them—moving in his direction. Since he had programmed the tricorder to alert him to the presence of survivors, Data turned and sloshed off in that direction.

A few minutes later, he strode out of the swamp and was once again slogging through thickets and thorn bushes. There was no doubt that the huge crowd of humanoids was headed in his direction, almost as if they, too, were following a tricorder.

He looked forward to meeting more survivors and finding out how they had fared in this bizarre new world. At last he saw a wall of blue-skinned figures, tromping through the woods. They were unusually quiet for humanoids—he heard breathing, but no talking. Mixed in among them were a few humans and other species, but the vast majority were Bolians. Data quickened his step, and so did they, until he was almost on top of them.

At that moment, it was too late. He didn't see the moss draped all over their backs, growing into their ears, noses, and mouths until they were on top of him. Although Data was as strong as fifty humanoids, he was surrounded by thousands of them, all crawling over the others to get to him. They beat and ripped at the android—with bare hands, knives, or whatever tools they had. Some sunk their teeth into his body in a frenzy of destruction.

With great struggle, Data just barely managed to stay on his feet. Five beefy Bolians had a hold of each limb, while a wild-eyed human bounded over the others, flattening them. With disappointment, he recognized the female with the auburn hair and thick muscles, although her vine-covered face and bloodshot eyes were barely recognizable.

"Mission Specialist Dolores Linton!" he snapped. "Attention!"

Dolores twitched for a moment and stared at him, while moss curled around her head and entered her ears, plugging them tightly. Opening her mouth wide, showing fungus growing over her teeth and gums, she lunged viciously at the android's face.

eleven

"The moss creatures are able to control their hosts' mobility . . . and drive them to attack," said Data into his tricorder, speaking until the device was ripped from his hand by one of the thousands of mindless Bolians who were trying to tear him apart.

Dolores Linton was gnawing at his face, but he was able to hold her at bay; still the others kept coming in their mindless attack. Fortunately, the android had been prepared for this exigency. With a superhuman effort, he wrenched an arm free from the clutching Bolians and drew his phaser pistol, which he had modified. As soon as he pressed the trigger, the weapon emitted a stun field instead of a single beam, and the attackers closest to him collapsed to the ground, unconscious. He caught Dolores Linton as she went down, then he retrieved his tricorder.

Outside the stun field, about ten meters away, the infected Bolians kept coming; but Data finally had room to take a leap. With Dolores Linton and a pile of moss in his arms, the android bounded upward and sailed in a mighty arc over the advancing horde.

He barely missed landing on two of the Bolians, and the others shifted direction to chase him. Carrying Dolores as if she were a large pillow, Data dashed between the disorganized humanoids and the trees, moving much faster than they could. Although the possessed Bolians were formidable in numbers, individually they were slow to react. Jumping and leaping through the forest, Data was able to get far away from the mindless throng.

As soon as he was able to find a clearing, he laid Dolores on the ground and began ripping the moss from her ears, nose, and other orifices. Pulling thorns and suckers from her skin, he detached the moss from her back and cleared away all of it that he could see. Data was concerned that the sudden separation from the parasite might harm her, and that she would become ill from fungal infection, but he wasn't going to leave her in this condition.

As soon as he cleared her trachea, she gasped and with difficulty began to breathe. "Please wake up," he said, gently shaking her, but she refused to comply.

He held her tightly with one hand. With his other hand, he tapped his combadge, sending a signal to the waiting shuttlecraft orbiting the planet. A simple signal was the best communication he could manage, but it worked. The two of them immediately disappeared in the blazing swirl of a transporter beam.

Mot sat perched on the top of the sanctuary, not feeling too confident about the makeshift scaffolding that supported him. The tiled dome was still a slippery slope, although enough vines were creeping upward from the ground that he could probably catch hold of one if he slipped. What he wouldn't give for a level balcony and a folding chair, thought Mot, as he gingerly shifted his weight.

Using the sanctuaries as shelters had been a good idea, Mot decided, but using the sanctuaries as forts against the demons outside wasn't such a good idea. The sanctuaries weren't built securely, and they had no good vantage points. The survivors finally had to smash out the skylight and use a ladder to climb out onto the roof. Then two house painters had built the scaffolding for him.

As usual, Mot felt indebted to be the first one to try the new watchtower, because of his limited experience on the *Enterprise.* "I'm a barber, not a security officer," he muttered to himself, but in truth he didn't resist.

Maybe, he thought glumly, *I'm trying to escape responsibility by always being the first one to volunteer to go outside.* It was getting rank inside the sanctuary, both in odor and in civil discourse. There were constant arguments, complaints, and recriminations, especially against Starfleet.

The survivors couldn't say that Starfleet had sold them a bill of goods, exactly. It had all happened so fast—the warning, the panic, then the destruction—that they hadn't had time to consider what they getting themselves into. The Federation had done what they said they would do, which was save lives, with no thought as to what would happen afterward. Although most of them had lived, their planet had died a grisly death—to be replaced with a cold, smelly mire of horror. Thus far, no one who had entered the gruesome forest had ever returned, and no one had visited them, except for Data. They seemed to be all alone, abandoned on this quagmire of a planet.

And there was nothing Mot could do for his charges. All the good cheer and brave words he had employed in the beginning now sounded deluded. There was no happy spin he could put on the situation, not after what they had seen coming out of the trees.

All in all, he had good reason to hide up here on the roof. It was almost better to face the monsters than forty thousand embittered Bolians. What could he tell them? That Starfleet was on their way, ready to ride to the rescue? No, they knew Starfleet had one android and a handful of technicians on the planet, and that was all they were going to get for the foreseeable future.

When a clump of moss floated down from the trees, Mot lifted his phaser and blasted it into gray confetti. Something moved in the thick brush below him, and he took a long look and decided it was more moss, which he disintegrated with one blast. The barber was getting good at destroying the vile plant, but what good did it do? The moss was all around them, hanging from every branch; it seemed to mock him as it waved in the damp breeze. Only a raging forest fire could get rid of all of it.

Hmmm, Mot thought to himself, a forest fire. That was the way the enemy had fought, with their dastardly Genesis Wave. Why should the survivors show them any mercy? They hadn't shown any to the inhabitants of Myrmidon.

Suddenly a head popped out of the hole behind him, startling Mot. He nearly fell out of his perch, but he managed to grip the ropes and hang on, clattering noisily on the golden tiles.

It was his father, looking very worried. "Son, you had better get in here. Ten of our number have hung themselves in the rectory."

Mot gasped, hoping his father was mistaken; but the elder Bolian was a practical man, not given to exaggeration. Mot sighed and lumbered back into the hole, stuffing the phaser into his father's hand. "Stand guard on top."

"But I . . . but I don't know what to do!" protested the elder.

"Neither do I, but I'm trying anyway," answered the barber. "Just keep watch and let me know if anything unusual happens. A few moss creatures aren't unusual, but thousands would be. If there's any sign of Starfleet—"

"Right," said his father, not sounding very confident about that prospect.

"Where did you say they are? The rectory?"

The old Bolian nodded, and Mot climbed down the ladder to the main attic, which was crowded with surly, frightened people, including his mother. Even children were hanging from the exposed rafters that bolstered the dome. The barber said nothing—what was there to say?—as he brushed past them and descended a flight of stairs, which was packed with people at every step.

Finally he made his way to the rectory, which had been the humble dwelling of the Mother in charge of this Sanctuary. On the first day, she had fled into the woods with the Crown of the First Mother tucked under her arm, never to return. So they had given her little apartment to ten people to share.

Holding his breath, Mot pushed open the door, and it thudded against something heavy. Pushing hard against the door, he managed to squeeze inside, but he wished he hadn't. They hung from the rafters like blue punching bags in a gymnasium.

He bumped into a child at the door, and she peered curiously into the room.

He pushed her back and said quickly, "No, little girl, I don't think you should look at this."

Big black insects hovered around the bodies, and the smell was like the sweat and waste in the rest of the building, but with a sickly sweet smell added in.

"Are we going to eat them?" asked the little girl. "My mother says that when we run out of food, we'll have to eat each other."

"No," muttered Mot through clenched teeth. "Nobody will be eaten."

"What are we going to do about this?" cried another voice. The outer hallway quickly filled with grumbling.

Mot squeezed out of the room and closed the door behind him. "We're going to cut them down, then vaporize them."

"After that?" snapped his interrogator. "If you don't *do* something, more of us are going to choose the path of no suffering."

Mot frowned and looked at the closed door. "I don't know if strangling to death is a 'path of no suffering.' "

"What *are* we going to do?" shouted someone else, and a sea of angry countrymen pressed toward him.

Mot stammered, trying to find some words that would mollify

them. "I . . . I have a plan to kill all the monsters . . . and clear the forest."

"What?"

"How?"

"We're going to burn it down!" vowed Mot, righteousness surging in his veins. "I don't know what we're going to use for fuel, or how well it burns, but I'm tired of that ugly forest and the foul beasts within it!"

"Right! Burn it!" bellowed the man who had interrogated him.

Soon everyone took up the chant, and the dome reverberated with the cry of "Burn it down! Burn it down!"

People began running around like children on a hunt for treats, and Mot soon realized they were looking for articles that would burn. Rags, oil, perfume, trash—it was suddenly a monstrous scavenger hunt.

The barber recoiled, a bit startled from the frenzy he had unleashed. His mouth dropped open as he realized that they were going to carry out his vengeful idea right now, without any further discussion.

"Wait a minute! Just a minute!" he shouted, waving his hands in the air. But no one was listening to him now.

A weeping woman stuck a large knife in his hands and said, "Can you cut them down?"

Mot gulped, realizing that he had lost control of the situation, even as he had finally given the distraught survivors a reason to live.

"Cut them down," begged the woman, her hands wrapping around his hands, encircling the knife handle.

He nodded solemnly. "Yes."

It was almost with relief that he sought the company of the dead inside the rectory. In truth, Mot envied them. They were the only ones not making demands, not girding for revenge, not eaten with fear and doubt. They were the only ones at peace.

However, they were also defeated—failures, nothing but unnamed casualties of war. Maybe they could have been saved if he had just been stronger, or wiser. The barber shook his head miserably; he felt like a failure, too.

The woman ducked her head into the door, looking distraught. "There are no stools—they've taken all the furniture outside!"

"Stay here," ordered Mot. "I'll get the phaser."

He stepped back into the hallway and climbed the stairs to the attic, which was now empty and completely devoid of furniture. His father was descending the ladder from the roof.

"Son!" he called with relief. "I was just coming to get you! What are they doing? They're dragging furniture, clothing, everything they own outside! And the moss creatures are active."

"I need the phaser," said Mot glumly. "Go on back up and keep watch. They're starting a fire in the woods—let's hope they start it far away from the building."

"A fire? Are you sure that's wise?"

"I'm not sure of anything anymore." Once again, Mot descended the stairs, which were also clear for the first time since the wave struck. He returned to the rectory to find nothing changed, except that the woman who had given him the knife was sitting in the corner, weeping softly.

"Which one is yours?" asked Mot, staring numbly at the suspended corpses.

"That one," she rasped, pointing a trembling finger at a large male.

"I'm just going to vaporize them here," said Mot, "with your permission."

"The words?" she said hopefully, twisting her hands together. "Who will say the words?"

"I don't know the proper chants," said Mot. "If the Mother had returned to us . . . but she hasn't."

Seeing her flooded eyes, he took a deep breath and plowed

onward. "Let us say this about these brothers and sisters who now swim in the Vein of Mystery: they were spared suffering. They died with their minds calm."

The woman wept even louder, and Mot checked his phaser. Starting with her loved one, he vaporized the hanging bodies, until there was nothing left in the room but a sickly smelling fog, and the buzzing insects.

His shoulders hunched in dejection, the barber climbed the stairs and then the ladder, to join his father on the roof of the dome.

It was bedlam all around the building, with numerous groups try-ing to start fires, some succeeding, most failing. A few were way too close to the building, and others were so far away that Mot feared for their safety. All of them made a great deal of noise, whooping and hollering. There was something so primal and satisfying about starting a fire that he couldn't resent their elation. Fire represented warmth, relief, and sovereignty over their environment.

Smoke drifted upward, polluting the haze. He saw two moss crea-tures stumbling through the underbrush, already on fire. They burned like walking torches. Where the flames were spreading, the underbrush shook with the movement of unseen animals trying to escape.

"What is happening to us?" his father asked. "Now we're the destroyers."

"As in most wars," Mot said, miserably, "we have sunk to the level of our enemy."

They continued to watch the smoke curl upward through the moss-covered boughs, while flames consumed the underbrush and licked at the tree trunks.

Data held Dolores Linton's body against his shoulder. She was coughing and gagging, and she had about as much control over her bodily functions as a baby. But she was still alive, against considerable odds. Undoubtedly, a doctor in a fully equipped sickbay would be able to do much more for her, but Data had at least nursed her through the initial stages of her withdrawal from the parasite and its deadly euphoria.

Without warning, she groaned, followed by rasping words. "Where am I? And why are you carrying me like a sack of potatoes?"

He let her down gently into a seat on the Romulan shuttlecraft. "You are coherent."

"No, not really," she murmured, wiping her mouth. "I feel like I ate a compost heap."

Data motioned to a few sprigs of moss he had saved in a sample bag. "You were covered by a moss creature. They are cryptogamic parasites, and they use a symbiotic fungus as well as telepathy to control the host organism—"

"That's enough," grumbled Dolores, grabbing her stomach. "Are you saying . . . I was a host organism? To a bunch of moss?"

"I am afraid so," said Data. "Humanoids are very susceptible to their powers. You do not recall falling prey to them?"

She rubbed her head. "Oh, I remember walking in the woods . . . it was getting dark, and I was trying to keep everyone together. The moss fell out of the trees. Was Geordi there?"

"No, but perhaps a facsimile of him appeared to you."

"Is Geordi all right?" she asked with concern.

"By now, he is aboard the *Enterprise*, along with Admiral Nechayev," answered Data, checking his instrument panel. "That is odd—the forest on the surface of the planet is burning in several regions."

"Because of volcanoes?" Dolores asked, rubbing her neck. Her fingers gingerly touched the sucker and thorn scabs where the creature had attached itself.

"No, these fires appear to be spontaneous, close to several shelters." The android peered curiously at his readouts. "The pattern of the fires is odd, unless they were set deliberately."

"By these moss creatures you talk about?"

"No, they have no reason to set the forest on fire, since it has been grown to their specifications. In fact, they have the most to lose, since they could not outrun a moderately moving blaze. I am most concerned about the flammable gases extant on the planet, such as methane, hydrogen, and methyl formate. Those swamps may be highly flammable. We should return to the surface."

Dolores sat up wearily. "Before I see other people . . . is there any-place on the vessel for a girl to freshen up?"

Data pointed to the rear. "Yes, there is a fully equipped 'fresher, plus clothes are available from the replicator. This Romulan shut-tlecraft, *Raptor*-class, is quite well appointed, and it is eleven per-cent faster than our fastest shuttlecraft."

"But we're not going anywhere, are we?" asked Dolores, rising unsteadily to her feet.

"No. My orders are to remain here and assist the survivors until I am relieved. Besides, it is uncertain that we could leave the planet's atmosphere without being destroyed. This craft is not equipped with phase-shifting."

Dolores grimaced as she stretched her back. "Yeah, but the planet's got hundreds of interphase generators lying around."

"That is true," allowed Data with a cock of his head. He filed that observation away for later use. Dolores Linton was one of the most practical humans he had ever met.

The geologist shuffled off, then she stopped and looked back at Data with a grateful smile. "Thanks for saving me. All those other people with me—"

"I have only the resources you see here," answered Data, motion-ing around the gaudy but cramped shuttlecraft. "We will have to hope the infected survivors will be able to live until help arrives. I believe the moss creatures will want them for their mobility . . . if they hope to avoid the fires."

Dolores shivered and pulled her filthy, ripped jacket around her body as she stared at the mottled planet taking up most of the main viewport. In a quavering voice, she asked, "What did we do to this place?"

"It was not us," answered Data. "It was a species who used our technology as they use everything else—without thought."

"Humans were once like that," murmured Dolores.

"Yes, I have often wondered what change occurred in your history to set you upon a different course," said the android with honest curiosity.

"We had to hit bottom—the last big war." Touching the scars on her neck, Dolores shuffled to the aft compartment.

"Our enemy has not hit bottom," said Data to himself.

Behaving like her personal valet, Commander Jagron carefully removed the heeled boots worn by his intelligence officer, Lieutenant Petroliv. Bending over like a toady, he massaged the statuesque Romulan's feet, until she lifted a foot and kicked him onto his back. Jagron rose quickly, trying to maintain some of his dignity, but it was difficult when he was so hungry for his lover. It had been days since they had been able to escape to his quarters.

"My Lady, I haven't cleaned your uniform yet," he said apologetically.

Petroliv looked at him with pity and held out her arms. "You may remove it now."

With extreme care and tenderness, he lovingly undid every button on her intricate uniform, allowing himself to get close enough to smell her astringent odor. Petroliv kept herself very clean.

She sighed with impatience as he took his time. "I need that sonic shower. I've had a difficult day."

"I know." Jagron gave her a sympathetic bow. "Before we departed, did you check the bomb you planted on their bridge?"

"Yes!" she snapped at him. "Unlike *some* on your staff, I follow through on my projects. The device is still responding to signal, and its miniature phase-shifting is working well."

"I worried that the android might detect it," said the commander, "but he is gone now." With trembling hands, he slid one of her sleeves down her bare arm and over her wrist, and he watched her fine black hairs rise to the cool air of his quarters.

Jagron ran his hand over her arm, and she slapped it sharply. "Are you getting familiar with me, Servant?"

"No, Mistress," he responded, giving her a respectful bow. The commander was careful not to touch the back of his hand where it stung.

"Just remember who runs this ship," said Petroliv, eyeing him disdainfully.

"I tremble at your command." Jagron dropped to his knees and prostrated himself before the haughty woman, who towered over him, half undressed. "I accept your punishment. I am unworthy."

"I know," she answered with a sneer. "Don't worry, you will still become the youngest Senator in the Star Empire. Just make sure you obey me."

twelve

Protus was an oblong asteroid that looked like a burnt potato that had started to sprout. Its appearance belied its enormous size—it was a planetoid with the lazy orbit of a comet. As the *HoS* drew closer, Leah Brahms could see that what looked like sprouts were in reality drill sites, huge light poles, communication arrays, solar collectors, and docking bays. The darkest spots were actually tunnels with monorails and conduits running into the depths of the gigantic asteroid. Dilithium freighters scooted back and forth in a monotonous pattern.

"Things look normal here," said Leah.

Beside her, Maltz scowled. "Yes, they are groveling for money as usual. The mining companies are mercenaries, and so are the freelancers. They'll sell to anyone with enough latinum. The Federation is supposed to be in charge here, but this colony predates the Federation—and the traders know how to get around their restrictions. On Hakon, we had traders who bought dilithium legally from Protus and sold it illegally to anyone. They would claim it was for domestic use, or for approved customers, but it was not."

"Why, Maltz, I'm shocked," Leah said with a smile.

"I wasn't responsible," the old Klingon protested. Then his shoulders slumped, and his leathery face took on a few more wrinkles. "But I turned my back on what was happening. I let the documents go through my office and took the fees. This is what I was reduced to—a money-grubbing civil servant."

"Have you ever been to Protus before?" asked Brahms.

"No," answered Maltz, "but I have heard they do not like people coming here unless they have business. We should have a reasonable story." He grinned slyly. "Let us say we want to buy dilithium for the Cardassians, who are not approved but need it badly. With Hakon destroyed and our usual sources gone, we were forced to come here directly."

"Then why do we need to ask about Lomar?" Brahms queried.

"We want to use Lomar as a secret dilithium refining station. We need a planet that's out of the way but near here." Maltz beamed with delight at his own cleverness. "I am almost as devious as a human."

"If you say so," answered Leah. "Helm, contact their operations and request permission to dock."

"Yes, sir."

A moment later, the young officer reported, "They wish to know our business."

Leah looked at Maltz and shrugged. "We're dilithium buyers. We normally go to Hakon, but it doesn't exist anymore."

The officer relayed the message, then listened intently to his earpiece. "We have been cleared to dock—bay seventeen."

The captain and her first officer watched with interest as their helmsman piloted the Klingon cruiser between two sparkling metal gantries that extended a kilometer from the dark asteroid. A sophisticated system of blinking lights guided them into a force-field bumper, and giant clamps emerged from the structure to secure the ship. A moment later, a giant tube snaked outward and connected to their main hatch.

"You and I should go, Captain," said Maltz, "plus some security."

"Is the security really necessary?" asked Brahms.

"We are Klingons in Federation space," Maltz reminded her. "Besides, I don't trust these people."

Leah nodded. "Very well."

There were five of them waiting to disembark when the main hatch opened. Leah led the way into the giant tube, which functioned as a gangplank, and she saw a tow rope moving at a slow speed over her head. She grabbed the rope, as did the four Klingons, and they were soon moving weightlessly down the length of the tube.

In due time, they reached the end of the gangplank, which opened onto a monorail car with artificial gravity. With relief, Leah took a seat in the sleek conveyance, as did her entourage. Soon they were hurtling along a dark tunnel into the bowels of the giant asteroid. Every so often, they caught a glimpse of mining operations.

The Klingons looked a bit out of place riding in such luxury, but Leah enjoyed it. This was the first time since losing her husband and coworkers and fleeing from the Genesis Wave that she felt relaxed. It wasn't peace exactly, but it was rest. Leah sat quietly, turning off her mind and letting the monorail do the work.

With a shudder, the conveyance came to a stop, jarring her from a light sleep. The Klingons rose to their feet, looking anxious about being so deep inside this Federation rock, and Maltz motioned them to the door. "Look lively," he growled. "Remember, we are Klingons. Honor with discipline."

They all nodded, except for Gradok, the hulking weapons master. He grinned. "Do they have ale here?"

"I hope so," said Maltz, "or we're going to smash the place up." His fellows grunted their approval at that sentiment.

Leah shook her head, thinking that she couldn't be in safer company, or more dangerous company. But they hadn't come to Protus to have fun—they had come here to find out about Lomar. Anything else that happened was immaterial.

She led the way off the monorail into a bustling underground city. The high ceilings gave her the impression that this was a hollowed-out mine converted to public use. Much to the delight of her entourage, there were bars, taverns, and restaurants everywhere, as well as storefront offices with signs proclaiming, PUREST DILITHIUM, BEST PRICES. And CURRENCY BROKER—PRECIOUS METALS ACCEPTED. Plus the ubiquitous, MINERS WANTED. INQUIRE WITHIN.

The low gravity inside the asteroid gave her step a definite bounce, but it also reminded Leah of her lab back on Seran-T-One. She tried to shake her melancholy, but it was difficult to see this happy, humming city when her own world had been reduced to a foul swamp. She tried to concentrate on their fact-gathering mission, but they weren't exactly inconspicuous. Although there were representatives of numerous races among the inhabitants, there were no other Klingons. People glanced suspiciously at them and gave them a wide berth as they strode through the underground complex.

"These people act like they've never seen a Klingon," muttered Gradok, casting an appraising eye at a Bajoran female, who hurried away.

"We're a long way from Klingon space," answered Leah.

"How well I know that," replied Maltz. "I've lived in this region for ten long years—never saw another Klingon myself."

Leah looked at him with newfound sympathy. "That must have been difficult."

He shook his head. "No. Being imprisoned on my own ship ninety years ago—*that* was difficult. Ever since then, being an outcast has been my life. It came easily."

"Can you ever redeem yourself?" asked Gradok.

Maltz nodded forcefully. "I will redeem myself when I wash my hands in the blood of Carol Marcus."

"We have to find her first," said Leah, trying to keep their minds on the task at hand. "What's that?"

She pointed into the distance, where a golden fountain was shooting a beautiful plume high into the air, almost to the roof of the great cavern. Leah altered course to head toward the fountain, and as they drew closer, she saw it wasn't water but golden glitter shooting upward. Force fields or magnetic fields must have controlled the golden flow, because it rippled back into a pool of gold in a varying array of patterns. Leah felt like she had never seen anything more beautiful in her entire life, and she was drawn to the fountain as if to a magnet.

"Isn't it lovely?" Leah said breathily, staring at the massive piece of art.

"If it were ale, that would be lovely," Maltz said to the appreciative laughter of his fellows.

"They're flecks of gold-pressed latinum," explained a voice behind her. "Ostentatious, but it shows how rich we are."

All five of them turned around to see a short, chubby human dressed in gaudy plaids that would do a Tellarite proud. He held his hand out to Leah and said, "Welcome to Protus. I'm the chief administrator, Colin Craycroft."

"Hello," she answered, "I'm Captain Leah Brahms, of the *HoS*. We just got in—"

He chuckled and held up his hand. "Oh, I know that. Word came down that a Klingon ship had docked, and I frankly couldn't believe it. And now you tell me that *you're* the captain?"

"You have a problem with that?" grumbled Maltz, eyeing the smaller man ominously.

"Oh, by no means, no," Craycroft answered swiftly. "I take it . . . you're not part of the Klingon fleet?"

"No, we're independent traders," answered Leah, feeling funny about lying. But they needed information, and if they could get more information by pretending to be dilithium traders, then so be it.

"This is my first officer, Commander Maltz," she said, giving her comrade a field promotion. She went on to introduce Gradok and the rest of them, priding herself on having finally learned all their names.

"You're a long way from home," observed Craycroft.

"We were on Hakon and barely escaped when it was destroyed," Brahms answered, injecting a bit of truth into their story.

The administrator shook his head and clucked his tongue. "Yes, terrible tragedy that. So many planets gone—I hear Earth is next."

"I think Earth still has a few days left," answered Brahms, "although not many. Maybe someone can do something."

"We're lucky it passed us by," Craycroft said with a shiver. He glanced again at the quartet of strapping Klingons. "I don't suppose any of you would like to work as miners for a few weeks? The pay is excellent."

"Work in a hole in the ground? That is not the life for a warrior." Maltz rubbed his lips and looked around. "Do we have to stand out here and talk?"

The little man smiled. "Of course, you must be thirsty and hungry after your narrow escape. Let me introduce you to my favorite place, the Pink Slipper."

Gradok grimaced. "I'm not sure I want to drink in a place called 'The Pink Slipper.'"

"They have fifty different types of ale," answered Craycroft.

"Why didn't you say so!" exclaimed Maltz, wrapping his arm around the little man's shoulders. "Where is it?"

"Nearby." The administrator led them around the fountain and across the plaza toward a large establishment that beckoned with the sounds of laughter and music. Catching sight of the tavern, Maltz said warily, "Maybe we should check it out, Captain?"

"Go ahead," she answered. The Klingons surged ahead, leaving Leah Brahms and Colin Craycroft to bring up the rear.

The little man gazed at her. "You must be quite a remarkable woman to lead a band of Klingons."

"They're a good crew," she answered, "and people don't usually try to cheat us."

He chuckled. "No, I wouldn't think so. I don't believe I've ever heard of Klingons who were dilithium traders."

Leah said nothing in response to that, and they strolled into a large but dimly lit tavern with several gaming tables, dining tables, and an old-fashioned bar. But the main attraction seemed to be scantily clad men and women swinging on trapezes suspended from the high ceiling. Seeing the performers' footwear, Leah knew where the Pink Slipper got its name. Although their acrobatics were quite tame, the novelty of having these artists flying overhead was apparently enough to fill the place.

Maltz and the other three Klingons had already commandeered the bar, shoving the other customers aside. Leah began to wonder whether bringing all of them along had really been a good idea, but they were here now. The sooner they got out, she decided, the better.

Bluntly she asked Craycroft, "Have you ever heard of a planet called Lomar?"

He gazed at her thoughtfully. "I believe I've heard of it, but I can't recall any details. Is it near here?"

"Not too far, only a light-year away. I thought you might know something about it."

"There can't be any mining there," said the administrator, "or I'd know about it."

"Maybe some freelance miners know the place," Leah said hopefully.

Now Craycroft looked curious. "Why? Are there precious metals there? Fuel crystals?"

Leah shook her head, thinking this was pointless. She meant to grill *him* about the place, not the other way around. With Craycroft in tow, she wandered toward her crew, who were laughing loudly and hoisting mugs. By the time she got to the bar, Maltz had already drained his first mug and was calling for a second.

She rose on her tiptoes and whispered in his ear, "Go easy there—we're here on business."

"I know. I'm just trying to fit in." He pounded a beefy fist on the table. "You! Barkeep!"

Gradok suddenly leaped high, swiping giant hands in the air, and Leah realized that he was trying to snag one of the trapeze artists as she flew past.

"Gradok!" she snapped. "Honor with discipline."

The weapons master looked dumbly at her, then his craggy face broke into a smile. "Sorry, Captain. It's been a long time since we were in port."

"I know, but we've got business." Leah glared pointedly at him.

"Right." Loudly he bellowed, "Does anybody here know anything about Lomar?"

Leah cringed, thinking there was a reason why Klingons didn't make very good diplomats, or spies. The tavern suddenly grew quiet, and the only noise was the whooshing of the trapezes over their heads. After a few moments of this uncomfortable silence, the conversation and gaming began again.

From the shadows crept a bent old man—a Tiburonian, judging from his giant, elephantine ears. He shuffled up to Gradok, barely coming up to the Klingon's chin, although he must have been taller in his youth. "You want to know about Lomar?" he asked in a gravelly voice.

Leah inserted herself into the conversation. "Yes, we do," she answered. Unless someone demanded to know why they were curious about Lomar, she wasn't going to use their cover story.

The grizzled Tiburonian licked his thick lips. "I don't suppose you could give an old miner a little drink."

"Gladly!" exclaimed Maltz, shoving a fresh mug into his hands. "Have you been there?"

The old miner nodded. "Yeah. Only once." He took a long chug of ale, as if the memory of Lomar made him thirsty . . . and afraid.

"What's your name?" asked Leah, trying to cut the tension between them.

"Krussel," he answered hoarsely.

"Why did you only go to Lomar once?"

He stared at her with haunted black eyes. "Because that's a bad place."

"What do you mean?"

"I mean, most people who go there . . . never come back." Krussel took another long swig, and he set the mug on the bar with a trembling hand. "More, please."

"A man after my own heart!" Maltz bellowed, slapping the old miner on the back and nearly knocking him over. "Barkeep, two more here!"

Leah rubbed her eyes, hoping they had enough latinum to pay for all of this. She also noticed that Mr. Craycroft had not gone away; instead he was lurking behind her, trying to be inconspicuous while he eavesdropped on the conversation.

"What's so dangerous on Lomar?" she asked.

"Evil, ugly place. Nothing of worth there," answered Krussel. He lowered his voice to add, "There are carniverous plants on Lomar."

Maltz laughed heartily. "A true warrior is not afraid of any plant."

"Then you're a fool," said the old miner.

Before Leah could blink, Maltz had grabbed the Tiburonian by the collar and lifted him off his feet. "Who are you calling a fool?"

"Maltz!" barked Leah. "Put him down—he's trying to help us. Besides, there *are* carniverous plants in the universe."

Delicately, Maltz set Krussel down and brushed off his clothing, but the old miner spent several seconds coughing. "I apologize," said the Klingon. "I got carried away. Here, let me buy you another ale."

"No, no!" The miner tried to escape, but Gradok swiftly grabbed him and held him in place.

"You do not refuse a Klingon when he wants to show you hospitality," the weapons master said sternly.

Sandwiched between and Maltz and Gradok, the old Tiburonian had little choice but to nod helplessly. "Y-yes, another one, please."

The bartender, who had barely had a moment to deal with his other customers, quickly rustled up more mugs of foaming ale. Leah Brahms tried not to roll her eyes and look discouraged, but she felt as if they were getting nowhere . . . but drunk.

She felt a tug on her sleeve, and she turned to see the administrator, Colin Craycroft, who had been all but forgotten in the interrogation. The rotund little man smiled at her. "Why don't you and I go to a private booth and discuss business?"

Leah knew they were already discussing the business she had come here to discuss, but she couldn't say that. Maybe it would be good to get away from her boisterous entourage. With a sigh, she answered, "All right."

She look pointedly at Maltz. "I'll be right back. Behave yourselves."

"Always," he answered with a lopsided grin.

Once again, Leah tried not to roll her eyes. She let Craycroft take her arm and lead her away from the laughter, music, and trapeze artists to the back of the tavern, where it was even darker. Giggles wafted from secluded compartments hidden by red curtains. Suddenly she wished she were back on the *HoS*, plowing blindly ahead. Perhaps this detour had not been such a good idea.

Craycroft nodded to a tall Andorian waiter lurking in the shadows, and a silent communication passed between them. The waiter drew open the red curtain on one of the booths and motioned them inside, then he quickly hurried away.

The booth was uncomfortably intimate, with luxurious lounge chairs and a small antigrav table, which floated in the air and could easily be pushed aside to make more lounging space. As she slid into the compartment, Leah was glad that she had four hulking Klingons outside, willing to protect her, although Colin Craycroft didn't look particularly dangerous.

He folded his hands and smiled pleasantly at her. "How many cubic meters do you want?"

"Pardon me?"

"Dilithium. You did come here to buy dilithium, didn't you?"

Brahms had her lie carefully prepared, but it suddenly seemed pointless to lie when time was so precious. They were already on Protus and couldn't be turned away, so this was no time to mince words. Still she surprised herself when she blurted out, "We don't need any dilithium. I really came here to find out about Lomar."

"Why? The old miner said it had nothing of worth."

"That's not *our* information," Leah answered cryptically.

Craycroft clapped his hands on his thighs. "Well then, why don't we organize an expedition to find out what's there?"

"Um—" Leah tried to think of a good reason to head off this idea. Before she could reply, the curtain parted, and the Andorian waiter appeared with an open bottle of champagne and two fluted glasses.

"This isn't really necessary," Leah said with embarrassment.

"Why not?" asked Craycroft, grabbing the bottle and glasses and doing the pouring himself. With a wave, he dismissed the waiter. "This is champagne . . . from Earth. You'd better enjoy it, because there may not be any more where this came from."

Leah couldn't dispute that grim assessment, so she took the proffered glass and put it to her lips. The fizzy beverage tasted incredibly delicious—tart, fruity, and alive—and she felt herself relaxing as it coursed down her throat. Still there was a feeling of guilt, as they lounged in this opulence while millions died or were left homeless.

"You were saying," said Craycroft, "there is something of value on Lomar?"

Brahms opened her mouth to deny it, but she suddenly felt lightheaded and extremely tired. Her mind tried to form a quick lie, but her mouth betrayed her—speaking slowly and deliberately, she answered, "The Genesis Wave . . . comes from Lomar."

Craycroft peered at her and snapped his fingers. "Rakber, get in here!"

Through a blurred haze, she saw the Andorian waiter stick his head through the curtain. "Yes, boss?"

"I want you to listen," he said. "Her speech is getting slurred, and I don't want to miss anything."

The Andorian slid into the seat beside her and gently took her hand. "Just relax," he said in a deep, soothing voice.

Oh, I'm relaxed, she wanted to say. *I'm about to pass out.* She could see and hear them, but she felt like she wasn't really there—as if her body were floating above them, looking down. She understood everything they said when they spoke directly to her, but their conversation with each other came in fuzzy pieces.

"I . . . gotta . . . go . . ." Leah tried to rise to her feet, but the muscles in her legs refused to work. She tried to shout, but her voice came out a hoarse whisper. "Maltz—"

"Your friends are doing fine," Craycroft assured her. "They're very happy, and they want you to tell me everything you know about the planet named Lomar."

"Lomar . . . source of Genesis Wave . . . maybe."

They waited for her to say more, but she didn't seem to know anything more. Leah felt like a video lens—able to see and hear . . . but unable to react or participate. She had to concentrate to understand what they were saying, and she still got only the gist of it.

"That's all she knows?" Rakber asked in amazement.

"Well, it's something," said Craycroft thoughtfully, "although what it is, I'm not sure. What are the Klingons doing?"

"Drinking," answered the Andorian. "So far, the drug hasn't had any effect on them. Or very little effect."

"See if you can pick a fight with them," said Craycroft. "We need to have them arrested."

The Andorian gave him a sidelong glance. "You don't pay me enough to pick fights with Klingons."

"Go tell them that you saw the two of us leave through the back door," the little man said with a smile. "That should keep them drinking for a while. I'll take her downstairs."

Rakber shook his head doubtfully. "Remind me to ask you for a raise." The dour Andorian slipped out of the booth and through the red curtain.

Craycroft gripped Leah tightly around the shoulders. Although she wanted to scream and slap him, she was unable to do either one. "I'm not really the chief administrator," he said apologetically. "But I'll take you to him, if you cooperate."

He reached behind the couch and pressed a panel. At once, the wall behind her slid open, and the booth began to rotate. The soft cushions dropped away beneath her, and Leah felt herself falling into darkness. This time she screamed involuntarily.

thirteen

Through a hazy fog and blaring music, Maltz thought he heard something troubling—a scream. He looked around the Pink Slipper, but he wasn't able to focus on anything in the dimly lit tavern—not the laughing patrons or the grinning trapeze artists floating overhead. It was all a fuzzy blur.

The old Klingon had been drunk many times in his life, especially the last few years on Hakon, so he knew the feeling well. This wasn't it. With a lunge, he slapped the mug out of Gradok's hand, and it went banging across the bar into a row of bottles, resulting in a loud crash.

"Watch it!" the weapons master bellowed, his words slurred. "Why did you do that?"

"There's something wrong," muttered Maltz. He looked around, blinking to clear his eyes. "Where's the captain?"

Gradok snorted. "Oh, she went off with that popinjay. When it comes to mating, she must prefer smooth-heads. *jIyaj.*"

Maltz looked around more thoroughly, and he spotted the Tiburonian, Krussel, lying at his feet, blissfully passed out. Their two younger comrades, Kurton and Burka, were leaning over the bar, semiconscious.

Angrily, Maltz grabbed Gradok and whirled him around to face his fallen comrades. "Have you ever seen two Klingons get drunk so quickly? Have *you* ever gotten drunk so quickly?"

Gradok gave him a smile that was missing several teeth. "Good ale!"

"No, *bad* ale! Drugged ale." Now he looked around for the bartender, who had suddenly disappeared.

At that moment, a gangly Andorian approached them, an insincere smile plastered to his narrow face. "I bring word about your captain. She has gone off with Mr. Craycroft to see the—"

In a flash, Maltz whipped out his knife and shoved the point under the Andorian's chin, while gripping his antennae with his other hand. "I've never gutted an Andorian before," whispered Maltz. "Are your intestines as blue as your skin?"

"I . . . aghh . . . I can't talk this way," complained the waiter, trembling.

"I bet you can, and speak the truth," hissed Maltz. "What is in these drinks?"

"Regulan ale."

Maltz pressed the knife point home, drawing a drop of blue blood from the Andorian's quivering chin. "I'll tear off your antennae with my bare hands, so help me Kahless. Where is our captain?"

With a trembling finger, the Andorian pointed to the back of the tavern. Gradok removed the knife from his chin and prodded the Andorian's back. "Lead the way. One false move, and it's the last move you'll ever make. Gradok, wake up those two children. Bring the Tiburonian, too."

The big Klingon picked up the remaining mugs of ale and dumped them over the heads of Kurton and Burka, who jumped up sputtering and swinging their fists. "*Qeh!*" he barked, then he grabbed the old Tiburonian and tossed him over his shoulder like a sack of *targ* food.

With the terrified Andorian in the lead, the wary party of Klingons stalked to the back of the tavern. By now, it was very quiet inside the Pink Slipper; the blaring music and gambling tables were stilled, and customers scurried out of their way.

"Watch our backs!" Maltz told the younger Klingons, never taking his eyes or his blade off the Andorian. When they reached the rear of the tavern, they could hear the giggling coming from the curtained booths. Gradok dumped the Tiburonian onto the floor and began throwing open the curtains, eliciting many shrieks and much scrambling for clothes.

"Which one?" snarled Maltz, letting his knife make his point for him.

"This one," said the waiter, pointing to the only booth that had been empty. "There's a secret panel behind the cushions."

Suddenly, there was a commotion and a stampede of footsteps coming from the front of the tavern. "Security!" shouted a deep voice. "Nobody move!"

"Help!" screeched the Andorian. With a quick thrust, Maltz made sure it was the last sound he ever made.

Maltz shoved the body headfirst into the emtpy booth and motioned to his comrades. "Hurry—in here! Grab the Tiburonian! Lay down cover fire!"

Gradok picked up the old miner, while Kurton and Burka drew their disruptors and sent scarlet beams streaking across the tavern. The place erupted in screams and chaos, and trapeze artists tumbled out of the air onto the advancing security guards. That gave the two younger Klingons time to duck into the crowded booth with their comrades. They closed the curtain behind them and waited to fire the moment anyone opened it.

Maltz was busy ripping cushions away from the walls. "If that worm was lying, I'll kill him again!" Finally he uncovered the panel and pressed it without a moment's hesitation.

At once, the plush booth turned into a carnival ride, swirling around and dumping all of them—four Klingons, a sleeping Tiburonian, and a dead Andorian—down a long chute into the darkness.

A wild howl erupted form Maltz's throat, but it was silenced with a thud when he and his comrades landed in a sea of soft cushions. Flickering artificial candlelight barely illuminated a circular chamber; pillows covered the floor, and lewd paintings of debauchery covered the dark stone walls. There was a bar, a viewscreen, the chute they had fallen down, and two doorways, but no sign of Captain Brahms or Colin Craycroft. Both doorways led to rustic passageways carved from the black rock and lit by more flickering lights.

"Get up!" Maltz growled at his men. "Kurton, Burka—cover the chute and the doorways. Gradok, hide that body in the cushions."

The weapons master quickly burrowed through the pillows and cushions to the floor beneath, where he deposited the dead Andorian. Grabbing handfuls of cushions, Gradok wiped the pale-blue blood off his thick chest and his pitted metal sash, then he tossed the stained cushions over the body.

Meanwhile, Maltz went to the viewscreen and pressed buttons until he activated the device. The view on the screen showed the empty trapeze above them, and he pressed more controls until the scene switched to a sweeping view of the central tavern, now lit up. Security officers were clearing out the customers and searching the place, to no avail. They apparently didn't know about the saloon's secret passageways.

Maltz hurriedly tapped his combadge. "First officer to the HoS. Come in, Kurok!" There was no answer. "taHqeq! We are too deep inside this infernal rock to contact the ship."

"We told them to leave at the first sign of trouble," answered Gradok.

"I hope they are able to leave," said Maltz. The old Klingon continued to bang on the controls of the viewscreen, cycling through various other sights until he found a plush bedroom with a woman lying prone on the bed. It was difficult to tell, but it looked like Leah Brahms.

"Which way?" he bellowed, now wishing that he had kept the treacherous Andorian at least partially alive. Maltz drew his disruptor and motioned to his younger comrades. "Burka, Kurton—you take the left-hand passage and look for this room . . . where they hold the captain. If you find her, try to contact us via communicator, and we will do likewise. If we can't communicate, try to make your way back to the ship. If that's impossible, return here. Do not allow yourselves to be captured."

The two young Klingons nodded in acknowledgment and hurried down the assigned passageway. Maltz motioned to the old Tiburonian, who was snoring peacefully, and Gradok heaved a sigh and picked him up.

With a worried frown, Maltz leveled his disruptor and led the way down the right-hand corridor. They hadn't walked far when they heard whining, grinding, and clanging sounds. Ahead of them, it appeared that the corridor widened, but it was hard to tell in the flickering light. Maltz slowed his pace and motioned Gradok against the wall, which was a difficult maneuver for the big Klingon burdened by the unconscious Tiburonian. Cautiously, Maltz made his way toward the rhythmic noises in the distance.

Within a few paces, the corridor expanded into a much larger chamber, with gleaming walls of yellowish crystal, buttressed by shimmering force fields and narrow walkways at different levels. Flashes startled him, and the Klingon dropped into a firing crouch; a moment later, he saw that the flashes were industrial, robot-controlled phasers carving their way through the glittering crystals.

Workers in lightweight environmental suits and hoods manned these weapons and other more primitive tools, like grinders, airhammers, and saws. Most of them wore green suits, but a few of the bosses wore white. Although the walls appeared to glisten like solid facets, Maltz could see that many of the cuttings were waste. Harried miners had to physically chop and grind the rubble in order to find crystals large enough to be saved. These crystals, about the length of a Klingon's hand, were carefully placed in pressurized conduits, which whisked them away. Other workers shoveled the debris left by the process into biofilter bins, where the inert black rock disappeared, to leave only dilithium chips. All of these materials were carried away in conduits.

Portable light stands lit the cavern all too brightly, making Maltz nervous. He slipped back into the shadows of the tunnel and motioned Gradok to go back the way they had come. After a moment, Maltz stopped to listen.

"Are you sure where you're going?" the weapons master asked, dumping the Tiburonian onto the ground.

Maltz shook his head. "Who can tell? Was the captain transported somewhere? There's a busy mine this way, so we have to backtrack. Pick him up."

"Why can't we *wake* him up?" The brutish Klingon reached into his belt and removed a small capsule, which he broke under the old miner's nose. At once, the Tiburonian gasped and waved his arms feebly.

Maltz reached down and pulled Krussel to his feet. "You're all right, be calm. They drugged us in that evil place . . . the Pink Slipper."

"*Me?* I've never been drugged in there before. You must be *very* important." Krussel sniffed the air and looked around the rustic passageway. "Where are we?"

"Near a dilithium mine." Maltz scowled at the bent old miner. "They drugged us, kidnapped our captain, and tried to arrest us. Since they outnumbered us, we fought until we could make an escape."

The Tiburonian trembled. "Oh, dear, what have you gotten me into! Don't you know you'll be sentenced to the *mines?* It will take you twenty years to work off your sentence!"

The grin faded from Gradok's face. "What are you talking about?"

Krussel motioned toward the noise coming from the depths of the artificial cavern. "*Listen* to them—a lot of them are prisoners leased out to the mines. That's where you're going to go! Work makes the time go faster, and you can earn a little money while you're in. But I don't want to go back! You made a big mistake . . . because Colin Craycroft is the *owner* of the Pink Slipper. He's a powerful human around here."

Maltz grunted in anger. "I'll kill him later. First we must find the captain. Back to the pillow room." Pushing the other two ahead of him, the grizzled Klingon stalked down the corridor.

They hadn't walked far when the Tiburonian froze and held out his hands, his big ears twitching. Maltz almost ran over him, but he was able to catch himself. Then he reached out a long arm to catch Gradok.

"What is it?" asked Maltz.

"Voices," whispered the old miner. "Ahead of us, not the way we came."

"Stay here." Maltz motioned both of them to remain while he scouted ahead. It took several moments of stalking through the shadows, but he finally heard the voices, too. They were angry, busy, and officious—security voices. It sounded as if they had found the Andorian's body, which they could have done with a tricorder. If they had tricorders, they would soon investigate the corridors, too. Maltz hurried back down the corridor.

Into his communicator, he whispered, "Maltz to Kurton. Kurton, respond." He waited, but there was no answer, which didn't surprise him. Plunging ahead, he reached Gradok and the Tiburonian. "The authorities are back there. We have to think like humans."

"Oh, do we try to talk our way out of it?" asked Gradok.

"No. We use human subterfuge." Maltz pointed back down the hallway toward the distant sounds of mining. "I know . . . what about those environmental suits the miners wear?"

"They're actually more like cleanroom suits," said Krussel, "to keep the crystal from being contaminated."

"They will disguise us," said the Klingon. "Where can we get some?"

"Off their backs," Gradok answered with a shrug.

"Better yet, from the clothing bins or the locker room," Krussel said, craning his neck to look around the corner. "They should be nearby."

Maltz leveled a jaundiced eye at the old miner. "Are you going to help us get out of here, or are you going to betray us?"

Krussel snorted. "If I'm in your presence, I'm in as much trouble as *you* are. We need a diversion."

Suddenly they heard voices behind them—loud enough for anyone to hear. Maltz reached into his sash and pulled out a tiny chunk of pliable explosive, which he affixed to one of the flickering artificial candles.

"Go ahead of me," he ordered. "Walk slowly, as if you belong in there. Find suits and disguise yourselves, then look for me. Move."

Gradok pushed the old Tiburonian down the corridor, while Maltz backed away from the charge he had rigged. He rounded the corner and stopped at the farthest distance he could go and still see the light fixture, then he aimed his disruptor. The moment the guards appeared, he shot the light with a narrow beam. The guards ducked, but it didn't help them. The explosion blew out a ton of rocks and rumbled through the caverns, filling the passageway with smoke and dust. Lights went out the length of the corridor, plunging it into merciful darkness.

Somehow the explosion ricocheted along the power lines into the main chamber, where several light standards exploded, causing even more panic. There was chaos on the narrow catwalks, and one or two miners fell off their perches as a third of the mine was plunged into darkness. "Cave in! Cave in!" sounded the cries.

Maltz emerged into the larger room to find total confusion, with miners discarding their tools and rushing for the staircases and tur-bolifts. He didn't waste time getting a disguise—he hid in the smoke until a miner passed by, then he jumped out and clubbed him with his disruptor. Maltz dragged his unconscious victim into a shadowy corner and ripped the hood off his head.

He emerged a few moments later, looking like all the other pan-icked miners, except that he carried a Klingon distruptor in his hand. After making sure the security guards were still delayed by the explosion, he crept along the wall, looking for two miners who were not running as fast as the others. He noticed them lurking in the doorway of a small closet—a towering hulk who strained the material of his suit and a bent one who barely filled his out.

He motioned with his disruptor, and they waved back. Soon all three started in the direction of the mad rush. They had to practi-cally carry the old Tiburonian, he was trembling so badly.

"You there!" someone shouted. "If he's injured, get to the emer-gency transporter!"

It took a moment for Maltz to realize that the white-suited boss was talking to them, thinking the Tiburonian was wounded and they were assisting him. "Thank you!" he muttered, turning away. Although the hood completely covered his head and the suit his body, the faceplate was transparent.

The figure in white pointed impatiently, and the trio scurried in the indicated direction. They got into a line with other miners waiting to enter a large tube. At first Maltz was worried that they would be whisked away in some kind of pressurized conduit like the crystals; then he saw two wounded miners enter the tube ahead of them and disappear in the swirl of a transporter beam. It was proba-bly a short-range transporter, he decided, which wisely avoided passing through the dilithium-loaded rock.

While they waited, Maltz tried to ignore the alarmed shouts all around them, thinking that the miners weren't very disciplined. Of course, working underground was conducive to panic, especially when tunnels began mysteriously collapsing and exploding. He had already decided to go down fighting rather than risk being slave labor in this glittering hole.

Nevertheless, he hid his disruptor from view and told Gradok, "Limp. Pretend to be injured."

Finally they reached the tube, where the operator waved all three of them aboard. With relief, the trio stepped upon the transporter platform, only to have their molecules scrambled and reassembled at an unknown destination.

Still groggy, Leah Brahms was hauled rudely to her feet, and she looked longingly at the soft bed she had just left. Then she realized that she didn't know where she was. She blinked at the little man in the plaid jacket who had dragged her to her feet; she knew him, but she couldn't place him. The details of his identity were lost . . . somewhere in the cobwebs of her brain.

"Wake up!" he said urgently, shaking her by the shoulders. "We have to get out of here! The tunnel alarm has been set off."

Leah mumbled something in agreement, but instead she dove back onto the soft bed, curling up with a silky sheet. "No!" shouted Craycroft. "Oh, to hell with you. What do I care if you get arrested? I'll beat you to Lomar."

Suddenly Leah was left alone . . . nobody tugging on her arm, nobody yelling in her ear. Still she could hear the Klaxons and sirens at an indistinct distance, and she knew waking up in a strange bedroom was never good. The guy who had been shaking her was no good either—that stood to reason.

Despite all attempts to go back to sleep, her analytical mind took over, and Leah Brahms slowly accepted the notion that she should be awake and coherent. At least for a while. In her condition, she wanted to reserve the right to go back to sleep.

She rolled over and tried to find the floor with her feet. *Oh, this is* bad, she realized. *Whatever landed me in this state . . . in this place . . . had better be worth it.* There were lewd paintings on the walls, and the room was decorated with mountains of lacy pillows and billowing curtains. The curtains hid only small air vents, not windows. Despite its posh accessories, the bedroom had the feeling of being home-made, like a spare room in someone's basement. Maybe it was the lack of windows that gave it such an eerie quality—it was definitely a hideaway.

The bed lay between two doors at opposite ends of the room; they were solid metal, and both were ajar. Brahms had her choice of exits . . . or of not leaving at all . . . but a vague feeling of urgency propelled her to her feet. She knew she couldn't wait around to answer questions. Swaying unsteadily on her feet, she closed her eyes; when she did, gnarled, grizzled faces floated in her mind's eye.

The Klingons! *My crew.* A rush of memories came flooding back, giving her such a headache that she slumped back onto the bed. That was when she heard loud voices and hurried footsteps near the door to her right.

Flashes of light slashed into the metal door, ripping it apart in a hail of sparks. Two figures collapsed against the metal debris and tumbled into the room. To her horror, Leah witnessed the final sec-onds of life for the young Klingons, Kurton and Burka. They died in a conflagration of crisscrossing beams, and their bodies disappeared in a sizzling red haze.

Leah had no time to do anything but hurriedly pull the covers around her and cower in the bed. Phaser rifles leveled for action, a detail of four security guards burst into the bedroom. They instantly focused their attention and their weapons on her, and she pulled the covers up to her chin.

"Out of the bed!" ordered the one with the most stripes on his sleeve. He pointed his weapon at her head. "Hands up!"

"I am naked!" she pleaded, letting them see only her face. Luckily, Leah had long ago mastered the innocent-but-sexy gamine look, and she had no problem mustering real tears after seeing two of her crew killed. "The *awful* things they did to me . . . the *animals!* You wouldn't believe—"

The hardened guards looked sympathetic but still wary, and she added, "There were *two* more Klingons! They went out the other door. If you hurry, you can catch them!"

The ensign looked back at a subordinate, who was carrying a padd. "That's the report," she said. "*Four* Klingons."

Leah felt for the small hand phaser she kept on her belt. It had been part of her tool kit ever since Gradok had cornered her in the bowels of the ship. She forgot where in her travels she had picked up the phaser, and she hoped it was set on stun.

Doubt left the leader's eyes, and he barked, "Squad, continue pursuit! Keep alert, and use your tricorders. Lady, when we leave, you get dressed and wait here for us. We have questions for you."

Leah relaxed and gave him a warm smile. "Thank you, sir. I look forward to seeing you again . . . soon."

He flashed her a quick grin, then signaled. "Move out!"

Seconds later, the security detail was gone, passing through an unfamiliar door that led to parts unknown. At least they were unknown to Leah. She assumed they were still on Protus, but that was all she knew—although she had a strong feeling that she shouldn't wait around to be questioned. She hoped she hadn't inadvertently sent them after Maltz and Gradok, wherever they were.

Throwing off the covers, Leah rolled out of bed, her head still groggy. She would have to come to her senses on the run, she decided, so she staggered toward the door where her young crewmen had died. After all Leah had witnessed, she ought to be immune to the effects of death, which had chased her over half the quadrant; but she was terribly saddened by the loss of these two. They had been young, eager to follow orders, and dependent upon superiors to use them wisely. It was her idea to come here, and they had probably been trying to rescue her when they died.

Leah had forgotten that humans were often the worst predators.

Then again, Burka and Kurton had gone down fighting—their fellows would say they had achieved honorable deaths. Leah wasn't ready for that yet, because she wasn't done fighting.

Taking a deep breath and getting her wobbly feet under her, she plodded out the door into a narrow tunnel carved from black stone. Dim lights flickered along the length of the winding tunnel, and Leah tried to combat a pounding headache as she walked. Finally she picked up her pace, noting the pits in the wall and the scattered pebbles where the recent phaser battle had left its mark.

She wracked her brain. *What do I remember? What do I know?*

Nothing about this place or how I got here, came the answer. *No matter how hard I try to forget, I remember too much about Seran, Hakon, Myrmidon, and the other planets that have already died.* Leah plunged onward into the gloomy passageway, certain only that she needed to survive and keep moving, just like before.

fourteen

Maltz, Gradok, and the feeble Tiburonian, Krussel, inched toward a huge underground chamber that was outfitted with at least fifty beds, a hundred blinking displays, and two dozen medical workers. Still disguised in green mining suits with hoods, they had been shepherded into this line the instant they stepped off the transporter platform. There was no apparent way to escape from the underground chamber. The corridor went straight from the transporter tube to the trauma center, and it was awash in a sea of blithering humans and their allies, all convinced that they needed medical attention.

There had to be a lot of mining accidents on Protus, thought Maltz, because they were prepared for a large influx of patients. He fought the temptation to fight or run from the close-pressed horde, because the Klingons were outnumbered and stuck inside this subterranean labyrinth. They would have to wait for an opportunity, but they couldn't wait long. Despite hanging back as much as possible, the threesome were being pushed toward the medical workers. Soon they would have to take off their hoods to be examined, revealing their identities.

Think! he ordered himself. *What would a devious human do?*

When he couldn't come up with an idea, he merely looked around. The workers in the center were extremely calm as they dealt with the influx of patients. Did they even know or care what kind of emergency it was? Escape would be much easier, he decided, if the people on this level were in a cowardly panic like the miners below.

With a smile under his disguise, the cagey Klingon bent down to the old Tiburonian. "Krussel, take off your hood and shout as loud as you can that the Genesis Wave is going to hit Protus."

Krussel threw his head back and gasped. "Is that true?"

"Yes," he lied, thinking the old miner was either addle-brained or still drugged. "The collapse in the tunnel was just the beginning."

"Oh, my! I'll tell them." With difficulty, the Tiburonian pulled the hood over his big head and floppy ears. Then he shrieked at the top of his lungs, *"Doom!* Doom is here! The Genesis Wave is headed toward Protus!"

"What? Where! Says who!" bellowed the workers, most of whom were already frightened by the explosion, smoke, and dust below in the mine. Maltz grabbed his confederate, Gradok, and pulled him away from the mob that was starting to collect around the ranting coot.

"The Genesis Wave is going to hit Protus!" the Tiburonian shouted, believing it more thoroughly each time he said it. "That's what's causing the tunnels to collapse!"

Worried cries erupted in the medical center, and Maltz decided that panic was a very good weapon indeed. The combination of the Genesis Wave and collapsing tunnels was an effective rumor on Protus, judging by the reaction. He was sorry that they had to desert the old miner, but escape was crucial.

While most of the people in the corridor surrounded the Tiburonian and bombarded him with questions, the two Klingons plowed against the current of bodies. Maltz was bound for the only visible exit, the transporter tube on which they had arrived. Keeping their hooded heads low, they approached the transporter as two injured miners limped off.

"What's going on down there?" asked the transporter operator, craning his neck to see over the surging mob.

"Word just came down that the Genesis Wave is going to hit us!" answered Maltz, trying to sound like a worried human. He nodded to Gradok, who stepped behind the operator.

"What? Are you kidding me?" the worker exclaimed. "Says who?"

"Look! You can see for yourself." Maltz pointed into the chaos at the door of the medical center. While the human was distracted, Gradok brought a heavy fist crushing down on the back of his head, and Maltz caught the man as he fell.

"Taken ill," said Maltz in case anyone was watching. But no one was. He dragged the human behind the transporter console and propped him up as best he could, while Gradok bent over the controls. The human must be nicely thick-headed, thought the Klingon, because he was still breathing.

"There are many preset destinations," Gradok said with confusion as he studied the complex board. "No time to look up coordinates."

"What destinations are there?" the elder Klingon asked, rising wearily to his feet.

"There they are!" cried an agitated voice. Maltz whirled around to see that the Tiburonian had spotted them and was pointing in their direction. "They can verify it! They're the ones who told me about the wave coming!"

"Pick a place!" Maltz shouted, leaping into the transporter tube.

Gradok punched the board a couple of times, then he jumped into the transporter just as their molecules were collected in a spinning flurry of light.

Once the tingling of the transporter beam had stopped, Maltz warily opened his eyes; he found himself in a sumptuous booth that was decorated with lacy curtains and golden tassels. Gradok peered curiously at him, but neither one of the Klingons could offer a guess as to where they were.

With dread, Maltz pushed open the curtain, and he and Gradok stumbled out of the booth into the middle of a lady's lingerie shop. A fashion show was in progress, and both the models and the customers gasped at the sight of two hooded miners in their midst.

"What is the meaning of this?" demanded an indignant matron, as the models bounced off the stage and rushed for cover. "You're not supposed to be on this level!"

Wide-eyed, Maltz stared at the women. "Everybody, run for your lives! The tunnels are collapsing! The Genesis Wave is headed toward Protus."

That brought even more abrupt gasps from the audience. Maltz considered pulling out his disruptor and trying to destroy the transporter booth, so no one could immediately follow them; but he had created enough havoc already. They had to slip away unnoticed, not draw any more attention.

Gradok was craning his neck, trying to locate the scantily clad females, and Maltz grabbed his collar and barked, "We have to keep moving!"

"Why?" muttered the weapons master with disappointment.

People in the crowd peppered them with questions and demands, but Maltz just shoved his way through them, while keeping a close eye on Gradok. Running, the Klingons quickly outdistanced their pursuers and exited the clothing shop into the busy subterranean mall. Maltz whirled around as they walked, searching for the Pink Slipper, but he didn't recognize any landmarks. Even the golden fountain wasn't in sight—there was no telling where they were in this maze of an underground city.

The old Klingon looked around for signs, easily reading the Federation tongues he had learned during his dipomatic career.

Finally his eyes lit up behind his clear faceplate. "Look! There's a sign for the space docks."

"You want to return to the ship without our captain? Our men?" Gradok gaped at him.

The old Klingon glared at his comrade. "Remember this well, the Blood Oath is more important than any one of us. If the others are worthy, they will find their way back to the ship."

Maltz slapped his comrade on the back of his tight-fitting suit. "But we will do what we can to help them. Perhaps we should continue to spread panic."

The climb was slow and laborious, because Leah Brahms had to stop every meter or so to burn more handholds and footholds with her phaser. Then she wrapped rags around her hands in order to endure the heat of the handholds. In this tedious fashion, she continued to scale the metal slide she had found in the pillow room. She could vaguely remember plunging down this slide to reach the plush chamber below.

It helped that the gravity was light inside the asteroid, so she could make good progress up the metal incline once she got started. Still it was slow having to carve footholds as she went, but it had to be done. If she ever lost her hold on the slippery slope, she'd slide all the way down to the bottom and would have to start again.

Only a hint of light trickled down from above, but it seemed to be getting brighter the higher she climbed. Leah was also relieved that her memory was coming back to her—now she recalled entering that secluded booth in the Pink Slipper. That was really the last thing she remembered clearly, other than drinking champagne, making mindless conversation, and riding down the slide.

With determination and patience, the engineer climbed to the top of the metal incline, where she found a shattered wall with a hole big enough to climb through. She emerged into the same private booth she had visited before, only now it was torn apart. With the pillows and curtains ripped to shreds, she could easily inspect the mechanism of the tilting booth and its attached chute. The gears and springs looked ancient and grimy, and she wondered if the slide was really an old piece of mining equipment, discarded then put to a use for which it was not originally intended.

As she caught her breath, Leah noticed something even more unusual—silence. Earlier, the Pink Slipper had been full of raucous noise and behavior, but now the tavern was eerily quiet. Bright lights illuminated every square centimeter of the place, which gave the garish decor a sickly pallor. She stepped out of the booth and looked around, verifying that the huge chamber was deserted. Several of the gaming and dining tables were overturned, and empty trapezes hung like dead vines from the cathedral ceiling.

Leah strolled through the abandoned playground, which looked phony and tawdry in the glaring light, and she wondered what could have cleared it out so totally. Then she remembered that she had left four Klingons behind, and two of them were dead. Maybe all four of them were dead, she thought with a pang of remorse. They had probably caused a commotion while looking for her.

It's all my fault, she decided gloomily. *I brought them here. All this time, I was worried about their conduct, when my conduct was what endangered the crew and the mission.*

Still distracted, Brahms reached the front door of the Pink Slipper and nearly crashed into it when it didn't open automatically. She pushed on the door, but it refused to budge. Peering out the smoky-glass windows of the tavern, Leah discovered that the door was locked from the outside with a blinking contraption. She was locked in!

When she saw three people run past the tavern in a panic, Leah wondered what was going on. The mall itself seemed to be deserted, or at least in the process of getting cleared out. Gone were all the amiable shoppers and merrymakers, and most of the businesses appeared to have closed their doors.

It was tempting to stay in the relative safety of the empty tavern, but she had to return to her ship . . . and hope she still had a crew. Leah stepped back and aimed her phaser at the window. The beam was already set to melt solids, and she had no problem carving a hole in the window big enough to crawl through. An alarm went off, but it only added to the surreal atmosphere in this part of the subterranean city.

A moment later, Leah was loping through the mall alongside members of the populace. She singled out a woman, who appeared to be a Coridan by her distinctive hairstyle. "Where is everyone going?" asked Leah.

"You haven't heard?" asked the Coridan in amazement. "We're all getting out of here. The tunnels are collapsing, and the Genesis Wave is supposed to hit us any minute!"

"We're not in the path of the Genesis Wave," declared Brahms. Even though she knew that to be true, just the idea panicked her. "Lots of planets are in danger, but not Protus."

"What makes you such an expert?" The woman picked up speed, pointedly running away from Leah.

The engineer stopped jogging and stepped into a recessed alcove, so as not to be run over by the stampede. She pulled out her communicator badge and barked, "Brahms to the bridge of the *HoS*. Come in! Kurok, are you there?"

When there was no response, she scowled and put the device away. It wasn't going to be that easy to get out of here, but she had to keep trying. Studying the signs overhead, Leah saw that most of the riot was headed the same way she was—to the space docks.

As she walked, the underground city looked oddly familiar—like a hundred space stations—yet it was alien and unfamiliar, too. Leah had no idea where she was, so she just had to follow the trickle of frightened citizens.

That trickle became a sluggish throng as they neared the monorail station. She was soon bogged down in the crowd and could do no more than move with the flow, trying to listen and stand on her tiptoes to see. Through the bobbing heads, she got a glimpse of security officers surrounding the monorail track, where a train waited. They were wearing riot gear and gas masks. Not a good sign.

Angry shouts rose over the anxious murmur of the crowd, and she could make out a few phrases: "The monorails are overloaded! Go back. There is no emergency!"

Just as loudly came the responses: "Then why can't we get on board? I've got to get back to my ship! Let us go!"

Like a wave sloshing toward the shore, the crowd pressed forward, and Leah found herself carried along. With a feeling of dread, she turned and tried to fight her way against the tide, but it was futile. Once again, she was sucked into the frenzy. Although this had to be a false alarm, the panic was just as real as it had been on Hakon. Besides, thought Leah, for all she knew, the tunnels really were collapsing—this much chaos didn't happen in a vacuum.

The verbal exchange between the guards and the mob became heated, when suddenly a projectile came lofting over their heads. It landed amid the crowd, and a big plume of red smoke went up, followed by cries of alarm. But the people nearest the red smoke sat calmly on the floor looking blissful. Despite the innocuous effect, the shouts turned to shrieks, and everyone in the crowd tried to run in a different direction. Leah held her breath and kept low, managing to avoid the fumes; still her eyes watered. *Dazzle gas!* She had heard of it, but she never thought she'd ever see any.

Brahms fought the temptation to drop to the floor and curl into a ball. Instead she jumped upon some poor soul's back and tried to peer over the choppy sea of heads. Now the security guards were arguing with each other as well as the rabid crowd, and pushing and shoving broke out. Another gas canister lofted over the crowd, exploding in a burst of colorful smoke, and the screams reached a higher pitch.

It was like the guards were inciting the riot, thought Leah. *What idiots!* Without warning, she was dumped off the broad back she had been climbing, and she barely landed on her feet. Finally the crowd had figured out that they could only escape from the dazzle gas by going in the opposite direction, away from the monorail station. Exhausted and bruised, Leah joined the sluggish flight.

Using her elbows and shoulders, she worked her way over to the wall, looking for an access panel, a ladder, anyplace where she could gain a handhold and pause in this mad flight. She heard a burst of screams as another canister was lobbed into the crowd, raising the panic level. Leah pushed toward her objective; her step quickened when she saw the familiar black and yellow colors of a fire hose box.

Fighting against the press of the mob, she lunged for the handle of the box and gripped it as she flew past. With a click, the door opened, and she swung back on the hinges into the wall. Leah didn't quite get the breath knocked out of her, but it took all her effort to hold on and keep from blacking out.

Finally she was able to squeeze against the wall and use the open door as a shield. It was a good thing she was small. Some of the overzealous guards in their gas masks were fighting their way through the crowd. For what purpose? she wondered. Everything they did just made things worse.

Leah glanced inside the box on the wall and saw a lever beside the coiled fire hose. She had an irrational urge to fight back against the heavy-handed security officers and their dazzle gas. Besides, if she got arrested, maybe she could tell her story to someone in charge. So she grabbed the nozzle of the hose. Her actions did not go unnoticed, and two of the masked security guards veered off from the others and headed in her direction.

Angry over the way she'd been treated—and the way all these people were being treated—Brahms reached inside the box, grabbed the lever, and pulled it down. At once, the recoil from the fire hose slammed her against the wall, but she gripped the nozzle and managed to maintain control of a powerful jet of fire-fighting chemicals. The stream blasted the advancing guards, who slipped to the ground. It also knocked down a few frightened citizens, but they were no worse off than when they were fleeing from the tear gas.

While Leah was watching, she lost track of the guards. One of them jumped to his feet right in front of her and tried to grab the hose from her hands. She fought with all her might to hold on, but he was strong, almost berserk, in his determination. When his partner gripped her wrist, she was helpless to stop them from wrenching the hose from her hands.

"You come with us!" ordered a gruff voice, and she was pinned rudely against the wall.

fifteen

Leah Brahms was certain that she was about to be arrested—or beaten—in the sodden mall deep inside the asteroid named Protus. To her surprise, the two guards who had assaulted her suddenly let her go, and the one with the hose turned it back upon his fellows, several of whom were trying to advance to their position.

"It's *us*, Captain!" barked a voice in her ear.

Leah whirled around to stare at the snaggle-toothed face under the gas mask and hood. "The hose was a brilliant idea!"

"Gradok?" she asked in amazement.

He nodded. "First officer Maltz, too."

She looked at the wiry warrior manning the fire hose, keeping dozens of locals at bay. "Have you seen Kurton and Burka!" he shouted over the din.

"Yes . . . they're dead!"

"How!" roared the Klingon.

"I'll tell you about it later," she answered. "Can't we get out of here?"

"Yes! Follow me." Using the powerful jet as a battering ram,

Maltz surged into the crowd, cutting an impressive path with the water bolt.

When a few phaser beams streaked over their heads, Gradok drew his disruptor and returned fire in deadly fashion. At least three of the guards dropped, and the others were soon in retreat. It seemed as if they didn't want to fire for fear of hitting the onlookers, but Gradok had no such compunction.

They fought their way toward the monorail station until the length of hose ran out. Maltz let it go, and it snaked around violently, whipping a stream of chemical spray into the cascade already pouring down from above.

Disruptors blazing, the Klingons ran toward the closest empty monorail car. Brahms could do little more than try to keep up with them. She realized they were shooting to open a hole in the conveyance. Their bold actions were lost in the general pandemonium, and no one rushed forward to stop them. However, the car began to move.

"Hurry!" yelled Maltz.

Shooting on the run with his disruptor, Gradok drew a crude oval on the side of the car, then he crashed into it at full speed. The Klingon and a chunk of the car fell into the cabin with a crash, and Maltz and Leah dove in after him—just as the monorail picked up speed and tore out of the station.

"We can't stay here!" shouted Brahms. "We'll lose pressure and oxygen!"

She charged toward the front of the car, which was connected to another car; and she grabbed the wheel to open the hatch just as a sudden rush of air yanked her off her feet. It almost sucked her backward out the gaping hole, but Maltz steadied her. Gradok took the wheel, twisted it easily, and opened the hatch. They ducked into the air lock and slammed the door shut behind them just as the last of the air rushed out of cabin.

Calmly, regaining his composure, Maltz opened the door to the next car. It was full of what looked like dignitaries, the rich and beautiful people of Protus, who all turned around to stare in amazement. Maltz stepped into the cabin, leveled his disruptor with one hand and pulled off his gas mask with the other. At the sight of the crusty old Klingon, there were audible gasps among the thirty-or-so passengers.

Maltz sneered. "We are taking a slight detour."

A well-dressed human frowned at him. "Are *you* the ones who have thrown this entire operation—the whole asteroid—into an uproar?"

"None other," said Maltz with a sense of accomplishment. "So imagine what we could do to this one car if you don't cooperate?" Without taking his eyes or weapon off the passengers, he nodded toward a console at the front. "Captain, you might want to see if you can get us back to our ship."

"Right," answered Leah, striding down the aisle, ignoring the looks of contempt from the passengers. "We didn't treat you people any worse than you treated us," she muttered to no one in particular.

While Leah settled in at the controls of the speeding monorail, she heard Maltz say, "Do any of you know Colin Craycroft, owner of the Pink Slipper?"

Now came vehement words of disgust, and more than a few people observed, "Of course you would know *him!*"

"Tell Craycroft to make his peace, because he will die the next time I meet him," replied the old Klingon.

That somber proclamation brought much of the conversation to a hush, and Brahms was finally able to concentrate on the readouts. She located dock seventeen and found that she could reroute the monorail to get there.

She heard Maltz say, "I need crew. Who wants to sign on?"

Now there were disbelieving looks all around, followed by nervous tittering. Someone asked pleasantly, "Where are you going?"

"To find the fiends who created the Genesis Wave and kill them." That brought the muttering to a complete stop, and the only sound to be heard was the whisper of the rail overhead.

It took a while, but finally a human youth stood up. "I'll go," he said shakily.

"Herbert, sit down!" shouted the woman with him, probably his mother. She clutched his arm. "They'll kill you!"

"No, boredom will kill you," declared Maltz. "Step out here, young human."

The lad gently pulled away from the woman's clutches. He looked down at her with sympathy and love, but also with the coldness that comes with a streak of youthful independence. "Aunt Patricia, I'm old enough, and this is what I want to do. Please don't stand in my way."

"To go off with these—" She glared at the Klingons, then lowered her head and sniffed. "If your parents were alive—"

"Well, they're not and it's because that thing, that Genesis Wave, killed them and destroyed our home. I'm not going to let the same thing happen here. Good-bye, Aunt Patricia." The lad stepped forthrightly into the aisle, and Maltz and Gradok sized him up. He looked like a well-groomed teenager, with a slight build, sandy hair, about sixteen years old.

"A little skinny," said Gradok with a frown.

"I'm a good rock climber," declared the boy proudly.

"We accept you," answered Maltz, slamming a beefy hand onto the lad's scrawny shoulder. His aunt shrieked and tried to charge up the aisle, but her friends wisely stopped her.

Leah turned back to her board, and she made a decision, too. "There's a maintenance station coming up," she reported. "It's empty, and I think we should stop and let everyone out there."

"Except the lad," said Maltz.

"Crazy volunteers exempted," Brahms said with a glance at the boy. "Just don't expect a long career and a pension." She wanted to slap him and tell him he was insane, but they needed the crew. The rest of his life might be short, but it would be exciting.

"Captain," said Maltz hoarsely, "how did Kurton and Burka die? Was it a warrior's death?"

"Oh, yes," she answered. "There was a fantastic battle in the tunnels. They were trying to protect me, but they were outnumbered. They went down in a blaze of phaser fire."

"Their bodies were not desecrated?" asked Gradok.

"No. In fact . . . they were vaporized by all the phaser beams."

"Let's announce them to *Sto-Vo-Kor*," Maltz said with a tear in his rheumy eye.

The Klingons threw back their heads and roared to the heavens with frightening howls. The passengers shrunk back and covered their ears at the unearthly sounds. It went on for such a long time that even Leah grew edgy, and she finally decided that the only way to accept it was to join in. She cut loose with a gut-wrenching shriek, which only caused Maltz and Gradok to yell all the louder, until their voices collided in an anguished chord.

When they stopped at the maintenance station, the passengers bolted off without being told, while the howling went on. Herbert's protesting aunt was dragged off by the friends, and Leah glanced back to see if their newest recruit was still aboard. He was.

"Last chance!" she shouted over the din. He stood perfectly still, rooted to the spot, and Leah shrugged and put the monorail into forward motion. She no longer cared who lived and died anymore, as long as the ones responsible for the Genesis Wave were on the rolls of the dead.

This is quite an impressive hologram, Carol Marcus mused as she gazed around her spacious laboratory on Regula I, with its 360-degree view of the stars and an impressive collection of nebulas beyond. One of them was the Mutara Nebula, which shouldn't exist in this timeframe.

No wonder all of it seemed so familiar—they dredged it up from my mind, warts and all. The old woman looked at a scratched microscope screen, which she had always meant to replace. She remembered how she had made that scratch ninety-five years ago with a pair of dropped tongs; in many respects, her memories had never been clearer.

Her captors had spared no effort in producing this recreation for her benefit. Still, parts of the lab were undoubtedly real, such as the computers and test chambers; other areas had to be fake. This whole space station couldn't exist—*didn't* exist—in the current year. Besides, she was convinced that they were on a starship. There was something in the familiar sounds and sensations—delicate whirs, the vague sensation of motion—that conveyed the impression they were headed somewhere.

As always, Marcus was able to compartmentalize and put all other considerations aside while she worked. It had felt wonderfully sinful to be immersed again in her Genesis discoveries and designs, all returned home to roost in her mind like long-lost children. But she no longer had to imagine the most soulless and evil purpose to which Genesis could be put, because she saw it outlined in front of her. *The doomsayers had been right for once,* she thought miserably. *Imagine that.*

Keep working, she ordered herself. "Computer, activate personal log."

"Log activated," said the officious voice.

She rubbed her eyes and continued: "Dr. Carol Marcus, general notes for Genesis Wave, test two. The goals are to implement three improvements over the first discharge. One will be a solar analyzer built into the matrix; this will analyze suns in the path faster and more accurately than before. Suns meeting criteria will undergo mild conditioning instead of drastic conditioning. These two improvements should cut down on the losses of otherwise suitable planets when their suns were altered too hastily."

Carol shivered, trying not to think of how many worlds had been destroyed and then wasted when they couldn't exist with their new mutilated suns. She hurriedly went on:

"The third change is increased resistance to phase-shifting, as found in non-Federation cloaking devices. Stage two will incorporate a random pattern of tachyons, which are known to disrupt temporal fields. Although this theory should work, we lack both the raw data and the time needed to test it, even in a simulator. I believe we have about a fifty-fifty chance of success."

Carol paused, wondering who had circumvented the original wave with phase-shifting. Romulans? Some other race? How many races had they destroyed in the deluge of horror she had helped unleash?

"End log." Sniffing back her emotions, Marcus tried not to grieve too much for the millions, probably billions, who had perished. She couldn't afford to—as far as she knew, she was the only one standing in the way of a second Genesis Wave, worst than the first.

There were ways she could sabotage this new trial, but she knew they could read her mind. She had to be honest with them whenever possible, which meant not attempting to keep a secret. Yet in their own way, they were as wary of her as she was of them. There was something in her captors' makeup that was oddly dependent . . . nothing like the real David Marcus or Jim Kirk. It seemed as if they would do anything to keep her alive, solely because she was useful.

I'll have to do something spur-of-the-moment, she decided, *and I'll probably have only one chance. Until then, I'll pretend they're my loved ones, while we all go through the motions.*

The door whooshed open, and Carol quickly turned back to the schematic of a tachyon cannon, wondering how they could mount it inside the emitter array. The fake Kirk swaggered in, wearing the protective cleanroom suit he wore almost all the time now. That suit was designed to protect the environment from the wearer.

"Do you like the new suits?" he asked rhetorically, reading her mind as easily as she read the screen. "I'm just giving it a test—see how it wears."

"I don't care what suits you wear, darling," she answered, peering at her instruments. "However, I would like to figure out how to time the tachyon burst with the variable speed of the wave."

Jim cocked his head under the pale yellow hood and stepped closer. "I thought you had that figured out."

"In theory," she answered, "the carrier wave will force the tachyon stream to keep pace, but I have to adjust for the drag coefficient when we're in active mode on a large celestial body. I mean, there's no way to try the changes before the test, so we'll have to live with the results. I'm also worried about matrix degradation, because this wave is already carrying a lot of data."

Innocently, she added, "If we could delay the test—"

"Impossible," snapped Kirk. He immediately softened his stance, and she could see a youthful grin behind his faceplate. "Hey, this test will tell us if the tachyons work or not, so let's just do it. There's no point in having *two* tests, now is there?"

"We *are* having two tests," she answered truthfully, "and it would help if I could see all the figures from the first test. Where are the long-range scans you and David were talking about?"

"You heard us talking?" said Kirk with surprise. "Your hearing is very good for—"

"An old lady?" Carol finished his sentence. But she was thinking about something else . . . that she had picked up their thoughts *mentally*. Unless they were talking to each other for her benefit, which they often did, they had no reason to communicate in audible sound. She couldn't have heard them making verbal communication—she knew that for a fact.

"You're not old," said Kirk, mustering some of the tenderness with which he had enthralled her. With a gloved hand, he touched her cheek. "You know what you're doing here, don't you?"

"Getting a second chance," she answered, knowing that was true in more ways than they ever considered.

"You're worried about the target planets," Kirk said with mocking good humor. "I told you, we've taken great pains to avoid inhabited planets. We are doing this quadrant a tremendous service, terraforming useless rocks into a chain of beautiful paradises!"

Plastering a smile onto her face, Carol squeezed his hand in return and tried to concentrate on pleasant memories, of which there were many. "Believe me, I've been thrilled to see you again, darling . . . and to work with you and David. Whatever magic you used to make this happen, you won't get any complaints from me."

She turned back to her instruments with a sigh. "I'm sure you know what you're doing when you keep data away from me, but I warn you that my results may be less than perfect."

The fake Kirk held his palms up. "The data is . . . confusing. We just didn't want to confuse you."

"But you're also confusing the algorithms for the solar analyzer," she replied. "Those variables are dependent upon raw data, and we could use some more data for the simulations."

"You'll get the raw data," said Kirk, as if coming to a decision. "Let me go to the computer room and fire up the sensor logs. Quick thinking as ever, sweetheart." When he playfully tweaked her cheek, she tried not to grimace.

After the creature left the room, the elder scientist let out a sigh and gripped her console for support. It was draining—keeping up her guard while working around-the-clock at a high level . . . for a nefarious cause. But she had learned something valuable today—that the mind games seemed to be working *two* ways now. They had nearly killed her by accident, but their cure had left her with something of theirs. She had a feeling that she would only be seeing the two ghosts when necessary.

The worst of the damage has been done, Carol Marcus told herself, *both to me and the galaxy. The only thing left is to stop it from happening again.*

sixteen

All across the mottled plains, forests, and swamps of Myrmidon, massive fires burned out of control. Watching from orbit in the Romulan shuttlecraft, Dolores Linton thought it looked like a newly born sun trying to break out of its crumbling shell. Where the dense smoke and clouds allowed visibility, the forests blazed like glowing lava, and it was impossible to tell the chain of fires from the chain of volcanoes. In their zeal to fight the moss creatures, the Bolians had turned Myrmidon into an unholy inferno.

After taking a few sensor readings, she could tell that the smoke was winning the battle against the clouds to rule the blackening atmosphere.

"All readings getting worse," she told Data, who sat beside her at the controls of the Romulan shuttlecraft.

The android cocked his head and replied, "If current trends follow my predictions, most of the survivors will be dead in thirty-eight hours, when the air becomes unbreathable. However, the moss creatures will be neutralized."

"Small consolation," Dolores said miserably, as she looked out the viewport at the smoldering planet. "I feel like I'm a part of that place—I don't know why. It feels like *I'm* dying inside."

"You were a part of the natural order," answered Data, "before I rescued you."

"Yeah, and I can't thank you enough. But after all we tried to do . . . to lose all those people is hard to take."

"Perhaps they are not lost," Data said thoughtfully.

"What do you mean?"

"There may be a fleet of rescue vessels just waiting to come to Myrmidon," said the android. "Certainly the Federation must be very interested in the outcome here, since we have been unable to communicate. But this hypothetical fleet will not be able to come here unless they know it is safe to cross the residue of the Genesis Wave."

"How will they know that?" asked Dolores, already dreading the answer.

"We will have to pilot this uncloaked shuttlecraft back to unaffected space."

Dolores shifted nervously in her seat. "But I've already told you, there are interphase generators lying all over the planet!"

"However, using phase-shifting will not be a viable test. To assure the admiralty that a normally equipped fleet of starships can fly safely to Myrmidon, we need to accomplish the feat in a normal craft."

"But . . . but if the residue is still active, we'll be dead!"

"That is correct," answered Data.

"Do you have a Plan B?" Dolores asked hopefully.

"No, I do not," answered Data. "I suppose we could rescue a few more Starfleet personnel, five or six at the most, and wait until someone eventually contacts us."

"And everyone on the planet will be dead?" asked Dolores.

"There will be a small percentage who find a way to survive," answered the android. "Three-tenths of one percent, by my calculations. "

Dolores laughed with frustration and disbelief. "You know, I thought I would get used to your cold way of talking about this stuff, but I can't. Don't you *care* what happens to anyone? Even yourself?"

"I have an emotion chip," Data said with some degree of pride. "Would you like me to activate it?"

"Yeah, go ahead."

Once again, the android cocked his head slightly. His eyes widened in complete horror, and his frantic face went through every emotion known to humankind—joy, terror, rage, fear, hope, and about fifty more—in a few seconds. Dolores got exhausted just watching his rubbery face.

He turned to her with a look of complete panic. "What is the *matter* with you? We must save these wretched souls on Myrmidon! We must get *help!*"

Then Data trembled with fear. "But what if you are *right?* What if the effect has not dissipated? We will *cease* to exist. I am too young to cease to exist! You will have to make a decision!"

"First of all, turn off the emotion chip!" she cried.

"Done," he answered with a nod, his becalmed self once again. "I apologize—I seem to have many pent-up emotions concerning this issue."

"All right," muttered Dolores. "Set your course. I never expected to live forever, anyway."

"We should know very quickly," Data assured her as he worked his board.

"Well, that's a relief."

"I want you to know that you have been very good company these last forty hours."

"You, too," said Dolores, "although I wish I could hear you play the violin once more . . . before I go."

Data glanced to the back of the shuttle. "I do not believe the Romulan replicator is equipped to produce Terran musical instruments, although it does offer Starfleet uniforms."

"I'm wearing one," said the geologist with a smile. "I'll just *imagine* the violin music while we head off into space."

"I could hum for you," said Data.

"Just make it quick, like you promised." The geologist stiffened in her seat and screwed her eyes shut. A moment later, she felt them banking as the shuttlecraft pulled out of orbit.

She waited stiffly, but she felt nothing unusual. Shakily she asked, "Tell me when it's going to happen."

"Nothing happened," answered Data.

"We're alive?" whispered Dolores. She opened her eyes to see nothing but a beautiful sprinkling of stars floating in the darkness. It didn't look as if this sector of space had been ravaged by the Genesis Wave.

"Enough time has passed for the effect to have dissipated," said Data, "although communications are still unresponsive. Our destination is the rendezvous point where we met the Romulans."

The android rapidly worked his console, then reported, "Going to warp drive."

Dolores Linton sat back and breathed her first relaxed breath in what seemed like weeks, but she didn't feel relaxed. There were too many people in danger, too much to do, too much undone. People were spread out all across the quadrant, battling this scourge. Where were Geordi La Forge, Leah Brahms, Admiral Nechayev, Captain Picard, and all the others? She didn't bother to ask Data, because she knew he didn't know. Even if they had survived a risky gamble, they were still just two beings who had been left behind to witness a disaster. She tried to shake the fear that Myrmidon was a lost cause—a planet that should be left to fester and die alone.

"We have arrived," said Data, pulling Dolores out of her melancholy.

With excitement, she sat up to look out the viewport, but all she saw was a nondescript array of stars and distant dust clouds. No ships.

Dolores looked down at her sensor readings, but Data was way ahead of her. "There are no ships in the vicinity. We will have to use delayed subspace to communicate."

"Where the hell are they?" muttered the geologist, banging her fists on the console.

"Unknown," answered Data. "If I were to make a supposition, I would say Earth."

"Earth?" echoed Dolores. Feeling spent, she slumped across the console, her head resting on her brawny arms. "It's hard to imagine Earth being gone."

"Not for another twenty-three hours," said the android.

"Are we going there now?" Dolores asked wearily.

"No, we could not reach Earth in time to be any help. We will follow the *Enterprise* and the *D'Arvuk* to the Boneyard."

"What about all those people on Myrmidon?"

"We are one small shuttlecraft," said Data. "I will send a report via subspace, but their fate is out of our hands."

"Damn," muttered Dolores, dropping her head back onto her arm. "This thing just stays messed up, doesn't it?"

"Yes, it does," agreed the android.

As seen from Earth, a band of bright stars and glowing nebulas swept across the night sky. Near the Southern Cross, this dazzling belt of light was interrupted by a jagged hole—a black nebula called the Coal Sack. Not a true nebula, although there were plenty of opaque dust clouds in its depths, the Coal Sack was a huge chunk of space that was relatively empty. Compared to the brilliant starscape surrounding it, the Coal Sack was a desert. It was a good place to put something you didn't want, thought Admiral Alynna Nechayev.

Standing alone in the stellar cartography room aboard the *Sovereign*, the admiral had her choice of viewing any known object in the heavens, from any angle. She moved a tiny jumpstick on a device in her hand to enlarge her view of the Coal Sack. Her feet clacked across the raised platform as she inspected the contents of the dark nebula.

In its mysterious heart floated an even darker body—the Furnace. This opaque object was classified as a nonstandard quasar, as if there were such a thing as a standard quasar. Its pronounced redshift on the spectrum made early Terran astronomers think it was much farther away than it had turned out to be. It put out enormous amounts of radio and electromagnetic interference, and some said it should be classified as a pulsar. Whatever it was, the Furnace obliterated anything that came too close, including most varieties of light waves.

For Nechayev, it was the ultimate incinerator, and she was assigning the dirtiest garbage to it. That is, if the La Forge theory worked and their forty thousand starships did their job.

If the plan didn't work, a certain planet named Earth would not exist—as anyone recognized it—by this time tomorrow. And they would probably be at war with the Romulans.

Nechayev tried never to second-guess herself, but she couldn't help but wonder if she could have done anything differently. After all, she knew Carol Marcus had been kidnapped, and she should have been ready for some deployment of the Genesis technology. But she wasn't expecting something of this immense scope.

Should she have sent more ships to find the source? Nechayev had thought the task force of *Defiant*-class vessels would be enough, but they had disappeared without uncovering anything. After that, her dependence on a defensive strategy of evacuation, shelters, and now the Ring of Fire had necessitated hanging onto to all the ships at her disposal. She was still mired in the ramifications of that quick decision.

It was clear by now, thought Nechayev, they were fighting more than the Genesis Wave itself. There were signs of a ruthless, clever enemy behind all of this. By now, a dozen ships had reported back from the Boneyard, and no one had found anything unusual. The enemy had covered their tracks, as any sensible foe would do, and sending more bloodhounds wouldn't be useful. By dealing with the wave, she felt they were attacking the most immediate threat to the Federation. If their homeworlds were wiped out, what did vengeance or justice matter?

After so many failures and partial successes, we finally have a plan to neutralize the wave, Nechayev assured herself. *I still don't see what I could have done differently, except to protect Carol Marcus better.* As in so many games of war, the early mistake is often the most costly one.

The door whooshed open, mildly startling her. The admiral turned to see her main attaché, Lieutenant Kelly, stride into the domed room.

"I have the latest dispatches," he said.

She nodded brusquely. "Make it fast—we only have an hour."

Her subordinate nodded and consulted his padd. "Commander Data has sent word that the forests of Myrmidon are on fire. He says the devastation is almost total. There's a detailed report in your inbox, but the gist of it is that the survivors have set most of the fires themselves—in an attempt to drive out the moss creatures."

The admiral's face hardened, and she said nothing. Her subordinate cleared his throat and went on, "Commander Data requests aid for the survivors within the next thirty-eight hours, maximum. He says we can navigate the space around Myrmidon safely now—the effect is over."

"That's good," Nechayev said simply. "Adjust the orders for the Klingons, so that they'll go to Myrmidon as soon as we release them. Make sure *all* orders for the cleanup stage get out as soon as possible."

"Yes, Admiral," the young lieutenant said, making a note on his padd. "The *Enterprise* reports that it has almost reached the Boneyard, but sensors don't find any sign of the Genesis Wave or its origin."

"Not surprising," answered the admiral. "Go on."

Kelly glanced down at his padd, and a smile crept over his youthful face. "I don't know what to make of this one. The mining colony on Protus says that they were invaded by Klingons."

Nechayev laughed despite herself—an unexpected release of tension. Her face and tone quickly turned somber again. "I don't see how. Every Klingon ship is here with us."

"I know, sir," Kelly answered, scrolling to the end of the report. "They haven't furnished many details either, except that the commercial district and mining operations were destroyed."

"I've been to Protus," said Nechayev. "I don't blame them one bit. Ask for more details—in triplicate. We are sending Klingons in that direction, so maybe they're just repeating a rumor they heard."

"That's probably it," agreed the lieutenant. She looked up and caught him gazing at her face, and he quickly diverted his eyes. Half of Nechayev's face was wrinkled and full of character, while the other half was youthful and smooth—a result of having been treated with mutagenically active soil on Myrmidon.

She would get it fixed when there was time—until then, she was a walking billboard for the power of the Genesis Wave. As usual, Alynna Nechayev didn't mind grabbing attention—that was how she got things done.

"Anything else?" she demanded.

"The Romulan third fleet reports that they're in position," answered Kelly.

"Good thing. They're only an hour and five minutes behind schedule." The admiral stared at a blazing ring floating in the middle of the three-dimensional holographic representation of the region. She had dubbed it the Ring of Fire—forty thousand starships, assembled from all the powers and fleets in the Alpha Quadrant.

"It's an extraordinary feat," said Kelly. "Just getting them all here."

She scowled. "That's just issuing orders and having them followed. The feat is yet to come. If I'm wrong, it will be the greatest failure in the history of the Federation, and Earth."

Kelly started edging to the door. "I'll be on the bridge. Are you . . . are you going to stay down here alone?"

"For the duration," answered Nechayev, regarding the celestial charts hovering in midair. "Do you remember my telling you that, as a commanding officer, you must never say 'Oops!' And you must never let your forces see you cry?"

"I remember that," Kelly answered, forcing a smile.

"Well, I intend to heed my own advice. Just tell the captain to keep feeding data to my charts. Dismissed, Lieutenant."

"Yes, sir." The young man nodded, then bolted for the door.

After he left, the admiral's shoulders slumped, and she let her guard down. Wearily, she walked away from her charts to sit at the master console, where a small viewscreen cycled through various views of the forty thousand warships under her command. Great Romulan warbirds, massive Klingon birds-of-prey, starships of every class and description, freighters, scows, and junks—it was the greatest fleet ever assembled. Like their enemy, they hoped to be victorious without firing a shot.

But the wave was now four million kilometers wide, and it took no prisoners and gave no quarter. The idea of stopping it with a ring of ships and a network of force fields was almost absurd. *But it has to bend,* she told herself. *Everything has to bend eventually, doesn't it?*

Allowing herself the luxury of a yawn, Nechayev realized how weary she was. Stress, lack of sleep, and an abbreviated recovery period from her injuries had all led to bone-deep exhaustion. She would like to sleep, but she couldn't—she had one more chore to do.

"Computer, take a memo. To Admiral Brud'khi, Chief of Starfleet Command, San Francisco." She paused, thinking that there might be no San Francisco by the time this message was delivered. "Computer, correct address to fleet at large," she went on.

"Admiral, with deep regret, I hearby tender my resignation from Starfleet, effective immediately," Nechayev said, her voice cracking. "If you have received this, then our strategy to divert the Genesis Wave away from Earth was a failure. I take full responsibility, as I have from the beginning. I let the genie out of the bottle, and it was my duty to recapture it. I tried every way I could in the time allotted, but I made decisions that might have been wrong. If I have failed, then I have failed the uniform, the honor, and the purpose of Starfleet. Sincerely, Alynna Nechayev."

She caught her breath, then went on, "Computer, hold this message for forty-five minutes, then send with my approval only."

"Acknowledged," answered the computer. Her viewscreen went back to revolving views of the ships waiting for action. Each was so distant from the others that the ring was indistinct—there was no video log big enough to capture it.

Nechayev glanced back at the holographic representation of the Ring of Fire—a massive circle of vessels and space stations, anything that could be towed or flown into position. Every vessel had to be capable of producing a force field or tractor beam. Young Kelly had been wrong—assembling the ships had not been the hardest part of the operation—matching the strength and synchronizing the timing of the beams had been the hard part. There was no room for error—if one ship was off, the entire network would fail.

She wondered if the Romulans and Klingons realized how vulnerable the Federation was at this moment. It was lying in front of them, its throat uncovered—but that was just one more leap of faith they would have to make. The admiral wished they'd had time for at least one test, but the last segments of the circle had just fallen into place. There was no dress rehearsal, only the real thing.

To her surprise, Nechayev actually drifted off to sleep—or at least she was in a drowsy state when she heard the voice of the captain addressing the ship. "To all hands, the Genesis Wave has been spotted and is still on trajectory with an ETA of twelve minutes, twenty seconds. It's available on your viewscreens, and should be rather impressive as it passes through the Hag's Head Dust Cloud in ten seconds."

Nechayev shook her head with exasperation, thinking that captains always had to inject more drama into a situation than was already there. She had lived through the Genesis Wave once—barely—but she couldn't remember a thing about that experience. With reluctance, she turned to her viewscreen.

Moments later, she was grateful that Alvarez had drawn their attention to the sight, because the Genesis Wave truly was a marvel to behold. Like a primal force, it came roaring through the big multicolored dust cloud, exploding it like a dandelion blasted by the wind. Just as quickly, the debris coalesced into an amorphous, pulsing body, trying desperately to become a planet. It succeeded in becoming nothing but a stomach-churning oddity as it twisted in the grimy detritus of the Genesis Wave. Nechayev found herself recoiling from the sight, even though it was just inert rock and dust being mutilated. The smooth side of her face tingled with the memory.

"Beginning ten-minute countdown," added Captain Alvarez. "All stations, maximum synchronization."

Nechayev gripped the arms of her chair, and she didn't let go for the next ten minutes.

seventeen

"Ten, nine, eight, seven, six, five, four—"

Admiral Nechayev rose to her feet and began to pace the stellar cartography room, unable to watch the moment of truth on the viewscreen. She also turned away from the holographic images on the charts floating overhead. She would know if they succeeded—she'd feel it in her soul.

"Three, two, one. We have contact with the intruder," said the computer's voice. Nechayev held her breath. Against her will, she looked at the Ring of Fire circling the wave's target; at that moment, it illuminated brightly. Did the lights in the room dim, or was that her imagination? This ship, as well as all the others, was being taxed to its limits by the power demands of the force fields.

On the simulation, a red beam entered the Ring of Fire, and the admiral held her breath again. The image flickered for a moment—probably the real moment when the wave hit the ring—then the red beam went streaking off at a different angle. It blinked as it headed toward the dark desert in the sea of stars, the Coal Sack.

Still Nechayev didn't let out her breath, because these were only simulations—the real wave may not have behaved that way. She rushed back to the master console. Before she even sat down, the captain's voice sounded on the shipwide intercom:

"Mission achieved. The Genesis Wave has been diverted. Earth is saved!"

With a grin, Nechayev slumped into her seat, hearing in her mind the cheers that went up all over the ship—in every ship. The Romulans probably looked smug and rolled their eyes, but she was certain the Klingons were cheering. They loved a victory against overwhelming odds, and they loved the moment when the tide turned in battle.

She banged on her console and said, "Nechayev to Tactical Command, Ring of Fire."

"Yes, Admiral," came the prompt response. "Admiral Horkin here. Congratulations, gutsy call. Maybe they'll let you retire now."

"Don't count on it," she snapped. "Is the wave past, or is it continuous?"

"Sensors show it's past—nothing left but the residue we've seen before."

"Good, then we can start the cleanup. I know we diverted the wave, but did we also narrow it?"

"Affirmative on that," answered her fellow admiral. "It's on course to the Furnace, and we've diverted all traffic from its path. Worked like a charm."

"That's enough patting ourselves on the back," said Nechayev brusquely. "Get those fleets dispatched—lots of survivors need them."

"Yes, sir. And now you'll check yourself into sickbay, and get the care you need?" he asked hopefully.

"Not yet," answered Nechayev. "I've got a comrade out there, and I'm going to help him. Picard and I have had our differences, but if anybody is going to find the root of this evil, he will. It's time to go on the offensive. Nechayev out."

With a smile, she added, "Computer, cancel message to Admiral Brud'khi."

"Acknowledged."

A satisfied smile on her face, Admiral Nechayev rose to her feet and considered the holographic charts gleaming overheard, especially the red streak that represented the Genesis Wave. Without warning, the red beam went dim and faded away. Nechayev rushed back to the master console just as her combadge chirped.

"Nechayev here," she answered impatiently.

"This is Admiral Horkin again. I don't know if you noticed, but—"

"I did."

"Okay, then you won't be surprised to learn that the Genesis Wave just died."

"Died? Be more specific."

Horkin's words spilled out. "We've got the top minds here, including a Vulcan who has seen this wave before, and she feels that the Genesis Wave has expanded to its utmost potential. It weakened to the point where it dissipated, except for the unpleasant residual side effects we've seen."

Nechayev gulped and sunk down onto the chair. "Are you telling me that all of this was for *nothing*? That the wave was going to dissipate, anyway?"

"That's the way it looks," said the admiral, "although our actions may have hastened it. Alynna, that residual could have wreaked a lot of damage on Earth. You still did the right thing."

"I wonder," rasped the admiral. "Have I left them hanging out there all alone?"

In Beverly Crusher's research laboratory off sickbay, Captain Picard studied a clump of moss growing on a miniature willow tree. The moss didn't look deadly, but it was ensconced in its own octagonal growing chamber, transparent and totally self-contained. He could inspect the soil and the root system of the tree, thinking they looked healthy, but the moss hung on the branches like an evil fog. It took some intestinal fortitude, but Picard lowered his head close enough go nose-to-nose with the innocuous-looking plant.

"Go ahead, it won't bite you," said Beverly Crusher with a smile. "The chamber is protected by biofilters and force fields. In fact, we've updated all the ship's biofilters for the moss, the fungus, and the spores."

"It's hard to imagine that this little plant nearly brought the Federation to its knees," said Picard with amazement. "Where did you get it?"

"It's a sample that Data picked up on Myrmidon," answered Crusher. "I don't know if it always grows this quickly, or whether accelerated growth is a by-product of the Genesis Effect—but a day or so ago that plant was just a little sprig the size of your finger."

The clump of moss moved slightly, causing Picard to jump back. Beverly chuckled and tried to wipe the smile off her face. "I should have warned you about that. In its waking state, the plant is ambulatory. It's nurtured by a tree until it's the equivalent of an adult, then it goes searching for a meatier host. I don't need to tell you, that's when it's dangerous. I think it's warming up to go hunting for a new host."

"I'd like to post a guard on it," said Picard. "Around the clock."

Beverly frowned. "You know, I'm not real fond of having security in sickbay, but in this case—"

"They'll be here as soon as I leave." Picard bent closer to the plant, still keeping his distance. "Can it read our minds now, do you think?"

The doctor shook her head. "I don't know. Everything this creature does is parasitic—for its own survival, no one else's. The fungus, the telepathy, they're very impressive; but I don't know how much is learned behavior and how much is instinctive. You would think that an individual who could infiltrate a starship, posing as a crewman, would have undergone special training. In our culture, they would have to."

Crusher gazed at the twitching parasite. "Then again, maybe it's born with enough skills to dig into your mind and impersonate a loved one."

Picard smiled sympathetically at Crusher. "You weren't the only one who was fooled. In order to develop these specialized traits, it must have preyed on humanoids and large animals for millions of years."

"Enslaved them, then preyed on them," said Beverly somberly. "I don't think they're handy with tools, but they could easily enslave a whole population of humanoids to do their bidding. I'm very worried about the survivors on Myrmidon . . . and anywhere else we've left these things."

"However, when they created their dream world, they didn't program humanoids into the matrix," Picard said curiously. "From all reports, the animal life was decidedly sluggish and low level."

Crusher's jaw clenched, and she gazed with hatred at the plant. "I think they consider humanoids to be decidedly sluggish and low level."

"How do they reproduce?" asked Picard, trying to change the subject.

"I know they don't grow from a seed. Probably a spore. Of course, this one's mommy was the Genesis Wave."

Picard frowned at the captive. "When it gets larger, what are we going to do with it?"

"What do we always do with alien life?" asked Crusher. "We should try to communicate with it. Telepathically."

The captain looked at her. "Do you mean Counselor Troi?"

"We don't have any Vulcans on board," she said with a shrug. "Besides, I wouldn't allow anyone else to touch it or breathe the same air. But imagine, Jean-Luc. These creatures had the means to imprint billions and billions of their offspring with whatever they wanted them to know. What is that knowledge? Until a week ago, we didn't even know they existed, yet they stole our technology and used it against us."

Beverly's eyes grew distant as she stared at the moss. "On Myrmidon, people are burning them up . . . for their own survival. It makes you wonder who's the parasite, and who's not."

"We never would have used the Genesis technology the way *they* did," answered Picard. "Then again, who's to say what we would do under desperate circumstances? Maybe the council was right ninety years ago when they tried to keep it secret. This technology is not safe in anyone's hands."

"It really is playing God," agreed Beverly, her gaze returning to the innocuous clump of gray moss. "Right down to making the inhabitants in your own image."

The captain's combadge chirped, and a voice said, "Riker to Picard."

"Picard here."

"We've reached the Boneyard, Captain," said the first officer. "The *D'Arvuk* is coming out of warp right behind us."

"Short-range scans?" asked the captain.

"There doesn't appear to be anything unusual, but it's a big asteroid field."

"I'm on my way to the bridge," said the captain. "Send a three-person security detail to the research lab in sickbay. The doctor is growing one of the moss creatures there, and I want it watched. Picard out."

He headed for the door, then glanced back at Beverly and the octagonal chamber. "I'll talk to Troi about helping us communicate with it, but I won't take any unnecessary risks where these creatures are concerned."

"Understood," said Crusher. "See you at dinner."

After the captain left, Dr. Crusher picked up her tricorder and began checking the health of the willow tree. For a host plant, it wasn't doing badly, she decided; it might even live if the moss left it to pursue another host. But the young tree would certainly die if left alone with the growing parasite.

She looked up from her tricorder and gasped with shock, dropping the handheld device to the deck. Inside the chamber, it wasn't a tree and a clump of moss anymore—it was an innocent baby hanging by intravenous tubes! Unmistakably, she recognized the helpless infant trapped inside the chamber.

"Wesley!" she cried, pressing her face against the transparent case. Finally she shook her head and pulled away, knowing she had to be hallucinating. With a tremendous force of will, Beverly Crusher rushed out of the room and banged a wall panel to shut the door behind her.

As she was catching her breath, three security officers entered sickbay, asked for directions, and were sent her way. Crusher had a moment to compose herself before the security detail reached her.

"Dr. Crusher," said the ranking officer, "Lieutenant Kraner at your service."

She pointed to the door. "Guard this laboratory. Nobody goes in or out without *my* personal approval. That includes *you*."

The young lieutenant gulped. "Why, is something dangerous in there?"

"Yes." Crusher shivered as she looked back at the door. "By the way, don't let *me* go in there alone. If I want to go in there, insist upon accompanying me."

"Yes, sir," the lieutenant answered uncertainly.

"Don't worry, I'll be sleeping here in sickbay," said Beverly, striding toward her office. "I won't be hard to find. Don't let that door open."

"No, sir, we won't." The young lieutenant glanced at his comrades and gulped. "You heard what the doctor said. Look alive."

• • •

Geordi La Forge sat back in his seat, grinning broadly. Dolores Linton's face was on his screen at his desk in engineering, and the muscular geologist was talking a kilometer a minute. "So, Geordi, there I was, with this stuff growing all over me—yuck!—and Data comes along and saves my life!"

"Actually," Data said, sitting beside her on the shuttlecraft, "you were trying to bite my face."

"I'm sorry," she replied, "but I was having a really bad day. Anyway, this stuff was growing everywhere, and I was like a zombie. But Data brought me back. For once, I was glad to get off solid land and onto a creaky ship."

"Data saved *my* life on Myrmidon, too," replied Geordi. "He's a handy fellow to have around."

The android smiled modestly, then turned serious. "Unfortunately, there are millions we could not save. I hope help arrives in time. Do you know about the fires on Myrmidon?"

La Forge nodded. "I haven't had much to do except to keep track of dispatches back and forth. I'm sure glad the Genesis Wave faded, whatever part we had in that."

"An ironic end," observed Data. "But is it over? There is always the possibility our enemy may deploy the wave again."

"That's why we need you back here, Data," said the android's best friend. "The captain says we're going to wait at the Boneyard until you get back, but no longer. When is your ETA?"

"Three hours and fifty-two minutes," Data answered precisely.

"Geordi," said Dolores, leaning forward, "have you heard anything about Leah Brahms?"

He shook his head and tried not to show how concerned he was. "No, not a peep. She's not on a Starfleet vessel anymore. I've heard she's on a Klingon privateer, which is supposed to be in the area. If that's true, she's on her own. But if we hear from her, I'll let you know."

"Good to see you, Geordi," Dolores said with heartfelt sincerity.

"Look me up as soon as you get on board," said La Forge. "Out."

His screen reverted to a Starfleet logo, and the chief engineer sat back in his chair, frowning. If Leah was somewhere in the area, he sure wanted to find her. It was a big relief that Dolores was safe again, because he felt responsible for leaving her on Myrmidon . . . or letting her out of his sight. He wished he could've kept Leah Brahms in sight, too, but he had no control over her. If only he could see Leah one more time, maybe he would finally get it through his skull that she didn't love him, that they weren't going anywhere.

"Sir, here are the recalibration reports on the forward impulse thrusters," a nasally voice said, breaking him out of his reverie.

La Forge looked up to see a young ensign, a Benzite named Mahzanor. "You requested these as soon as possible," the ensign insisted, thrusting the padd toward him.

"Thank you." La Forge mustered a courteous nod, took the padd, and tried to read the missive. But he couldn't concentrate. He tugged at his collar. "I'll get back to you later. What's the temperature in here?"

The Benzite peered curiously at him. "Are you feeling all right, Commander?"

"Not entirely." La Forge rose to his feet at the instant that the ship was rocked by what felt like a strong jolt. He staggered to stay upright, although Mahzanor seemed to have no such trouble. The ensign reached out to steady La Forge, but Geordi's legs suddenly lurched out from under him. The office was spinning all around his ocular implants, and La Forge pitched to the deck with a dull thud.

eighteen

Roaring talons of flame curled upward from the tops of the trees, sending billows of black smoke hurling into the befouled atmosphere. The stench on Myrmidon was wretched, the air was as thick as a sandstorm, and the heat was like a blast furnace. The underbrush burned with an ethereal white flame, aided by geysers of methane covering the ground like a foggy napalm. Nothing could live in this inferno except for the scattered handfuls of Bolians who crawled into the cesspools, fighting the salamanders and lizards for shelter from the flames.

Mot grabbed one of the squirming monstrosities by the gills and slammed it onto the bank. With fury and primitive rage, the big Bolian throttled the man-sized amphibian until he broke its neck with a loud snap. The flapping tail and limbs finally went still. Behind him, he heard his mother weeping, while his father tried to comfort her—but that wasn't easy when they were submerged in a murky swamp full of squirming horrors.

There were more shouts and shrieks as the others in their wretched party battled with the rightful denizens of the swamp. One of the females had a slithering thing wrapped around her throat, another was trying to pry it off, while a third bashed its head with a stick. They finally pried the thing loose and heaved it into the blazing bushes. With the rage of the dispossessed, the Bolians battled the amphibians, either driving them away or killing them, until they finally took possession of the dank pool.

The leeches and sucker fish still plagued them, eliciting the occasional scream, but the largest of the beasts were gone. The flames and heat were so intense that they could see each other's blistered blue faces as if it were daylight, but the sky was as dark as the blackest night. They cowered in the brackish water, barely opening their eyes to watch the conflagration. They didn't need to see it—they could *feel* it. Mot hugged his parents as they all gasped for breath, trying to steal some oxygen away from the inferno.

Like a slow version of the Genesis Wave, the snorting fire finally moved on, leaving behind a dark, mutated version of what been there before. Instead of the towering trees, now there were just spindly, black sticks, denuded of branches, leaves, and the moss. The underbrush was completely blackened, and the crunchy remains crumbled into ash at the slightest touch. Smoke continued to swirl over the devastated forest, blocking out all light and making it so dark that it felt like the end of the world.

"That should suit those monsters!" muttered a woman, whose voice quickly degenerated into a coughing fit. Some of the other survivors managed raspy, hoarse laughs of appreciation, but Mot could only wheeze. For the second time in a week, Myrmidon had been destroyed in order to save it. They seemed to have been successful, but that didn't afford him any consolation.

Gingerly, Mot let go of his parents, who still clung to each other in wide-eyed shock. Like him, they were amazed just to be alive. The sight of the charred forest and smoldering ground only added to the surreal sense of *déjà vu*. It was hard to tell if this sooty winter was better or worse than the gloomy forest it had replaced. It still seemed like one big nightmare.

Mot's lungs were sore from breathing smoky air—what little there was of it—and he wondered how long the planet's oxygen would hold out. One thing was certain, they couldn't breathe methane.

Coughing and wheezing, Mot dragged himself out of the mire and pulled his muddy body across the ash and stubble until he flopped with exhaustion on top of a rock. The rock was covered in black soot, and it only added to the bedraggled mess he was—a pathetic creature without enough strength left to pull a leech off his cheek.

He heard muffled crying and moaning. With great effort, Mot lifted himself up on his elbows and crawled back to the slimy pool. First he pulled his mother out, then his father; and they lay flopping in the ashes like two fish in the bottom of the boat, gasping for breath. Moments later, others crawled out of the muck and lay on the ground, barely half alive.

Is there anything left? he wondered. *Probably even the sanctuaries are gone now.* The big Bolian began to weep.

After a moment, he felt a hand on his shoulder—it was his father. "Don't cry," breathed the elder. "We are still alive . . . still together. There's always hope."

"No!" rasped Mot. "I should have talked you into going with me on the *Enterprise.* Captain Picard said he would take us. What a fool . . . what an idiot I am! The ones who chose suicide are smarter than I." Tears spilled out of him and ran down his blistered flesh, burning like the fire.

"There's still time for suicide," his father said helpfully. "I wouldn't mind that either, as long as we are all together."

"I think trying to live here *is* suicide!" groused one old man, who might have been a young man under his scars. There was wheezing laughter at that remark, and even Mot had to chuckle.

"The First Mother taught us to suffer," said Mot's mother. "Maybe we were too comfortable."

The laughter died away as they considered that remark, and Mot began to sniff back his tears, wondering what they should do next.

Surely these idiots weren't still depending upon him for leadership? When it had been *his* idea to burn up the forest! He consoled himself that somebody else would have come up with that bright idea, once the awful nature of the threat was known. There were certain ways a Bolian would be quite happy to die, but hosting a parasite while living in a swamp wasn't one of them.

"So, Son, where are we off to next?" asked his father, while the air still hung with ash and soot.

Mot shook his head and gasped for breath. "I'm fresh out of ideas . . . maybe that's a good thing."

When no one else had the energy to speak, he went on, "You know, the humans I serve with always think you can 'get a break.' Something good will happen if you just hang in there."

"What a stupid idea," his mother said, aghast.

"Not born out by the facts," grumbled his father.

Mot wheezed. "I know, but I've seen it happen on the *Enterprise.* Let's test it . . . imagine that something *good* will happen next . . . like the First Mother will appear in front of us and guide our weary souls to safety!"

In a bright flash, a dark, towering creature appeared in front of them, dressed in studded black armor and a pointed hood, and holding a disruptor rifle with bayonet. As smoke swirled around the frightening apparition, he stepped forward, his rifle aimed at Mot. After a moment, he lifted the weapon.

"If you're still alive, raise your hand!" he demanded, his voice booming from his hooded head. Through the faceplate, dark eyes glowered at them.

Mot did as he was told, along with every other member of his tiny party. The mammoth figure suddenly jerked to the right, plunging his rifle toward the ground. Mot heard a squishing sound, and the armored man brought up a huge, squirming salamander, speared on the end of his weapon.

"Ah, good hunting here," he said with satisfaction. With a

heave, he tossed the creature into a swirl of smoke behind him. "Krombek to main transporter, nine to beam up from these coordinates. I will look for more."

Then he waved to the survivors. "The accommodations on a Klingon ship are not much, but they're better than this. *"HIjol!"*

Mot could do nothing but weep with joy and hug his parents as their molecules were whisked away to a ship orbiting high above the smoke and flame.

A mammoth tree towered above him—it seemed to be the ancestor of all trees—majestic, thick with bushy leaves, and unspeakably ancient. Its trunk was as wide as his engineering room, and the aged plant seemed to be just as complex and intricate. The forest itself was primordial, unsullied by civilization. Still, sunlight trickled cheerfully through the thick bows of the regal tree, illuminating a forest floor of delicate wildflowers and tiny ferns.

Geordi La Forge had never been much of a biologist, and he couldn't identify the mammoth tree, except to know that it had to be the grandest tree in all creation. He touched its weathered, flaky bark and felt himself in communion with growing creatures all over the universe. La Forge could feel the life-force in the tree, pulsing with as much raw energy as any antimatter reactor under his command. He realized without being told that this tree was the pinnacle of life—the wellspring from which all good things flowed.

He heard a slight crunching in the leaves on the ground, and he turned to see an ethereal figure in a flowing white gown padding toward him. Her head was lowered, in deference to the tree; when she looked up, her radiant face was bathed in a shaft of golden sunlight. It was Leah Brahms, looking impossibly beautiful, her soft mane of brown hair encircled by a garland of yellow flowers.

Geordi's already soaring heart went into warp drive at the sight of his beloved. Grinning broadly, he took her hands knowing that she had joined him in the forest—before the magnificent tree—in order to become his mate for all eternity. His throat was speechless at the sight and promise of her beauty, but his face and eyes blazed with unrestrained happiness.

A shriveled black leaf tumbled from the tree and drifted before his eyes, dispelling his giddy sense of joy. His mind uncovered a tiny shred of reality, and La Forge asked himself, *How am I seeing this so clearly? Where are my ocular implants?*

Geordi knew what normal vision was like, ever since their visit to the planet of the Ba'ku, where his eyes had miraculously begun to function. Once again, he was seeing through real eyes, but they had to be someone else's eyes.

Desperately fearful he would lose Leah, he gripped her hands all the more tightly until she winced with pain. Leah mustered a brave smile for him, and her voice whispered in his ear, "Not yet, but soon."

She touched his eyes—only they weren't his eyes, they were thick, bulging scabs! Now everything was black, and Geordi had no vision whatsoever—not even the artificial impulses he had come to depend upon. In the black ink, he flailed his arms, trying to touch something . . . anything . . . to find out where he was.

Strong, unseen limbs struck from the darkness, grabbed his arms and legs, and pinned him to the ground. He struggled, but he knew he was as good as captured—he was so helpless. Geordi had experienced temporary bouts of blindness before, but for some reason this was more terrifying. Maybe it was because he was anxious about Leah, and he couldn't do anything to help her in this condition.

"Calm down, Commander. You're among friends," said an authoritative but compassionate voice. Hearing her say his rank brought him back to another reality—that he was a Starfleet officer. Before he panicked, he always tried to remember that his job incurred unexpected hazards—he just had to live with the risks. Geordi let his shoulder muscles relax, and he tried to lower his hands to touch his face. There was some resistance by his captors to let his arms go.

"Let him feel the bandages," said the female voice. With trembling fingers, La Forge touched the thin, rubbery appliances over his eyes—they felt like a second layer of skin.

"Good," said the voice. "I didn't want to give you a hypo. It's Dr. Crusher, and you're in sickbay. I can't tell you how sorry I am that you can't see, but it's temporary."

"What's wrong with me?" asked Geordi. "Was the ship attacked?"

"Not in the usual sense," answered Beverly testily, "but the assault by that damn plant goes on. You're infected with the fungus."

"But how can I be infected?" he asked with alarm. "I had the vaccine."

"Originally, *you* weren't infected. It was the bionic component of your ocular implants that became infected. This fungus is bad and it's persistent—it looks for any opening. You got a strong exposure on Myrmidon. Although you passed through our biofilters and took our vaccine, your ocular implants were bypassed. I'd guess that the fungus lodged in the mechanical portion of the implant, where it was protected, then it migrated into the biological receptors, where it got to the rest of your body. Since there wasn't a creature involved to control it, the fungus ran wild. I'm going to have to revaccinate everyone on the ship."

"But how long will I be without sight?" asked La Forge, getting to the heart of the matter.

"The infection is centered in your eyes," Crusher explained. "Even if you were a sighted person, your eyes would be covered, and I wouldn't let you use them for forty-eight hours. We'll replicate you another set of implants, but I can't install them until you're well."

He held up his hand, and she jumped in. "Don't even ask. You're too sick to wear your old VISOR. The only break you get is that we caught this really early, and you shouldn't be sick for long. Your fever is already gone.

"Go get his visitors," she said, apparently talking to someone else in the room. He heard footsteps clacking away, and he tried to relax. *It's temporary . . . I'm in good hands.* Geordi wanted to tell the doctor about his dream, but that seemed so inane with all that was going on. *Let her deal with my illness, not my love-life.*

A moment later, he heard loud footsteps charge into the room, and his bed moved slightly as people sat beside him. Someone who smelled very good and very earthy planted a wet kiss on his cheek, and a cold hand grabbed his.

"Geordi, I am perturbed to see you ill," said a polite voice, shaking his hand.

"Thank you, Data," answered Geordi warmly. "Dolores, could I have another kiss?"

"Sure," she purred, this time pressing against him as she did the honors.

"Don't get my patient too excited," warned Crusher. "He's got to rest. I'm kicking you out in a few minutes."

He heard Crusher walk away, and he called out, "Thank you, Doc!"

"I hope we've seen the last of this," she muttered.

Dolores squeezed his shoulder and moved closer. "They say you'll be fine in a couple of days, Geordi, and I'm not going anywhere. But I don't know why *I* haven't gotten sick yet."

"You were taken over by an entire plant in a much cruder but quicker-acting form of symbiotic relationship," answered Data. "The inexperienced plants on Myrmidon treated the humanoids as they did the trees, whereas experienced individuals can indulge in elaborate ruses to gain a humanoid's trust. That is when exposure to the fungus is the most intense. I believe there may be numerous levels at which humanoids and these moss creatures can interact."

"Okay, Data, okay," said Dolores good-naturedly. "Sometimes you take all the pleasure out of asking dumb questions."

"Thanks for coming to visit," said La Forge, trying to muster some enthusiasm. "I wish I could enjoy this reunion more, but I'm really out of commission. Has anything happened since I've been in here?"

"I don't know," answered Dolores. "We just got back twenty minutes ago. But it doesn't sound like much has happened."

"I take it we're on our way to that planet . . . Lomar?" asked Geordi.

"We have not yet left the Boneyard," answered Data. "Our departure is under discussion. I believe your illness had caused some concern to our Romulan escort."

"I don't blame them," said Geordi glumly. He barely listened to what else they said in the mixture of scuttlebutt and small-talk. At Dolores's urging, Data agreed to do another violin concert, to lift the crew's spirits.

Dr. Crusher was true to her word and returned to throw them out. La Forge accepted more sympathy and another kiss, then was left alone . . . in the dark. Even though he was a blind man, darkness was something he seldom experienced, thanks to the devices he usually wore. The engineer didn't care for it one bit, although it certainly made him notice his other senses. He could smell the antiseptics and hear the slight whirs and gurgles in the equipment. Distant, muffled voices were audible but maddening—in that he couldn't make out distinctive words. *Maybe with a little more effort,* he thought.

Geordi's hands rubbed nervously against the bedding, which felt course and clammy—much like his emotions. Just when he was getting over Leah, she had to return in that startling and wonderful dream. Of course, that didn't mean that he would ever see her again in real life, or that she cared if she ever saw him again. The dream was just his subconscious telling him he hadn't gotten over her at all.

I have to be practical and really try to forget her, he told himself, *and give Dolores a chance. Why couldn't I have met Dolores sometime when Leah was nowhere around?*

Leah was unfair competition, at least for *his* heart. Geordi tried to forget about all of it and go to sleep, while his body and the medications fought the fungus. It was ironic to become ill from an eye infection, when his eyes were normally no more useful than his appendix or his tonsils. Still, they were a part of his body, and he had to accept that they were still his weakest part.

So La Forge lay there in the darkness, his sightless eyes swathed in bandages, urging sleep to make the darkness less frightening.

Captain Picard sat at the desk in his ready room, trying not to let anger creep into his neutral expression. He knew he had to undergo this tirade if he wanted to come to any kind of agreement at all.

The narrow, scowling visage of Commander Jagron of the Romulan warbird filled his computer screen. "Captain, I simply cannot believe that you are unable to control this fungal disease infesting your vessel. Perhaps you need some of our doctors to attend to your patients, as your medical staff seems woefully incompetent."

At that, Picard bristled. "Our medical staff is perfectly competent, and we only have one patient. It was a bionic component of his that became infected. I hope for your sake that your ship continues to avoid infection . . . and the moss creatures."

"Certainly it behooves us to keep our contact with *you* at a minimum," the Romulan said snidely, "but we can't ignore the fact that we are wasting valuable time. The one good thing that came from your ship being infiltrated by the enemy is that we have the name of a planet. It may not be their homeworld, but it's a start. So now we are off to Lomar, correct?"

Picard took a deep breath and replied calmly, "All of our indicators say that the source of the Genesis Wave is here, in the Boneyard."

The Romulan rolled his eyes. "We've had twelve hours to run sensor scans and have turned up nothing."

"We could run sensor scans for twelve *years*—"

"I know," said Jagron with a conciliatory gesture. "This asteroid field is immense, and I agree with you that one of us should stay here and continue observation. So I propose that we split our forces, and I will take my ship to Lomar. You are the logical choice to stay behind, while you fight your ailments. If this is agreeable to you, we leave immediately."

Picard almost replied that he never asked for the Romulans to come along, anyway. Instead he smiled and said, "Good hunting."

"Thank you, Captain. Jagron out." The lanky Romulan nodded, and the screen went blank.

Captain Picard sighed and sat back in his chair. Although their enemy was despicable, he wasn't sure if they deserved to have the Romulans turned loose against them, without any supervision. There was no doubt that the Romulans could be unusually cruel in their own right. Nevertheless, the *Enterprise* couldn't be in two places at once, and both the Boneyard and Lomar required investigation. He took some consolation in knowing that more Starfleet ships were on the way.

He leaned forward and tapped the companel. "Picard to bridge."

"Riker here," came the familiar reply. "I see the Romulans are leaving."

"Yes, they're on their way to Lomar. We're going to stay here and investigate. You know what we're looking for. Have Data put together a plan that will make the most of our resources."

"Yes, sir," answered Riker. "Counselor Troi is waiting to see you."

"Send her in."

The door opened a moment later, and the dark-haired Betazoid entered the captain's ready room. "You wanted to see me, sir."

"Yes, Counselor," he answered, rising to his feet. Picard searched for words for a moment, then explained, "Essentially, we've captured one of the enemy, and we need to interrogate it. Did you know that Beverly is growing one of the moss creatures in her lab?"

Deanna's already pale expression lightened two more shades. "Yes, I knew before anyone told me. I went down to visit Geordi, but I couldn't get two meters inside sickbay before I started to feel nauseated and dizzy."

The captain frowned. "Then you couldn't help us communicate with it?"

"No," said Troi emphatically. "I get violently ill around that creature. It's really incompatible with our kind of telepathy."

Picard nodded understandingly. "Then we'll just have to find some other way."

Deanna's dark eyes flashed. "We could always do what I did with the other one—strap an overloaded phaser to it."

"I'm sure you could find many people who would support such a solution," said the captain dryly. "However, I must say I'm a bit surprised to hear the suggestion from you. I don't believe I've ever seen you in such a vengeful mood."

Her jaw clenched for a moment, but then she seemed to will the tension away with a sigh. "Telepathy should be used as a tool, not a weapon to deceive and kill. I can't even begin to describe what I saw on Persephone V, what it tried to do to Will—"

"All right, Counselor, I get your drift."

"I have a bad feeling this war is not over," Deanna Troi said grimly.

nineteen

Lomar looked like a planet captured in ancient black-and-white photography, thought Leah Brahms. Every bit of color and life had been drained from its jagged features. Gray and foreboding, it looked like an oversized moon with a wispy white halo of sickly atmosphere. Its own moon, although distant, appeared to be half as large as the aged planet itself. Lomar had towering peaks and dingy gray poles. The forbidding terrain would have given the planet majesty had it not been for the great black bogs that pocked the ashen landscape.

The black holes were tar, concluded Leah, checking her readouts at the science station on the *HoS*. It was natural asphalt, like the sticky detritus in the La Brea Federation Park. Geysers of methane, ammonia, and other noxious gasses leaked from the putrid surface.

No one said anything as they assumed standard orbit. The mood aboard the *HoS* had been stark since the deaths of Kurton and Burka. With a small crew, the loss of two was devastating, even if they had picked up one young, raw recruit. But Herbert was human, like Leah, and that was suspicious in the light of the events at the Pink Slipper on Protus. Worse yet, they had lost two crewmen while gaining no information about Lomar, except that they had carnivorous plants. From this distance, it didn't appear the place had any plants at all.

For the first time, she sensed some real hostility from the Klingons; even Maltz was a bit distant. None of this could be serious, she thought, because Klingons tended to exhibit their emotions openly. Then again, perhaps they were beginning to question their captain's decisions and qualifications. She couldn't blame them, because she was searching blindly for the enemy, making decisions by the seat of her pants. Coming here could be a huge waste of time, worse than going to Protus.

"Herbert," she asked her newest crew member, "there are supposed to be carnivorous plants down there. Do you see anything that looks like vegetation? Plant life?"

The sixteen-year-old bolted to attention at his console, where he was tracking a chemical analysis sensor. He was looking specifically for chlorophyll, chloroplasts, magnesium, and other signs of plant life. "Yes," he said, his voice squeaking. "A little vegetation in those bogs, if I read this right. Not much."

Leah frowned in frustration. In the records, Lomar had looked like one of the planets created by the Genesis Wave. Close up, it seemed to be a dead version of that model—desiccated and all used up. She continued to search for energy sources, cities, anything that resembled civilization, but it seemed pointless.

"Maybe this *was* the enemy's homeworld," said Maltz. "A long time ago."

Gradok, the weapons master who was now on tactical, called out, "There is a shuttlecraft on the surface!"

Maltz jumped down, and Leah hurried from her station to tactical. They peered over Gradok's shoulder at what was unmistakably a vessel, nestled in a relatively level and dry crater. "Federation, civilian class," said Gradok. "Speed-rated for warp two."

"Colin Craycroft," muttered Leah Brahms, shaking her head.

"What?" snarled Maltz. "From the Pink Slipper?"

"Yes, I remember now—he said he was going to beat us here. And he did."

"What is *he* looking for?" asked Maltz.

"He thinks there's treasure here, given our interest in the place." Brahms shook her head with confusion. "I wish I could remember our conversation better."

Maltz rubbed his hands together. "Good, we will kill him and be done with it before we go on. Ready away team." The old Klingon glanced around at his sparse crew and lifted an unruly gray eyebrow. "Gradok and Herbert, you come with me."

The lad looked startled, as if he hadn't expected such an assignment. "Yes, sir!"

"I'll go, too," declared Brahms.

The old Klingon lowered his head. "As you wish, Captain, but we won't be talked out of killing him."

"I'm ordering you *not* to kill him," responded Leah. "If we find him, we have to question him. Then I—and only I—will decide what to do with him.

Maltz narrowed his eyes and scratched his stubbled chin, but he answered, "Yes, sir."

Gradok lifted a beefy fist clad in leather and shook it at his board. "Give me the word, Captain, and I'll destroy his shuttlecraft right now! A small torpedo will do it."

"Is there anyone on board?" asked Brahms.

"No. No life-signs in the area," the hulking Klingon answered with disappointment.

"For all we know, it's a wreck, abandoned," said Leah. "It may not belong to Craycroft at all. But it's the only interesting thing we've found so far, so let's inspect it." She looked pointedly at Maltz, as if telling him to get his landing party moving.

"Kurok, you have the bridge. Keep shields up except when transporting. Use caution."

"Yes, sir," answered the second officer, a quiet sort who did as he was told.

"Away team, follow me!" growled the old Klingon. As they filed off the bridge onto the turbolift, Leah fell in beside the youth, Herbert.

"We're going to have to wear environmental suits," she said.

He nodded several times. "I've done that before—I can do it."

"I don't know what to tell you to expect," Brahms said with sympathy. "Just follow orders, and you'll be fine."

The lad wrung his hands together nervously. "But I *know* Mr. Craycroft. He's a family friend."

"Good, then you can kill him," Maltz said as the turbolift door slid shut.

Carol Marcus pretended to be sleeping on her laboratory cot. She had left the newest algorithms for the solar analyzer on her screen, without sending it to her captors, and she was fairly certain they would want to see the solutions immediately. It was an impressive piece of work, if she said so herself, and it would undoubtedly increase the number of custom-made planets and organisms they were able to spread across the galaxy. Try as she might, the old woman couldn't do anything less than her best, and that was pretty damn good.

Unfortunately, Jim and David were closer than ever to discharging the Genesis Wave a second time—in a different direction—and she still had no idea how to stop them. They had done their best to stay away from her, except to compare notes and talk business. Neither side made an effort at tenderness anymore. She was still a part of the team, turning in good work, so they let her live while they concerned themselves with the biological portions of the matrix.

Still Carol sometimes had the sense that they considered her to be indispensable, like a good-luck charm. At times, their neediness was palpable and a bit chilling.

The scientist felt them in her mind before she heard the door to the lab open. As she had practiced in so many naps, she tried to become a receptor—putting out nothing, giving them nothing to suspect, taking in everything. She was an old woman; they were used to her naps. Thanking the fates for all those yoga classes she had taken some forty years ago, Marcus managed to clear her mind.

They stole into the room, anxious needs filling their thoughts. Sometimes she could hear them speaking words as plainly as day, like two people sitting at a table behind her in a restaurant. Other times, she felt only impressions and emotions. They weren't cold and impassive, as she had thought, but hungry and desperate—it was like the center was missing from their lives.

Still dressed in their cleanroom suits, the two of them shuffled like old men to her computer station, which was about fifteen meters away. Eagerly they began poring over her results, and she felt their excitement.

"This will work," said the phony Kirk. "We must incorporate it immediately."

"Is she asleep?" asked the one she knew as David.

Carol willed herself into an empty-headed meditation. "Yes," answered Kirk. "We are ready now."

"But the test area is guarded by that ship," said David. "We can go no closer."

"Then we must discharge from here."

"No, the preparations will attract their attention. Please do not worry—we have other means." As if frightened by their argument, the verbal exchange degenerated into a lot of touchy-feely cama- raderie between the two, and Carol almost felt a stirring of sympa- thy for them. But not quite.

They shuffled out of the room as laboriously as they had shuffled in, and Carol waited until the door closed—then a few heartbeats more—before she started thinking again. It was clear, a ship was stopping them from docking in the ideal position to discharge the second Genesis Wave. Perhaps that would buy her some time, thought the scientist, but she had better do more than simply eavesdrop. She had to break out of this hologram and see the rest of the ship—where they really were.

Four figures shrouded in dark suits that resembled armor, and hoods that looked like horned helmets, appeared in a flash in a barren crater on Lomar. Wispy ammonia fog with ammonia sleet swirled around them, and it was hard to believe this had once been an almost breathable atmosphere. Leah Brahms stepped forward to inspect the shuttlecraft, which sat in a black scorch mark at the bottom of the crater. Half-covered in frozen sleet, it was hard to tell how old it was. The craft looked dark and lifeless, and her tricorder gave no indication of activity inside.

Maltz motioned them all back while he cautiously approached the shuttle, disruptor leveled for action. From the way he scrutinized the ground, Leah got the idea he was looking for tracks. When he found what he was looking for, he bent down and inspected a booted tread mark in the slush.

The old Klingon's voice was amplified in her ear. "I say they saw us coming on their sensors and ran like the cowards they are."

"I see only one track," said Gradok, peering over the elder's shoulder.

Maltz looked around, verifying for himself how many tracks there were. Without another word, he headed off in a northerly direction, bent over like a crab. Gradok fell in behind him. They were evidently hot on the scent.

Leah looked at Herbert and motioned him to follow. For some reason, she didn't mind bringing up the rear. The lad, armed with no more than a tricorder and a knife, padded carefully after the Klingons, and Brahms moved fast enough to keep up with them.

She really wanted to take readings and spend some time analyzing them, but slow and deliberate wasn't her crew's method of doing things. She pitied Colin Craycroft if they caught him, but not much—as long as they didn't lose sight of the mission. Of course, this excursion could be the second dead end in a row on which she had led them, and she might face a mutiny. On top of that, the shuttlecraft was probably a diversion they didn't need.

She checked her readouts and said, "Maltz, I don't see any life-signs on my tricorder."

"It wasn't a ghost who made these tracks," barked the old Klingon. "Sensors found a lot of kelbonite in these ridges, so your readings may be masked. Trust nothing but your eyes."

The party slowed down as they climbed a ridge with silty, ashen soil underfoot. It was a slippery ascent, especially in the sleet, and the Klingons forged ahead. Fortunately, Herbert was a good climber, as he had claimed, and he hung back to give Leah a hand. When they reached the top of the crusty ridge, everyone stopped to stare at the foreboding landscape beyond.

Spread before them was a vast black bog of natural asphalt, with seething bubbles shooting little puffs of smoke into the murky air. Around the edges of the bog were a few plants that looked like cat-tails, and in the center of the bog was a blackened tree trunk sur-rounded by brackish scum. At least, it looked like the remains of a tree, thought Leah, but one that had died eons ago.

Maltz and Gradok were stopped at the edge of the bubbling pitch. They would be scratching their heads if they could reach them, thought Leah. "The trail ends here," said Maltz, his gravelly voice booming in Leah's helmet.

She and Herbert reached the bank a moment later, and she glanced at her tricorder, even though Maltz had dismissed its read-ings. Signaling to each other, the two Klingons split up and went opposite ways along the bank, while Leah collected readings.

The lad stepped closer to her and asked, "What are we looking for?"

"Originally, it was the bastards who set loose the Genesis Wave," answered Leah. "But now it seems to be Colin Craycroft and the owners of that shuttlecraft. They beat us here, so maybe they know something. You have a pack of photon flares, don't you?"

"Yes," he answered uncertainly. "I'm not sure how to use them."

"Give me one," she said, holding out her hand. Behind her face-plate, she granted him an encouraging smile, but Herbert still looked shell-shocked by his extraordinary change of fortune. Finally the lad reached into his pack and pulled out a squat pistol with a large barrel, which he gently placed into her gloved palm.

She studied the device for a moment, gripped its awkward stock, then fired a bright stream of photons over the tar-encrusted bog. The dismal scene lit up like an amusement park on the Fourth of July, then a stream of live photons sprinkled down over the bog, which shimmered with strange energy surges. The tree trunk lit up like a Christmas tree in the glowing fallout, and it appeared to be a spiral staircase, not a tree at all. Some kind of boat or craft floated at the base of the tree.

"Holy cow!" said Herbert.

Brahms saw the two Klingons standing stock still, staring at all she had uncovered, and she couldn't resist broadcasting to all of them, "It's a holographic cloak. Sometimes you need more than your eyes."

"Is that a *boat* out there?" asked Maltz, jogging back to her.

"Hovercraft," she said, checking her tricorder. "A small one, probably two-person."

"How are we going to get there?" Gradok asked, dashing along the bank.

Leah pressed a button. "I just sent the coordinates to the ship. I think they can transport us there—one by one. Who goes first?"

"May I have the honor?" asked Gradok.

She contacted the ship and gave the order, and the weapons master was transported to the tree in the center of the tar bog, about seventy meters away. He had his knife drawn with a disruptor for backup, and as soon as he arrived on the tiny island, they saw his flailing silhouette fighting something invisible to them.

"Gradok, what is it?" demanded Maltz.

"A blasted net!" he grumbled. "Must be the holographic cloak!" There was a vivid burst of sparks, and they could make out Gradok kicking something on the ground. From the shore, they could see nothing but vague outlines and sparks, which finally died down to the normal gloom.

"Fine now," he muttered. "I see the hovercraft. Want me to bring it over? There's not much room to stand here."

"Do you see the staircase?" asked Brahms.

"I see a hatch. I think we can blast it."

"Belay that," ordered Brahms. "Don't destroy anything until we see what it is. We'll keep transporting over. *You* climb into the craft to make room for us."

"Yes, sir," grumbled the weapons master.

In an orderly fashion, they transported to the tiny island around the old tree trunk in the asphalt bog. Gradok had indeed destroyed a holographic mesh that covered the boat and the hatch. The cloak didn't do much but mirror the surrounding textures, but that had been enough in this gloomy place.

"I think visitors put this cloak up," Brahms said, holding the shimmering fabric between her gloved fingers. "Because the hatch was hidden without it."

"Craycroft!" said Maltz, seething. "How did *he* get in?"

The two Klingons scrutinized the small hatch at the base of the tree. Both of them tried their brawn on it, but there was nowhere to get a grip. The smooth, domed surface looked like it had to be opened from inside.

"Let me try," said young Herbert.

Glowering doubtfully beneath their hoods, the two Klingons stepped into the sticky tar to make room for the lad to approach. He peered intently at the dull hatch for several seconds, then he peered upward at the burnt tree trunk. With a quick move that startled Leah, the lithe youth jumped up and caught the burnt stump of a branch. When the branch tipped downward, the hatch opened like a camera lens. In the dim light, Leah saw a spiral staircase winding downward into darkness.

"How did you know to do that?" Maltz asked suspiciously.

"It just made sense," answered the lad. "If someone came over here in that hovercraft, he must have been able to let himself in."

"What if it's a trap?" asked Leah.

"Then it's a good one," said Maltz. "They have captured *my* curiosity. The honor is still yours, Weapons Master."

Gradok grunted and flicked on a light atop his helmet. Disruptor rifle leveled for action, the hulking Klingon tromped down the staircase, with Maltz on his tail. Leah nodded brusquely to Herbert, who took up the next position in the descent. She didn't know why, but she had a feeling that this was too easy, too convenient. Craycroft hadn't had that big of a lead on them. How had he found this place?

Before she could answer that or any other questions, Leah Brahms was clomping down a slippery metal staircase, plunging into the bowels of the dank planet. At this point, it seemed as if they had stumbled upon nothing but a pit under the tar bog, and she momentarily wondered if it was an excavation pit, maybe an archaeological dig. The walls of the stairwell seemed to be as hard and black as obsidian, and she figured some kind of process had been used to harden the asphalt.

Using the light on her helmet, Leah kept glancing at her tricorder as she descended. "There's oxygen down here," she told the others. "It's not breathable air, but it's getting close to it."

"There is more than that," said Gradok. Brahms leaned over the rail of the spiral staircase and looked down into the depths, where she saw the Klingons' lights. They had stopped descending and were standing motionless outside an open doorway, illuminated in a flickering light. Their weapons were ready for action, but they weren't firing.

When the two humans reached their position, Leah finally saw what had given them pause. Lying in the doorway, surrounded by his own dying light, was the old Tiburonian, Krussel. Gradok lowered his head to shine his beam at the frail Tiburonian, and Leah gasped out loud.

His face was frozen in a grimace of sheer terror, as if he had died of fright, and his fingers were curled into grasping claws. It might have been lack of oxygen that produced such terror, Leah told herself, because his headgear lay about a meter away from his paralyzed hand.

"Is that . . . the old miner?" she asked, just to make sure.

"Yes," answered Maltz. "He was going to be our guide, and he must have become Craycroft's guide instead."

Young Herbert turned away from the sight, while Gradok lifted his light into the blackness beyond. Leah turned to her tricorder, trying to get an estimate of how long he had been dead.

"Maybe it's the conditions in this pit," she reported to the others, "but he hasn't decomposed much. I don't think he's been dead long."

Gradok kicked the body out of the way, and he and Maltz continued plunging into the darkness. Herbert stood petrified on the stairs, as stiff as the dead Tiburonian, and Leah had to squeeze past him. "You can stay here if you want," she told the youth.

"No, no, I'll go," he insisted. "Captains first."

She rolled her eyes at him. "Thanks."

Brahms only gave the Tiburonian's body a passing glance as she walked by, concentrating on the uneven floor and her tricorder readings. They were in a dark tunnel that had also been carved from solid tar. This tunnel was different only in that some kind of moss grew on the walls at intervals, along with thick vines underneath it.

Brahms checked her tricorder but didn't note anything unusual about the plant growth—it was probably a natural occurrence from the dampness and the increased oxygen. These types of plants, including the fungus she was picking up, didn't need much sunlight. They may be getting sunlight from the surface, she surmised; maybe these were the roots of the cattails above.

"We see him!" said a sharp voice in her ear.

Leah jogged in her heavy suit to catch up with Maltz and Gradok. She instantly knew it was bad, because the Klingons were backed up against the mossy walls of the cavern. Her eyes followed their light beams to a frail form sitting on a rock, and the being turned around and gazed at her with blurry, indistinct eyes.

To her horror and amazement, it was the old Tiburonian, Krussel! Only this time, he was alive and grinning contentedly at them.

twenty

A phaser beam struck the grinning figure of Krussel and blew him apart in a haze of green confetti. His body floated down from above like a feather pillow torn apart in a pillow fight. Instantly, the Klingons dropped to a firing crouch, their disruptors aimed, looking for the source of the phaser blast in the dark tunnel. Leah glanced at Herbert, half-expecting that *he* was the one who had fired the unexpected shot, but the lad was cowering from the remains of Krussel, which were still floating down.

They didn't look like parts of a body, thought Leah, that was for sure. Unfortunately, there was only pitch blackness in the tunnel, and their pitiful lights did little to dispel it.

"Don't shoot! Don't shoot!" screeched a voice. From the blackness ahead of them, a phaser skittered across the floor, and Leah bent down to grab it. Then a figure emerged from the inky blackness, wearing civilian clothes and waving his hands frantically in the air.

"That wasn't Krussel!" shouted Colin Craycroft. "That wasn't *real!*"

Maltz kicked at the remains of the old miner, which looked like dried leaves, then he leveled his disruptor at Craycroft. His voice boomed from his helmet. "What in Klin was it? Speak fast, or I'll kill you!"

"Yes, go ahead and kill me! I beg you!" The crazed human opened his shirt and showed them his flabby chest.

Leah quickly stepped between them. "Hold your fire, mister. I have some questions for Mr. Craycroft here."

The old Klingon lowered his weapon and glowered at Craycroft. "Yes, I have some questions, too."

Brahms turned to the tavern keeper. "First of all, there's air in here? You can *breathe?*"

"Yes! No!" he answered confusedly. "Yes, there is air, but no, don't take off your helmets. They'll confuse you, like they did with Krussel. Listen, come with me, and I'll show you."

The little man rushed off down the corridor, and Maltz and Gradok were quick to follow. Brahms gave Herbert a shove, and they both made a wide path around the pile of leaves that had looked like a humanoid a few seconds ago. Leah could well understand the boy's fear; but this was a volunteer mission for him, so he had no reason to complain. Hearing a discussion ahead of her, she hurried to catch up with Maltz, Gradok, and their new guide, Colin Craycroft.

"You can't con a con artist!" Craycroft said with a satisfied chortle. "I knew they were fake. For his own protection, I sent Krussel back to the shuttlecraft, but then he picked up your ship on sensors. He panicked . . . forgot to put on the camouflage. But at least he told me where to look. Wait 'til you see it!" He skipped ahead of them down the gloomy corridor.

"Don't get out of my sight," warned Maltz.

But they needn't have worried about that, because they soon emerged into a vast, well-lit engine room. Huge, gleaming crankshafts and rods churned away, and massive silos towered dozens of meters into the air, turning slowly, gurgling softly. It was difficult to tell what kind of energy they were producing, or storing, but this was well-maintained equipment. Nevertheless, there were piles of dead leaves scattered around the expansive floor.

"What is this place?" asked Maltz suspiciously.

"I don't know, but I claim salvage rights!" Craycroft said, giggling. He dashed through the cavernous chamber, pointing at the piles of dead vegetation. "Don't worry, it's safe. I killed them all!"

"What has this got to do with the Genesis Wave?" demanded the old Klingon.

That stopped the crazed human in his path. "Genesis Wave? I thought that was just a rumor you were using to keep away the competition. This is a secret production facility—for what, I don't know. But if they want to remain secret, they've got to pay *us* to go away. And then a little stipend every now and then to keep quiet. Either that, or I file salvage claims . . . to these ruins."

"These aren't ruins," insisted Brahms. "And according to you, this place was inhabited . . . before you killed all of them."

"Besides, we're going to *kill* you." Maltz aimed his disruptor at the agitated human.

"Wait!" begged Craycroft, holding up his hands in supplication. "I *saved* your lives! I led you to this place! It wasn't just Krussel—I have sophisticated mine detectors on my shuttlecraft, and *I* was the one who spotted this underground complex. And I killed these creatures in self-defense!"

"Hold on," Brahms said quickly. She interceded with the old Klingon. "I said we're taking him prisoner. We could use his shuttlecraft, and he might be worth a ransom to someone."

Maltz scowled behind his faceplate, but he finally said, "Yes, sir." Pulling a coil of rope from his sash, he strode toward Colin Craycroft and grabbed him by his wrists. When the human put up a struggle, the Klingon smashed him in the mouth, drawing blood. After that, Craycroft went silently and allowed Maltz to tie him to a pole with his hands behind his back.

"This is a death sentence!" shouted Craycroft, spitting out a tooth. "You'll see. You *need* me!" He kept babbling, but it was incomprehensible.

"I've had enough of this." Without hesitation, Brahms drew a phaser—she now had two of them—and set it for stun. Then she drilled Colin Craycroft with a bright beam, and he slumped into a pile at the bottom of the pole. The cavernous chamber was much quieter without his ranting.

The Klingons again signaled to one another and started forward, inspecting the braces that held up the vats, looking for hidden enemies. At least the gleaming silos looked like vats to Brahms, and her tricorder indicated that they contained an unidentified liquid. From a quick glance at the chemical components in the vats, she guessed it was fertilizer. Leah wanted to find a computer terminal, or other high-level processor, so she concentrated her tricorder search on power sources and electromagnetic impulses.

Herbert walked around, gazing up at the ceiling, which was covered in a thick growth of moss.

"This place is the key!" crowed Maltz, his loud voice sounding deranged in her headgear. "I know they were here—I can *feel* them. This is the lair of the enemy."

"This complex is big—goes back a long way," Brahms said, amazed at the readings she was getting. "We could spend a week searching it."

Gradok suddenly ran to the wall and began ripping away the vines and moss. Slowly he uncovered a sealed metal doorway. The big Klingon tugged on the door and beat it with his fists a couple of times. "Youngster!" he called. "Do you have a way of getting this door open?"

It took Herbert a moment to realize that he was being addressed, and he stumbled forward. "Let me look at it." To her surprise, the lad didn't use his eyes but instead used his tricorder. On her tricorder, Leah was picking up impressive circuitry behind the door, and she was all in favor of getting it opened.

Before the young human could work any magic, they heard a gruesome scream from behind them. The mangled cry was enough to make them all whirl around. It had to be Craycroft, thought Leah, but their prisoner was too far away—behind too many poles and braces—for them to see him.

"You should have used a longer stun," said Maltz.

"Was *that* Mr. Craycroft?" asked Herbert. "It didn't even sound human."

"I'll go look," volunteered Gradok, lifting his disruptor rifle and trudging off toward the entrance to the mammoth cavern. A moment later, he disappeared in the forest of machines and silos.

"If we contact the ship," said Leah, "maybe they can transport us to the other side of that door. We're not that deep inside the crust."

Maltz nodded thoughtfully, but before they could act on the suggestion, they heard startled shouts; and disruptor beams flashed across the empty spaces of the cavern. A moment later, the entire complex was plunged into darkness, and all they had were the insufficient light beams on their helmets.

"Gradok!" Maltz shouted, trying to raise his comrade. "Gradok, respond!"

"Sir!" cried Herbert, pointing a trembling hand into the darkness, where a row of ghostly shapes had suddenly materialized and were slowly advancing upon them.

Brahms didn't wait to see more of this; she aimed her phaser and raked the front row of attackers. But the stun setting had no effect on them, and she cranked it up to full. This time, both she and Maltz cut loose with withering beamed fire, blasting the front row of attackers into flaming confetti. Lit up like a mobile bonfire with flames leaping off their backs, the mysterious enemy kept advancing.

Within seconds, Leah, Maltz, and Herbert were backed up against the door they had uncovered. Leah drew her second phaser and blasted away with both weapons at the advancing horde, while Maltz clubbed them to shreds with the butt of his rifle. Still the enemy kept coming from the blackness, reforming into ranks from the flaming debris.

Just when there was no place left to go, the door behind them creaked open, and a strong hand grabbed Leah and yanked her into the darkness. Herbert and Maltz wasted no time following her, as they ducked into the unknown.

Geordi La Forge bolted upright in his bed, sweat streaming down his face. His stomach was knotted, and his clothes felt clammy. For a moment, he was totally disoriented by all the alien sounds and smells—not *his* normal sounds and smells—and he was even more confused by the unfamiliar darkness.

I'm blind, he reminded himself. *I'm in sickbay, not engineering. No, I don't belong here, but this is where I am. But damn, that dream was awful.*

Before he had a chance to stop it, the dream replayed in his mind's video log. He was a prisoner in a transparent cage in a laboratory, which he could see much more clearly than his ocular implants should allow. He wanted out of this crystal cage in the worst way, because he could *imagine* a giant tree where he belonged. The great tree towered above him, offering sanctuary, shelter, nourishment, along with Leah Brahms and everything else that gave him comfort in life. The longing to escape his cell was the strongest urge he had ever experienced, and he felt totally bereft without that tree.

The tree—the answer to everything—was behind a door. He knew that. The object of his desire was behind a closed door that was very near—Geordi could feel it like the heat radiating off a fire.

After a moment, he lay back in his bed, trying to shake off the beautiful but disturbing images. Geordi didn't know which was worse—being a prisoner or feeling helpless. He supposed they were both related. At the same time that he saw things more clearly in his dreams than he ever had, he couldn't see at all in real life. Where was the door he was supposed to find? He felt its presence very near at hand.

Leah blinked in amazement, because in the bobbing light of her headlamp stood Gradok, half-naked with his suit and hood gone—but grinning broadly. She heard scuffling, and she turned to see Maltz and Herbert struggling to shut the door Gradok had opened for them. She leaned into the oblong metal hatch, but the forces on the other side were also determined. Thick vines crept around the side of the door and lashed at their arms, while a concerted force pushed against them.

It wasn't until Gradok muscled into the fray that they got the door closed and latched, chopping off dozens of branches, which fell to the earthen floor.

Panting so loudly it echoed in her own ears, Leah Brahms turned around. She didn't think she had enough breath in her lungs to gasp, but gasp she did. She was standing outdoors, with a starlit sky sparkling above her head—the stars looked like loose diamonds sprinkled on black velvet. In the distance, a ghostly horizon bathed in mists and lit by Lomar's huge moon beckoned with the enchantment of a fairy land. The tar bogs glistened like black pools of forgetfulness.

"How did we get outside?" she asked.

"Don't trust your eyes," said a voice as a hand thrust a tricorder into her view. She looked down to see energy readings leaping across the tiny screen, then she looked up at Herbert's youthful face. "It's a holodeck," he said.

"Gradok, how did you get in here?" Maltz asked with suspicion.

He pointed toward the door they had just closed. "Those creatures . . . they surrounded me, but I managed to cut a hole in the wall with my disruptor. It was just big enough for *me* to get through, not my suit. They took the suit, and I barely got out of it in time. Then I ran along the wall until I found the door."

"So a hole is open, and they're coming through?" asked Brahms.

"The hole is small," answered Gradok, "but we should keep moving."

"What happened to Mr. Craycroft?" asked Herbert with concern.

The big Klingon flinched at the memory. "Those plants were growing all over the human. He must be dead."

"Good riddance," muttered Maltz.

"You can take your suit off," suggested Gradok. "The air is good in here."

"Belay that," said Brahms. She lifted her phaser and shot a beam straight into Gradok's chest, and he promptly slumped at her feet, unconscious.

Maltz whirled on her. "Why did you do that?"

"To see if he was real," Leah answered. "Remember, the *two* Krussels we saw, and what Craycroft told us? They're shape-shifters . . . or something. He'll come to in a few seconds. Until we need to take our suits off for a specific reason, we leave them on."

The engineer began wandering through the starlit scenery, checking her tricorder. "Herbert, if this is a holodeck, then there's got to be a computer running it. Use your tricorder to help me find it. Maltz, cover us."

"But, Captain, we've got to get more people—explosives!" protested the old Klingon. "We've got to *destroy* these evil creatures."

"First of all, we don't even know if these beings set off the Genesis Wave," answered Brahms. "We've got to find proof, and I haven't seen any. If this is a conventional holodeck, then maybe they have a computer, which we can access. Until then, *we're* the intruders, and they've got every right to attack us."

"Yes, sir." Grumbling under his breath, the grizzled Klingon jogged back to his fallen comrade, Gradok. The weapons master sat up, slowly regaining consciousness.

Brahms shouted loudly, "Computer, end simulation!" Nothing happened, and the two humans continued to explore in the darkness for several minutes. Without warning, there were flashes of disruptor fire behind them, followed by Klingons howling in victory. Leah tried to suppress her fear and concentrate on the task at hand.

Herbert called excitedly, "Captain Brahms, there's a strong energy source over here!"

She rushed toward the youth, monitoring her own tricorder readings as she ran. Herbert had stopped at the edge of a cliff overlooking a rather picturesque black bog; it seemed likely that no one would progress much beyond this point. Leah could easily make out the energy surges that had attracted the lad, but she suspected it was an energy coupling or a conduit, not a computer station. That would be a start.

"Step back," she ordered, drawing one of her phasers. The boy didn't wait to be told again, and he scurried away. Without worrying about accuracy, Leah cranked up the phaser to a destructive setting and turned it loose on what appeared to be a methane mist floating over the bog. The mist started to shimmer, and sparks flew out of nowhere.

Leah stopped the phaser barrage. When the smoke cleared, she saw that she had wreaked enough damage to reveal a black-and-gold grid where there had been a distant horizon. After a few more flickers, the entire scene switched to a beautiful copper beach, complete with gently waving palms and a quaint beach house in the distance.

The Klingons staggered toward her, shielding their eyes from the sun-drenched scenery. "What is *this* supposed to be?" demanded Maltz.

"An island . . . on Earth. Or Pacifica." Brahms frowned. "Pacifica? Why should that mean something?"

She was startled out of her musing by the sharp buzz of her Klingon communicator. "*HoS* to away team!" called a frantic voice. It was Kurok, sounding more perturbed than she had ever heard the second officer.

"Brahms here," she answered for the team. "What is it?"

"A large Romulan warbird has just shown up, and they are demanding to board us."

"No!" bellowed Maltz. "Tell them to take their shoulder pads and stuff them up their—"

"Belay that!" cut in Brahms. "They're supposed to be our allies. Tell them we have an away team on the surface."

"I did," answered Kurok. "They are demanding that we transport to their vessel and turn over all records to them. They act as if they want to take us prisoner, but I have yet to lower shields."

"They want all the glory!" yelled Maltz in rage. "I am not leaving until I fulfill my blood oath. Listen to me, Kurok, do *not* lower shields to transport us. Or for any other reason. Get out of there as fast as you can! The Romulans won't pursue you."

Brahms caught her breath, wondering if she should override Maltz's rash orders. But she realized two facts—she didn't want to lose her ship to the Romulans, and she wasn't ready to leave this planet yet. "Go on, Kurok, get away from here. Come back when they're gone."

"Yes, sir," answered the second officer.

Herbert flapped his arms, looking incongruous in his bulky environmental suit on the sunlit beach. In a squeaky voice, he asked, "Captain Brahms, are you sure you want to defy the Romulans?"

"We've come too far to let anyone stop us," the engineer declared with grit in her voice. She drew one of her phasers and handed it to the young man. "Here, you may need this."

twenty-one

"Commander!" called the centurion standing at the tactical console on the bridge of the *D'Arvuk*. "The Klingon vessel is powering impulse engines. Shall I open fire?"

The cadaverous Romulan commander turned to his ornate view-screen and saw the outdated Klingon cruiser suddenly veer away from the ugly planet. "Are their shields still up?" asked Jagron.

"Yes, sir."

"Then don't bother. Unless we destroy them, it might cause an incident." The commander of the mighty warbird returned to his planetary sensors. "It is interesting that they would leave a landing party on the planet, unless that was a lie. Do we sense any life-forms?"

"No, sir," answered the centurion on tactical, "but it will take us several hours to complete a scan. Lomar would appear to have very little life . . . only a few plants."

"Hmmm, what kind of plants?" asked Jagron with interest.

"Unknown from these scattered readings. Shall we prepare an away team?"

"Prepare *ten* away teams," answered Commander Jagron, glowering at the gray, misty planet. "We are going to search every centimeter of Lomar. But use caution, and make sure everyone is vaccinated against the fungus. The creature that took over the *Enterprise* wanted to come here, and so did the Klingons. There *must* be something here."

"Sir," said the centurion with urgency, "I have just detected a shuttlecraft. Civilian Federation design."

The corners of Jagron's thin lips curled into a smile. "For a deserted planet, there's considerable traffic here. I will lead Team One myself."

Cautiously, Leah Brahms approached the front door of the quaint beach house just off the glittering copper beach. Neither one actually existed, because this was a holodeck; but the simulation had been done with considerable detail. If time were unlimited, she would have preferred to linger by the sparkling lagoon, watching the mysterious black shapes glide under the turquoise water. But she knew she had to access some real technology if she was going to learn anything.

As her gloved hand touched the doorknob of the front door, the knob suddenly turned from rustic wood to a glittering chunk of faceted crystal, and she found herself standing on the porch of an antebellum mansion. The scenery behind her also switched from the tropical isle to a flower-laden garden in the center of a quaint city, like New Orleans. On the other side of a hedge of flaming bougainvillea, she saw and heard pedestrians strolling by, filling the air with pleasant chitchat. Their voices only added to the rich sounds, which included birds and the gentle buzz of the bees as they darted among the colorful daffodils and petunias.

Disruptor beams suddenly tore into the strolling crowd, who completely ignored them and continued on their way.

"Don't fire!" she ordered, turning to see Maltz and Gradok, ready for action. "They're not real—they're part of the program. As much as I'd like to look around here, this holodeck is unstable. We need to get out of here."

"Holodecks," grumbled Maltz, his voice filled with disdain. "I know some Klingons use them for exercise and battle drills, but I never liked them."

"Holodecks are a favorite pastime among humans," agreed Brahms, walking across the porch and stopping at a setting of old-fashioned wicker furniture. "And this one is decidedly human. I would say this is a scene from Earth."

"And who do we know from Earth?" Maltz proclaimed triumphantly. "Dr. Carol Marcus!"

"It's incriminating, but it's still not proof," said Leah. "We need to find something definite to link this complex with the Genesis Wave."

"Captain Brahms!" Herbert's high-pitched voice said loudly in her headgear. "I think I may have found another exit."

It took her and the Klingons a moment to locate the lad, who was in a far corner of the garden, standing over what looked like a wishing well, complete with hand-cranked bucket and overgrown vines. Beside the well stood some small, weathered statues of garden gnomes. The wishing well was the only feature in the otherwise cheerful garden that looked at all foreboding.

Herbert stood over it with a tricorder. "According to my readings, this is a real hole," he declared. "Before the scenery changed, it was a sinkhole near the lagoon. If we want to explore it, I think the rope will support us." He gave the rope a forceful tug, and it didn't fall off the crank.

Maltz leaned over the well and aimed the light from his helmet into the pit. "It looks dark down there. And wet."

"I think the water is an illusion," answered the boy hesitantly.

"You *think?*" replied the Klingon. "Then you go first." He shoved the boy forward, and Leah said nothing. She was too busy watching a commotion on the other side of the hedges. The happy pedestrians were suddenly bustling about in agitation, running into each other, but she couldn't see the cause of the problem through the thick bougainvillea.

"Hurry!" she urged them.

Without hesitation, Gradok slung the disruptor onto his back and leaped into the well, grabbing the rope on his way down. He disappeared into the dark water without a splash, and Maltz shoved Herbert toward the opening. The lad hurriedly stowed his tricorder and phaser before he took hold of the rope and leaned over.

A rustling sound alerted Leah, and she whirled around to see the bougainvillea split asunder by a wedge of thick boughs. She wondered if the hedges had been programmed to move, until she realized that a horde of moss creatures were trying to break through. A distruptor beam sliced into them, cutting the shrubbery to shreds and filling the air with debris. At once, Herbert flung himself into the well with surprising agility in the bulky suit.

"I've got you covered, Captain!" insisted Maltz, laying down more fire. Moving seemed the prudent thing to do, and Leah rushed for the hole, swinging her legs over the side of the stone wall. As the bougainvillea completely disappeared—to be replaced by the inside of a physics laboratory—Leah grabbed the rope and plunged feetfirst into the watery hole.

Her feet hit the shimmering surface with absolutely no sensation. As she passed through the illusionary water, the rope disappeared from her hands, and Leah plummeted into darkness.

Strong arms caught her and yanked her out of the way, just as Maltz tumbled down from above, landing headfirst on the hard floor and smashing his lamp to pieces. The only light they had was from Herbert's helmet, and he tried to sweep the room while Gradok rushed to help Maltz.

The old Klingon sat up, shaking his head. He stared at the

weapons master, who shrugged apologetically and said, "I could only catch one of you."

"Where are we?" grumbled Maltz, gazing upward at the dark hole he had fallen down.

"I don't know, but it's cold in here," answered Gradok, his scarred body shivering.

"It's another storage area, I think." Leah turned on her light and directed the beam upward into the rafters, where what looked like sides of beef were hanging. That was her first impression, but the reality brought a gasp to her lips. They were not sides of beef but hundreds of naked humanoids in all shapes and sizes. They were encased in transparent bags, which expanded and contracted at the rate of normal breathing; the poor souls appeared to be in some kind of suspended animation.

As Leah looked more closely, her stomach tightened, because the bodies were being fed by vines and clumps of moss, snaking everywhere among the dark rafters.

"Holy cow," murmured Herbert.

"Do I see Klingons up there?" asked Maltz in rage.

"All kinds . . . all kinds of humanoids." Brahms guided her light to two small forms in a single bag, fed by twin stalks. "Look, there's a pair of Bynars."

"Are they still alive?" asked Gradok, his teeth chattering from the cold.

"Yes, according to the tricorder," answered Herbert.

"What fiends these are!" seethed Maltz. "If I were convinced the Romulans would do a good job, I would beg them to raze this planet. But they would more than likely befriend the devils and turn the Genesis Wave on *us*."

"We still don't know who *they* are," insisted Brahms. "Like the old miner said, this planet is riddled with weird plants, but who's in charge? Could a bunch of plants have built this complex? I don't think so. These beings, who are hanging in stasis until they're needed again, could have built this place. The question is, are they captives, or are they here of their own free will? This could be some kind of cult, or a conspiracy against the Federation."

"No Klingon would live like *that!*" shouted Maltz, shaking his fist at the gently breathing bodies hanging above them. "I say we cut one down and ask him."

They were hanging so low that Maltz reached a lanky arm upward and grabbed the foot of the closest encased humanoid. With his other hand, he drew his disruptor.

"Maltz, be careful," warned Leah. "I don't want a murder on our hands."

The Klingon nodded, then with pinpoint precision, he shot a beam into the vines and sheered them off around the head of the suspended captive. When the vines snapped, they spewed a vile, greenish sap all over the bag as it tumbled down. Gradok rushed to help Maltz catch the fallen dead weight, and he got the sap all over his bare skin.

"Aiyyagh!" howled Gradok, slapping at his skin as if it were on fire. That left Maltz to lower the body to the floor by himself, and he did so with surprising gentleness. Both Leah and Herbert moved forward, shining their lights on the naked humanoid in the bag, who was gasping for breath.

"Open the bag," ordered Leah.

The old Klingon reached for a small slit in the top of the bag, which was over the man's head. That feat alone wasn't easy, because the suddenly lively corpse was struggling for air and fighting blindly. Nevertheless, Maltz braved the onslaught long enough to get his fingers into the hole and rip it downward, tearing the squirming package open like a ripe banana.

"Oh, God!" croaked Herbert, turning away. The lad's action resulted in only half the light being cast on the afflicted man, but that was just as well, decided Leah. She cringed in horror but kept her eyes focused on the poor creature, whose mouth, ears, nose, and other orifices were plugged with moss and leaking vines.

Meanwhile, Gradok rolled around on the floor, writhing in pain. Brahms was glad that she had told the rest of them to keep their environmental suits on. She took a step toward the weapons master, but he motioned her away. "I will live," he said hoarsely. "A warrior can survive discomfort."

"Let me know if you need help." She turned to Maltz and motioned to the being he had cut down. "You've gone this far, so finish the job. Pull that stuff out of his mouth, so he can talk."

With a grimace that was clear even behind his faceplate, the grizzled Klingon bent down and began yanking weeds from the man's face. As he worked, Leah stepped closer to give him more light, and she tried to look beyond her disgust to see what species he was. From his high forehead and his black hair pulled into a severe ponytail, she assumed he was Antosian.

"Do you still think he's an accomplice, or a victim?" asked Maltz, panting from the exertion of clearing the man's windpipe and nostrils of the ubiquitous moss. "Even an Antosian is not so stupid as to agree to *this*."

Leah leaned in a bit closer to the afflicted man. As his breathing came more easily, he relaxed and stopped his struggles, slipping back into a comatose state. From a pouch on the side of her environmental suit, Brahms took out a small first-aid kit and quickly assembled a hypospray.

"What are you going to give him?" asked Maltz.

"A stimulant. We haven't got time to wait around here for him to wake up, do we?"

"No," agreed the Klingon. He gazed upward at the disturbing contents of the cold chamber. "Hurry, Captain."

Squelching her disgust at the slimy, naked body, Brahms bent down and stuck the hypo in his neck. Instantly his body twitched to life, and his eyes opened, staring around with shock and horror. Before the Antosian could focus his eyes on the frightening figures in dark armor, Leah said softly, "Try to relax, you're among friends. We're here to *rescue* you—to help you."

"Huh? Erghh?" His lips moved, and he seemed to want to talk, but the motion skills were just not there. "Mouth . . . sore," he finally croaked, working his jaw.

"That's a start," she said encouragingly. "Do you know where you are?"

He shook his head and looked around, then he curled into a fetal position and shivered. Brahms pulled out her phaser and shot it at the floor, heating a small area to a red-hot temperature—enough to warm both the Antosian and Gradok, who huddled near the spot.

"Captain Brahms," said Herbert with concern. "According to the tricorder, his vital signs are abnormally high, as if his system was racing."

She bent down in front of the Antosian, trying to get his attention. "What do you remember about being here? What did they make you do?"

He looked at her with confusion and puzzlement. "I . . . I thought I was somewhere else . . . my homeworld. My job . . . I did my *job!* I was never so happy."

"What is your job?" demanded Maltz.

"Biomolecular physiologist," said the Antosian, his eyes flashing with remembrance as he stated his title. "Where are my wife and children? They were here, too!"

Leah grimaced, because she didn't think his wife and children were here. At least she *hoped* they weren't. "Do you know what you were doing? What was the project?"

"Programming . . . theoretical." He shook his head. "We had synthesized several genomes into a matrix that could be exchanged over a carrier wave."

"Exchanged?" asked Maltz suspiciously. "Exchanged with whom?"

The Antosian shook his head. "Listen, I need some clothes . . . I need to get out of here!" He tried to stand, but his legs were none too stable, and he collapsed back to the floor.

"Do you *know* a way out of here?" asked Herbert, moving forward. "We'll be glad to save you."

With a trembling hand, the Antosian pointed into the darkness. "I remember . . . that way . . . I think."

Then he clutched his throat and began coughing and wheezing for breath. Leah moved to his side, as did Maltz, but they were too late. With a massive seizure that shook his whole body, the Antosian cried out in pain, then he went limp. The color drained instantly from his flesh, and he looked as if he had been dead for days.

Herbert spoke up, his voice cracking. "He's dead. He was dying even while he was talking to us."

Gradok leaped to his feet, rubbing his arms to keep warm. The Klingon jogged off into the darkness. "He said this way—come on."

As they followed, Maltz fell in beside Leah, and Herbert brought up the rear. "It sounds to me like he was working on the Genesis Wave," said the old Klingon.

Brahms nodded. "But the question is—what do we *do* about it? We're four strangers, lost inside this planet, with no ship and a Romulan warbird circling us."

"There is Craycroft's shuttlecraft," answered Maltz.

"If we can get to it," answered Brahms.

As they walked, the room began to narrow, and there were no longer bodies swinging over their heads. With Gradok leading, they moved quickly but warily, casting light ahead to look for dangerous plants in the shadowy corners. Soon they were inside a tunnel that appeared identical to the one they had passed through to reach the room with the crankshafts and silos. Moss grew at intervals, and vines snaked the length of the dark passageway. Although none of this vegetation was moving, it didn't look innocuous anymore, and they eyed the moss warily as they passed.

Brahms had the disturbing feeling that they were walking in circles when they saw light shining ahead of them. A few seconds later, they came upon a gleaming chamber with closed metal doors—it looked like some kind of secure portal. There was a small console standing at the side of the doorway, and Leah went straight toward it.

Herbert tagged along, still reading his tricorder. "It doesn't look like a hologram. It's giving off energy readings."

Leah shook her head and squinted at the small, unfamiliar console, which blinked at her with a cyclopean eye. She finally pressed the eye, and the door slid open. The inside of the chamber blinked and beeped invitingly.

"Maybe it's a turbolift," suggested Maltz. "Or a transporter."

"Or a disposal unit to disintegrate the bodies," said Herbert.

After a moment, Leah asked, "Are we going in there or not?"

For once, Gradok did not immediately volunteer, and Brahms didn't blame him. There was something unsettling about this gleaming metal compartment at the end of the dark tunnel, not far from where hundreds of helpless beings hung in suspended animation.

"If we only had some way to test it," said Brahms.

Without warning, a huge explosion sounded behind them, shaking the undergound passageway and causing dust to cascade down. The two Klingons and two humans whirled around and shined their lights down the corridor, where all they saw was smoke. Leah instantly drew her tricorder from her pouch and checked for lifesigns, finding dozens of them about a hundred meters away.

"What in Klin was that?" snarled Gradok.

"The Romulans," answered Leah. "They're in the chamber with all the bodies, coming closer."

"Romulans!" snarled Maltz, making it sound like an expletive. He lifted his disruptor rifle and assumed a firing crouch. "I am not going to be captured by Romulans."

"They're *our* allies!" said Herbert, his voice a strangled squeak. "Can't we make a deal with them?"

"There is no dealing with Romulans," answered Maltz. "I will not jeopardize my blood oath to please Romulans. In this narrow passageway, we can hold out against an army."

Another explosion ripped through the underground chamber, rocking the passageway again, but still there was no sign of the Romulans. Herbert drew his phaser, gripping it nervously. Without warning, the teenager turned and shot a beam that struck Gradok, and the big Klingon slumped to the floor.

"Traitor!" shouted Maltz. He fired his disruptor, but Herbert anticipated that action and ducked out of the way of the deadly beam. Then he scrambled down the dark tunnel, moving awkwardly in the bulky suit.

"Don't kill him!" ordered Brahms.

Maltz reluctantly lowered his disruptor rifle and just scowled instead. Then he turned on his heel and dove through the open door of the portal. No sooner had the Klingon entered the gleaming compartment than his body disappeared in a blinding flash.

Leah was about to follow him when another beam streaked from the darkness and struck her in the back. That was the last thing she remembered before she collapsed to the floor beside Gradok.

twenty-two

Maltz floated out of the chamber at the other end of the transporter link and gaped in awe at his surroundings. He was inside the most monumental space dock he had ever seen, a sphere containing literally hundreds of ships from every corner of the galaxy. As far as the eye could see were rows upon rows of sleek metal hulls, floating on moorings that expanded outward like spokes from a glowing central hub.

As he looked more closely, he realized that some of the vessels were centuries old, and others were partially disassembled, as if they had been salvaged for parts. But some starships looked brand-new and in perfect working order, such as the four squat *Defiant*-class vessels closest to him—no doubt the missing task force from Starfleet.

The old Klingon tried to turn around but couldn't do so while floating weightlessly, so he drew a small harpoon gun from his pack and shot it behind his head. After hearing a satisfying clink, he tugged on the rope and found it taut. Now he had an anchor with which to pull himself around. The effort was worth it, because the view behind him was no less remarkable. Through a somewhat clouded but expansive viewport, he could see a gray, foreboding planet, as close as if he were in orbit . . . or slightly farther out.

"I'm inside the moon!" he croaked to himself with amazement. He was at the outer edge of a hollow sphere that was easily as big as Lomar's moon, and he was looking through a camouflaged viewport. Like every other discovery, this one only reinforced his certainty that the enemy deserved no mercy.

"I am left alone . . . alone to destroy these monsters. It is my destiny." His blistered lower lip quivering and his rheumy eyes filling with tears, Maltz went on, "I will *smash* the wicked weapon and *kill* the woman who birthed this monster. If no living soul knows my glory, the heroes in *Sto-Vo-Kor* will know! Redemption will be mine . . . at last."

Maltz breathed deeply, trying to calm his war spirit for the immense task ahead. He looked again at the ugly planet in the window, thinking that if he watched long enough, he might see the hated Romulans cruise past. He chuckled with delight. It was funny that the overconfident Romulans were completely ignorant of this treasure trove of starships right under their noses. It had to stay a secret—at least until he made his escape.

Maltz let go of the rope to grab his disruptor rifle, which he aimed at the sleek transporter chamber. He unleashed a barrage of blazing beams, ripping the circuitry to shreds. Within seconds, the chamber exploded in a dazzling aurora, and the concussion propelled him backward, spinning at slow speed.

The Klingon flailed his arms for a moment, to no avail, until he realized that he would soon hit one of the vessels. The lanky warrior stetched his legs out straight, trying to time his collision, and he stuck feetfirst to the hull of a shiny *Defiant*-class small cruiser. After swaying on his feet for a moment, Maltz thanked Kahless for the magnetized soles of his boots.

The Klingon clomped across the saucerlike hull of the freshly minted vessel, looking for the gangway hatch. He finally found it on the underbelly of the ship, and he was relieved to see that the hatch had been left open. That was very careless of the enemy, but he loved it when an enemy was overconfident. They thought they had nothing to fear from these humanoid races they had fooled for countless centuries, but the Klingon would teach them otherwise.

Maltz opened the hatch and clomped inside the spacecraft, turning himself rightside-up in the process. Once inside the vessel, he carefully closed the hatch and looked around, the beam from his helmet the only light. He appeared to be in a storage area with photon torpedoes stacked all around him.

The Klingon found an access panel, which opened to a maintenance tube with a ladder leading upward, and he began to climb. He reasoned that he was down, and the bridge had to be up. It wasn't a large ship, and he found the heart of the vessel with no difficulty. The bridge had an efficient layout, with most of the stations facing forward as in Klingon vessels.

"Computer," he said loudly, "resume life-support."

At once, the lights blinked on, and the whir of air circulation sounded in his ears. Ah, it was wonderful that Starfleet engineers were such trusting souls, thought the old Klingon. Years of living in a Federation stronghold had taught him most of their terminology and technology, and he assumed he would have no trouble turning this discovery to his advantage.

He noticed a plaque on the bulkhead, which gave the name of the ship as *Unity*. That was ironic, thought Maltz, considering it now had a crew of one. The Klingon strolled up to the main viewscreen as he removed his helmet. It felt good to breathe freshly manufactured air again.

"Computer," he said with authority, "on main viewscreen, show me the most recent video log of activity on the bridge."

"Now displaying most recent log record before system shutdown," said the female voice of the computer. With that, the large screen came to life, showing images of a harried crew running around. Maltz sat in the pilot's seat, disturbed by the padded, contoured feel of a chair built for pampered humans, not for Klingon warriors. He stiffened his back, trying to make himself less comfortable, as he watched the drama unfold on the screen. Finally he would learn what had happened to the ill-fated task force, and he hoped to learn more about the enemy in the bargain.

Leah Brahms shook her head and painfully opened her eyes—only to focus with difficulty upon a pair of intense black eyes gazing down at her through a green-tinted faceplate. Slowly the cadaverous face pulled away from her, and she realized that she had been nose-to-nose with a Romulan, even though her own helmet had been removed.

"No lasting damage," said a voice behind her. "She will recover fully."

"Hello, Dr. Brahms," said a cultured voice. "Or should I call you *Captain* Brahms?" The hawklike face regarded her with mild amusement.

"Did you shoot me?" she asked hoarsely.

"No, that would have been our operative."

"Your operative," she echoed. "You mean . . . Herbert?"

The slim figure shrugged in his gleaming green environmental suit. "Yes, he is not actually human, nor is he young," answered the Romulan. "He was an agent we put on Protus for just such an emergency. We were very fortunate that he was able to join your crew when he did, or your refusal to cooperate would have resulted in casualties."

Leah gritted her teeth and sat up, anger flashing in her green eyes. "Where is Herbert now?"

"Aboard our ship, being debriefed by my intelligence officer. So is the Klingon we apprehended." The Romulan smiled like a snake.

"I am Commander Jagron of the *D'Arvuk,* and it's imperative that you cooperate with us. That is why we kept you on the planet—to help us. Where is the other Klingon?"

Her jaw worked furiously in anger, and she finally spit out, "I wouldn't tell you that, even if I knew."

"I see." Jagron's eyes narrowed into dangerous slits, and he motioned to the ornate chamber at the end of the narrow tunnel. "We know he went into this device, but our attempts to operate it have failed so far."

He gave her a pained smile. "I would hate to have to leave you here . . . now that you've been exposed to the fungus."

"Are you threatening me?" snapped Brahms. "I've been through more than you could possibly imagine! We didn't get here much before you did, and I'm sure your spy already told you how we found the shuttlecraft and a couple of crooks from Protus. Then we started exploring, and *this* is as far as we got. If you're here, then you've seen everything *I've* seen! So take your ridiculous threats and go somewhere else."

"Living with Klingons hasn't done much for your disposition." Jagron frowned under his hood and turned to the minions waiting behind him. "Team leaders, have all your teams concentrate their search in this complex. Tell them to exterminate the moss creatures as needed."

With nods of acknowledgment, several of the suited Romulans withdrew into the darkness, and Jagron turned to shake a fist at Leah. "If you've been lying to me, you will *pay.* Tell me how this chamber works."

"I don't even know what it does," she answered. "Maltz could be dead, for all I know. Why don't you walk in there and see?"

"I have," replied Jagron as he strolled into the empty chamber and turned to glower at the human. "Are you saying you haven't learned anything about the Genesis Wave from this place?"

Leah shook her head with frustration. "While you're standing here asking me stupid questions, maybe the enemy is getting away. Did you ever think of that? Or maybe they're planning another attack with the Genesis Wave. I don't care if you leave me here or not, as long as you *do* something."

"I feel we are closing in on our prey," Jagron said as he stepped from the empty chamber. "You'll be taken to our medical center and examined." He motioned to two more centurions, who hustled forward and picked Leah up.

Leah thought about saying something snide and spitting at this arrogant, two-bit potentate. But he was wearing an environmental suit, so it would be an empty gesture. Now that she thought about it, maybe this whole quixotic search had been an empty gesture.

Maltz sat back in his pilot's chair, his mouth hanging open at the image on the viewscreen. It was an oblong, brownish asteroid, which wouldn't have been remarkable except for one thing: It was fake! One after another, the other ships in the task force had been absorbed into an immense opening in the side of the asteroid, and the mostly human crew of this ship, *Unity*, were preparing to go next. They were total zombies, under the sway of several moss creatures, which lounged in the background, occasionally stepping forward to talk to the crew.

In those instances, the humans' faces registered absolute bliss when they talked to these monsters. It was sickening, but the video log wasn't fooled by their mind-clouding powers, unlike the weak-willed humans.

When it was over, Maltz checked the console where he had captured crucial data from the log. He had the warp signature of the fake asteroid, and he knew the exact location where they had captured these ships. It was incredible, but any force that built this fake moon could have done the same thing with an asteroid. It wasn't much different from a Dyson Sphere.

The Klingon had a burning certainty that Carol Marcus and the fiends behind the Genesis Wave were aboard that false asteroid. He was also certain that it was the location of the emitters that sent the wave on its genocidal onslaught. He would end the destruction and bathe in their blood.

Maltz rubbed his hands together and gazed at the Starfleet instrument panel. All of the security safeguards had been disabled, much to his advantage. Maybe he could use the ship's sensor to locate a Klingon ship in this mothballed fleet, and then transport over to it. That seemed unlikely, however, because they were awfully far from Klingon space, as he well knew. Better to use a shiny new Starfleet craft than a rusted hulk from bygone days. A more logical use of the sensors would be to find the exit from this immense cage, although he could always blast his way out if he had to.

That might be more fun.

Commander Jagron cringed behind his green-tinted faceplate and turned away from the desiccated, vivisected corpse they had found in what appeared to be a medical laboratory. It might have been a sickbay, but if so, it was one of the coldest and most heartless medical facilities he had ever seen. What had they been doing to this poor humanoid when they cut him up? Were they in such a hurry that they had to leave him here, opened up and drying like a carcass at the side of the road? Even for a man who could stomach a considerable amount of cruelty, this was a bit much.

"I'm detecting some of the fungus," said a science officer using a tricorder.

"I would imagine," answered Jagron distastefully. He turned to the specialists he had working on a computer terminal in the laboratory. "Have you retrieved anything?"

"Not yet, Commander," answered a gray-haired centurion. "They are using a high-level Federation encryption program, which we hope to crack in a few minutes."

The slim Romulan scowled, thinking that all this effort had better pay off soon. The complex was fascinating, but its infrastructure was clearly devoted to maintaining itself, not the Genesis Wave. Half of his crew was occupied with exterminating the enemy, and the other half lagged behind them, often exploring areas that had been damaged. If they weren't careful, they might be here for days, sifting through the layers of this eerie operation. In all they had seen, there was no direct evidence of the Genesis Wave.

"Bridge to Commander Jagron," said a familiar voice in his helmet. It was Petroliv, his lover and most trusted officer, and she sounded agitated.

"Go on."

"Commander, a Starfleet ship has appeared out of nowhere, and then has gone quickly into warp."

"Out of nowhere?" he asked doubtfully.

"We think they may have been hiding on the moon—or behind it," she explained. "From its warp signature, it's a *Defiant*-class small crusier. There are some anomalies around the moon that we should investigate. What should we do?"

Jagron cursed under his breath. "I would pursue this ship, but we can't get everyone back on board quickly enough. Put long-range scanners on it and try to track it. We may have to leave personnel here, with shuttlecraft for support, while we rejoin the *Enterprise*. What have you learned from our prisoners?"

"Nothing," she answered. "Even though they arrived before us, they don't possess any significant knowledge. Our operative confirms everything they say. Leah Brahms lost her husband and colleagues on Seran-T-One, so this is a personal matter with her. The Klingon we're holding is just a soldier. The Klingon who got away, Maltz, was at the Genesis Planet ninety years ago—he saw the original device."

"So he may have special knowledge," said Jagron thoughtfully. "And where did he go? This becomes frustrating, staying here. Ready two shuttlecraft for launch, and begin withdrawing the away teams. Start with my team. We'll decide quickly how many people to leave on the planet."

With disgust, the Romulan looked around at the cold laboratory, then at the gruesome, sliced-up corpse. "I am ready to leave Lomar."

"Commander," said Petroliv in the tone of voice she used when she was about to suggest something naughty, "I have an idea for our two visitors, Brahms and Gradok. They can't tell us anything, and they're really no threat. To return them to the *Enterprise* would only result in a lot of questions. Why don't we leave them here on Lomar, where we found them? We'll have a sizable force, and they'll be safe. Certainly Brahms can help our people with encryption and codes."

"Very well," answered the Romulan commander. "As always, I like the way you think. No one's government can squawk that we mistreated them, since this is where they wanted to be. Ready the prisoners for transport."

Geordi La Forge stared at a vast meadow with its gently waving grasses and shiny pools dimpling the landscape, all of it bathed in the golden glow of sunset. If this sight weren't magnificent enough, in the center stood a perfect, towering tree—the refuge he had always sought. At the base of the tree stood Leah Brahms in a flowing white dress, waving happily at him. He saw the gleaming meadow as clearly as he had seen sunset on the Ba'ku planet, when his eyes had functioned normally. Logic told him he shouldn't see this or anything at all without his ocular implants—or being immersed in a dream—but he was wide awake.

The engineer knew he had to rise to his feet and walk up that hill to the tree. Although it looked like a simple matter, a sickness had weakened him, and he knew it wouldn't be easy. It would require all his will and a major physical effort—he was certain of that. He gripped the sides of his bed, which was resting on the edge of the meadow, and he threw his legs over the side and climbed out.

At first, his legs were wobbly from spending too much time in bed; but since Geordi was normally on his feet all day his legs were strong. He willed himself to walk forward. His reward was a big smile from Leah Brahms, who waved encouragingly from the root of the tree. He could see her face vividly, too, for the first time, and he gasped at her angelic beauty.

There were unexpected obstacles in the way—trees and bushes that sprung up almost at the touch, blocking his passage. As much by feel as eyes, he guided himself around these obstacles, until he was again on a straight path to the proud tree. Geordi had heard the term "old oak" but still didn't know exactly what an old oak looked like, but he knew it represented something large, solid, and lasting. That described this big tree, beckoning like a lighthouse in the darkness. Its boughs were laden with fruit, leaves, and dew-covered moss, which glittered like emeralds.

As Geordi struggled up the hill, his legs weak from his sickness, gnarled vines erupted from the ground to block his way. As he struggled against these new obstacles, the vines wrapped around his arms and legs, catching him in place.

"But I'm so close!" Geordi shouted as he struggled. One vine rapped him on the jaw, knocking him to the ground. From there, the vines converged upon him—and that was the last thing he remembered before he blacked out.

When La Forge regained consciousness, the bed he was lying upon was much harder than his other bed, and the voices and hubbub were much louder. He reasoned that he was lying upon one of the examination tables in the outer triage, not the nice private area he'd had before. Geordi had to deduce where he was, because he was once again enshrouded in darkness.

"Hi, Geordi," said a familiar voice. "Do you know where you are?"

"Yes, Doctor," he answered, "I'm in sickbay . . . trying to get well."

"Is that all you remember?" asked an authoritative voice that he recognized as Captain Picard's.

La Forge shook his head, wondering why he felt as if he had holes in his brain. "Do you mean the dreams? I was having dreams."

"And walking in your sleep," added Dr. Crusher.

"I was?" asked Geordi with confusion. "I got up out of bed?"

"You certainly did," answered Crusher. "You got up from your bed, walked freely through sickbay—even though you're not wearing your implants—and then attacked three security officers who were stationed outside my research laboratory."

"I did?" asked La Forge in amazement. "I don't remember that—it wasn't in my dream."

"Security reports that you wanted to get into the laboratory very badly," said Picard, "and that you acted like you were awake. What did you think was in there?"

"A tree," answered La Forge, suddenly remembering—even if the image wasn't as vivid as before. "I know that sounds silly, but I could see a tree . . . at the top of this gentle hill with long grass and little puddles." He left out the part about Leah Brahms, because he knew she wasn't on board the *Enterprise*, which meant that his memories were more dream than reality.

Crusher's soothing voice broke into his thoughts. "You could *see* it? Don't you usually dream in your regular vision, from your implants or VISOR?"

"Yes, but I *saw* this. It was like seeing with eyes, which is an experience I'm familiar with." He didn't mean to sound defensive, but he was a bit weary from the questioning. Can't a sick, blind man have his dreams?

"Commander," said the captain sternly, "there is *something* behind the door that you were trying so hard to enter. One of the moss creatures is growing in there, and you seem to have made telepathic contact with it. It's grown to maturity now, and it's probably trying to find a new host."

Geordi recoiled in the darkness and pulled his bedding around him. He had never felt so helpless. "Why me?"

"It may be a residual effect of the fungus," answered Dr. Crusher. "The fungus enhances the telepathic connection, making the victim even more susceptible to suggestion. We thought we had everyone placed at a safe distance from it, but we were wrong. I myself can't go in the lab, because it has immediate control of my mind, offering more images of Wesley."

Crusher sighed, sounding like she was pulling herself together. "Your visions have probably been conjured up from your own mind, plus what it *wants* you to see. The fungus-telepathy combination has proven very effective on the rest of us, but you have an advantage over us. When you *see* something, you should know automatically that it's false. You can't physically see at the moment."

La Forge gulped, wondering what they wanted him to do. On one level, he would miss the beautiful visions if they stopped, but every fiber of his being urged him to battle these chimeras. Lovesick, blinded, recovering from an illness—he already felt helpless and vulnerable. Now one of those horrible plants was trying to control his mind.

"It's a disturbing organism," said Captain Picard, "but it's obviously intelligent. We'd like to find a way to talk to it. Perhaps more than that. Over what distances can they communicate with each other? Where is their base, where they launched the Genesis Wave? So far, these creatures have managed to manipulate *us*, and I'd like to return the favor. Will you help us, Commander?"

Geordi nodded forcefully. "Yes, sir, I will."

twenty-three

The more Carol Marcus saw of the fake Jim and David on the equally bogus Regula I space station, the more she hated them. Perhaps it was their condescending glances when she turned in her work, like a person looks at a cute puppy who has done a clumsy trick. They obviously didn't want to make her sick again, so they conferred with her infrequently, always encased in their cleanroom suits. Lately they had resumed making the occasional joke in character, and she could sense that their dark mood had lifted. This could only mean that they were close to unleashing the Genesis Wave again . . . and time was running out.

In her solitude, the old woman had figured out the basics of what she needed to do. She had to incapacitate Jim and David and get out of this holodeck long enough to sabotage their plans. Her only weapons were that she had been left with the power to read their thoughts, and she knew the real Regula I like she knew the rummage of her own brain. This simulation was impeccably accurate.

Ninety-two years ago, she had accidentally turned off the artificial gravity on Regula I by overloading the main superconducting stator with gravitons—an improvement that didn't work out. Although the holodeck program undoubtedly had safeguards built in, the lack of gravity wasn't life-threatening. The program should allow it to happen, she reasoned.

Ninety-two years ago, a chrylon gas leak had followed the gravity disruption a couple minutes later, but she was going to speed that up. She also intended to mix reality with illusion, as her captors had. Marcus had collected enough solvents, acids, propellants, and other chemicals to make a fairly noxious smoke bomb combined with an aerosol herbicide, the same kind she had used sparingly on her garden on Pacifica.

She had collected huge chunks of raw meat from the food replicator, which her jailers didn't seem to monitor, and she had stuffed one of the cleanroom suits with the slimy material. That suit full of dead meat was going to play *her* in the little scene she was directing; while she wore a lightweight environmental suit and stayed behind the curtain.

The preparations in her mind had taken days, but the old woman knew that the execution had to take seconds. There could be no hesitation. She had to perform each step precisely, never giving her captors a chance to realize that *they* had been fooled. For once.

If she were going to be stopped, fortunately, it would be at the very beginning—if the artificial gravity failed to go off inside this combination holodeck-laboratory. It was a good bet that these beings were more rooted to gravity than a spry old lady, and the weightlessness would affect them more.

As soon as she fastened her environmental suit shut, Carol Marcus leaned over the computer board and upped the graviton feed from the EPS conduits to the laboratory gravity system. With satisfaction, she watched the readouts—just like ninety-two years ago, then she stepped briskly away from the console toward the test chamber.

Carol reached the chamber just as the gravity actually cut out, forcing her to activate the magnets in her boots. That was cutting the timing a bit closely, and she sounded realistically out-of-breath when she hit her combadge.

"David! Jim! Help!" she implored them. "We've lost gravity in the lab! There's an overload in the superconducting stator!"

She pulled a melon-sized, papier-mâché ball from the chamber and lit the fuse with a lab burner. Within seconds, greenish yellow smoke billowed from the sputtering ball and flowed around the circular lab, obscuring the starscape in the surrounding viewport.

"And . . . and . . . now there's a chrylon gas leak!" she cried with alarm. "I'm . . . I'm losing consciousness . . . help me, David!"

Under cover of her crude smoke bomb full of homemade herbicide, Marcus reached into the test chamber and pulled out the cleanroom suit stuffed full of meat. She gently pushed the dummy, which was now weightless, into the center of the smoke. It was exactly like the kind of suit *they* had been wearing for weeks, and she had a feeling the meat would attract them.

With the curtain up and the action underway, it was time for the director to get off stage. So Carol grabbed the retractable pulley she had rigged to the door of the lab, hunched down, and waited.

The door whooshed open, and the two suited figures stood there, transfixed by all they saw. She cleared her mind as she had been practicing for many days, making them depend on their other senses, which were weaker than telepathy. Jim and David were loathe to enter a weightless room full of smoke, but they also knew this was a holodeck, where things were not as they appeared. They had to assume they could make this room go back to normal with a simple command.

However, the body floating in front of them was very real, and Carol could sense their worry and distress over the likelihood that she was dead. In unison, they made up their minds. They didn't rush into the room—they slithered in, keeping close to the floor, under some of the smoke, and using their hands like crawling vines.

It was slow, awkward going in their suits, and Carol held her breath, knowing that the cleanroom suits pulled air out of the atmosphere and filtered it. Even if they didn't remove their suits, they would still get a dose of poison.

When the fake Jim Kirk finally did remove his helmet, and she saw what was underneath, Carol tried not to gasp. But her mind reacted with horror, alerting both Jim and David. She turned off the magnetism on her boots, tugged on the retractable line, and flew across the room and out the door.

Her feet landed in a corridor with gravity, and she promptly turned around and grabbed the door of the hatch. Before she shut it, she saw Kirk shrivel up like a dried bush in a forest fire. Still wearing his suit and coping unsuccessfully with a lack of gravity, David crawled toward her, using his hands and legs like clawing vines.

Daggers of outrage and misery assaulted her mind. "Mom! Why are you hurting me?" screamed a voice, sounding exactly like David when he was little, getting a scraped knee bandaged. "You're going to leave me to die, just like you did before!"

That accusation cut deeply, and a pang of guilt tore at Carol's insides. Then she gritted her teeth and slammed the door shut on the creature who slithered toward her. Pulling down the latch, she closed the airtight seal, trapping her tormentors inside—one already dead, the other dying.

"Mom, don't leave me!" screeched a voice.

Covering her ears, Carol Marcus shouted to the stars, "You're dead, David! You're really, really *dead!* Killed by a Klingon blade . . . and nothing will ever change that. I can't see you again . . . not in this life."

Sniffing back tears, the old woman shuffled down the corridor, taking heart from the fact that she had been right—this *was* a starship. Now she was certain of it. Although it lacked specific signage, it seemed very much like a Federation vessel, or at least a vessel designed for humanoids to operate. It was very efficient, right down to the . . .

Blinking red lights and loud Klaxons that suddenly blasted and blared all around her. "Intruder alert!" warned a deep voice. "Go to red alert! Intruder alert!"

The creatures must have lived long enough to sound an alarm, thought Carol with frustration. If they were looking for an intruder, her only hope was to look like she fit in. She quickly shed her environmental suit and stuffed it behind a bulkhead joint, then she straightened her uniform, which she had pulled out of the replicator. Carol Marcus hurried down the corridor and rounded a slight bend just as a doorway to her left opened. When half-a-dozen people stepped into the blinking red lights, she realized she had stumbled upon a turbolift.

"Thank goodness, you're here," said Marcus, trying valiantly to hide her disgust at their appearance. They were all young humans in battered Starfleet uniforms, but they looked sick and malnourished. Still it wasn't their vacant-eyed expressions that chilled her—it was the greenery growing on their backs and necks like a lion's mane. In addition to this rich pelt of vibrant moss, tentacles reached into their noses, mouths, and ears. She caught an insignia on a shoulder that read, "Fifth Task Force Starfleet."

"There's been an explosion in the holodeck. There are casualties. Down there!" Marcus pointed down the corridor, where indeed there was smoke.

The afflicted officers just stared at her, dumbfounded, and she quickly reasoned they they were waiting for telepathic confirmation from their masters. She had learned to receive telepathically— could she send, too?

Believe this woman, she broadcast over and over again with her mind. *She is one of us. One of us. Trust her.*

They stared at the sincere elder, and the pathetic soul who was in charge snapped out of his stupor. "Thank you, ma'am. It might be

dangerous here. Will you go up to the control room?" He motioned
to the turbolift.

"Indeed I will," she answered, backing into the turbolift. "Thank
you." She shivered as the doors closed tightly.

Going to the bridge was tempting, but it seemed to her that
there might be more plant monsters on the bridge, keeping their
deluded crew in line. She was free, and the main objective was to
stay that way until she learned more. "Up one deck," she ordered
cautiously.

The door opened abruptly, making her jump. When Marcus
stepped out of the turbolift, she still found strobing red lights and
sirens, but there was no one in view. In fact, she seemed to be in
an unfinished part of the vessel that was now used for storage.
The vast room was divided into aisles by rows of raw materials, disassembled modules, and starship components. She noticed a row of
particle emitters exactly like those that would be used for the
Genesis Wave. Marcus walked past thickets of cables and conduits
until she reached the bare bulkhead, and she turned to look
around. They had enough stuff here to double the strength of the
Genesis Wave.

Without warning, the strobing red lights and Klaxons stopped,
and the large storage room reverted to normal ambient light. Maybe
they had stopped looking for her, thought Carol with relief; maybe
they had even accepted her fake body as real. With any luck, it
would take them a while to recover and inspect the meat in the
suit, plus they had to cope with the untimely deaths of the creatures
who called themselves Jim and David. She hoped that would be a
crippling blow to their plans.

It was tempting to stop here and rest a while, but Marcus knew
she couldn't stand still and wait for them to find her. She had to
keep exploring the ship. Judging by the size of this empty deck, the
vessel had to be rather large and an odd shape. As the scientist
walked down an aisle lined on both sides with shiny new equipment

and components, she looked for anything she could use as a weapon, or a bomb.

Her eyes lit upon a portable force-field generator, such as the kind erected outside an encampment for protection, or inside a cave to fortify the walls. If they had this kind of equipment, she thought with excitement, maybe they had gel packs to power it. Her heart thumping, Marcus rummaged through row after row of components until she found a case that was the right size. After prying the latches open, she lifted the lid and looked with delight at two deep stacks of gel packs and the fittings and tools needed to hook them up to just about anything.

Now she could turn this place into a fortress—or maybe turn herself into a walking fortress. But she had to work quickly.

"All right," said Geordi La Forge uncertainly, "can we go over exactly what you want me to do?"

"Yes," answered Captain Picard, sounding very patient and very serious. "So far, the mental exchange with these creatures has been very one-sided, with them probing our minds, stealing what they want, and regurgitating it back in a pleasing form."

"I know all about that," said Geordi. He grimaced as he recalled how one of them had kissed him while it was impersonating Dolores Linton. If Data hadn't saved him on Myrmidon . . . he tried not to think about it while he waited in the dark prison of his sightless eyes. Geordi wasn't even certain what room they were in, although his chair was comfortable enough.

"Dr. Crusher assures me that you've been cured of the fungus," the captain went on, "although you're still receptive to their telepathic overtures. Of all people, Mr. La Forge, you ought *not* to be fooled by their visions and falsehoods. You can contact them with a clear head, knowing nothing you see is real."

Picard took a breath as he seemed to collect his thoughts. "Since this plant is a young individual without much experience, we think you could even control the exchange. They have imparted a lot of false information to us, and we feel we can do the same to them. Counselor Troi has a few thoughts on the matter."

"You're doing my job for me," said the ship's counselor, "because I can't go anywhere near that thing without becoming physically ill. It's like a beacon that is always left on—putting out signals, trying to pick up signals. From what you've told us of your visions, you have invented a kind of symbolic language to speak to this creature. The tree isn't really *your* symbol—it's the moss creature's symbol of yearning. It's outgrowing its enclosure, and it wants a tree in which to roost. This is all it knows . . . for now."

"I know where you're going with this," said La Forge somberly. "You want me to give false information to this creature, instead of the other way around."

"That's right," said Picard. "For two days, we've scanned this asteroid field with sensors, and we could spend a lifetime doing that without success. We need to draw the enemy out . . . make them think it's safe to emerge from hiding. They're here somewhere—all our models show that the Genesis Wave originated in the Boneyard. But where?"

"The tree," said Geordi with realization. "You want me to tell this creature that the tree it searches for is here. And you think it will mentally contact other creatures nearby?"

"We're ready to try it," said Picard. "The evidence from Myrmidon is that they communicate with each other telepathically. They've lied to us with impunity, and now it's time to even the odds. But this is a controlled situation where we've minimized the danger to you as much as possible."

La Forge nodded solemnly, not relishing the idea of having to perform counterintelligence, but this ruthless enemy didn't leave them much choice. He was the logical one—if he could just remember that he was blind.

"Are you ready?" asked Deanna Troi. "Do you want some rest first?"

"No," said Geordi, rising slowly to his feet. "Let's go."

"Good luck," said Deanna, squeezing his arm. "I can't get any closer than this, but Dr. Crusher will be monitoring you by tricorder."

"Should I go into the room . . . with this thing?" asked Geordi.

"That's up to you," answered the captain. "The force fields will remain on, so it can't have physical contact with you. We'll be watching all the time. Remember, we want it to think it's safe here—that help is at hand."

In the captain's firm grip, Geordi allowed himself to be led from the room and down a long corridor. Before they even reached the laboratory, he felt the yearning and longing swell upward from unseen depths, striking him like a wave. Truly, it was the longing he felt so often—an emptiness that could be met by only one thing. For him, it was Leah Brahms; for the creature, it was an idealized tree. Not just any tree, Geordi knew, but a home where every need would be met.

He hardly felt the captain's hands on his arm or the voices talking to him, because his perfect sight had returned. In the golden meadow stood the majestic tree, and he knew instantly that he had to seize control of the exchange at this instant, before his opposite could dictate terms.

Instead of passively seeing, Geordi began to imagine. He imagined a tree even more wonderful than the creature's idealized tree, adding his own special impressions of a healthy infrared aura, coolly pulsing veins, and a vibrant electromagnetic glow. He had no trouble visualizing his favorite fruits—ripe and dripping with juice— along with plump leaves and vegetables. He also envisioned the hordes of moss creatures he had seen on Myrmidon, shuffling forward, claiming the entire planet as their own.

La Forge imagined an entire propaganda log for the benefit of their prisoner, extolling the wonderful day when hordes of moss creatures would cover the heavenly tree . . . all living in bliss.

With tears streaming down his eyes, Geordi pressed his face against the door, feeling the abject longing swell within him, then slowly dissipate. He knew instinctively that his message was getting through, and he joined the unseen creature in its unbridled joy at the idyllic outcome. The human had no trouble imagining a wonderful ending to their long, long search—he just had trouble making it happen for himself.

La Forge shook off this lapse of negativity, while he imagined the *Enterprise* giving up and departing. He played that scene over and over again—that they were safe, and all the enemies and bad times were gone. He imagined seeing the *Enterprise* zip into warp drive with such clarity that he knew it was his opposite regurgitating the visions he had fed it. They weren't so different, he and the creature, which didn't see in conventional fashion either. The parasite only saw through the eyes of others, which Geordi found tragic in a way. When it controlled others, it saw itself through a warped mirror.

Growing weak, the human slumped against the door and fell to the deck. Once again, he tried to concentrate on the beautiful tree, combining his unique vision with the brilliant clarity of the plant's view, creating the mightiest tree that had ever grown in rich soil and perfect climate.

Then his correspondent doubled the intensity, and the massive tree glowed with unearthly light. It put out wave after wave of warmth and nourishment, which washed over him like a cleansing rain. Geordi groaned with a mixture of ecstasy and fear. He could see himself turning into one of the moss creatures, with sprigs and vines spouting from his empty eye sockets.

Abruptly all vision and sensation ended, and Geordi felt himself being carried off on a gurney. Darkness reclaimed his world, and he struggled to return to the light. A hyposprary softly kissed his neck, and his anxieties melted away.

"You're fine," said Dr. Crusher, whispering in his ear. "But you were getting agitated, so we ended it. I'm not sure what happened to you, but your brain waves were very active."

"I lied to it," he said hoarsely. "But I think it told me the truth."

"What do you mean?" asked Captain Picard, his voice coming from the other side of the gurney.

"I think," said Geordi hesitantly, "that they're going to release the Genesis Wave again."

"What makes you say that?"

"Because they *showed* it to me," La Forge said with wonder and dread. "It's the only thing that can save them."

"Are you sure about this?" asked Picard.

La Forge shook his head helplessly. "You're asking me to describe an illusion inside a dream," he answered. "I believe I did as you ordered, sir."

In the silence that followed, Dr. Crusher remarked, "I think we can fit you with a new pair of implants, after you've rested."

"That's a relief," said the engineer, although he knew he would miss those vivid images of Leah Brahms waving to him from the golden meadow.

He heard the beep of a combadge, followed by the efficient voice of Data. "Bridge to Captain Picard."

"Picard here," came the response.

The android went on, "An asteroid on the inner part of the Boneyard has just changed positions and is emitting unusual energy readings."

"I'm on my way. Picard out." Geordi felt a squeeze on his shoulder. "Well done, Commander."

"I hope we're in time," answered La Forge worriedly.

Glancing at his instrument panel, Maltz suddenly bolted upright and lifted his unruly gray eyebrows, deepening his rugged head ridges. The asteroid he had been tracking had suddenly moved . . . when none of the asteroids around it were moving. It also gave off readings like a starship powering up weapons. The old Klingon watched with growing alarm as the huge oblong rock rose above the other asteroids in the Boneyard, giving it a clear line of sight in almost every direction.

"Come on, you Starfleet scow . . . *move!*" He pounded the board, taking the *Defiant*-class *Unity* from warp five to maximum warp, overriding the safeties. Even so, he knew it would take about a minute to reach the suspicious asteroid, and he began targeting photon torpedoes.

Without warning, the *Unity* was slammed by powerful beamed weapons, and the craft shuddered but stayed at warp speed. "What pathetic shields!" bellowed Maltz upon seeing that his defenses were already down thirty percent. Checking sensors, he verified that the barrage had come from the mysterious asteroid, which was humming with power.

The *Unity* couldn't take much of that kind of pounding, thought the Klingon, unless he took evasive maneuvers. "Blast evasive manuevers!" he roared. "Full speed ahead!"

Maltz diverted all power to shields and set course for the center of the asteroid. He knew that enemy fire would cripple the shields and bring the ship out of warp before he got there—he just hoped he would get close enough. The Klingon gathered up his weapons and gear, sticking as many disruptors, phasers, and tricorders as he could carry in his sash and belt. Then he dashed to the transporter room just off the bridge. As the *Unity* hurtled toward its doom, Maltz punched coordinates into the transporter console—coordinates deep inside the fake asteroid.

As the ship was again rocked by enemy fire, the Klingon yelled, "Hold together, you sand bucket!"

Quickly he entered a five-second delay into the transporter settings, knowing he was either going to be beamed off or blown to smithereens in that length of time. Another barrage slammed into the *Unity*—the lights dimmed, and sparks burst from burning consoles all over the ship. The computer issued a verbal warning, but Maltz knew without being told that the shields and warp drive were gone. He could only hope there was enough left of the impulse engines to get him in range.

As smoke and flames engulfed the dying ship, the old Klingon leaped onto the transporter platform and vanished in a brilliant flash.

A second later, the *Unity* disintegrated in a hail of silvery shards, which rained harmlessly against the craters and pits of the massive brown asteroid.

twenty-four

Maltz's eyes were scrunched tightly shut in anticipation of materializing inside a bulkhead or a vacuum. When he took a gasp of air and pried his eyes open, he found himself standing in the middle of a curved corridor—and he was still alive! The old warrior let out a groan of relief and slumped against the wall, but he allowed himself only a moment of self-congratulation.

Clomping footsteps alerted him, and the Klingon whirled around with a disruptor in each hand. Sirens sounded, and a strobing red light bathed the corridor, forcing him to concentrate on his aim. He couldn't see the foes clearly when they came tearing around the corner, so he relied on overwhelming firepower. His disruptor beams cut down the first row before they even spotted him. Although they looked humanoid, if they were in the service of these monsters, they were the enemy.

Roaring with rage, Maltz charged into the enemy lines. His foes were numerous but badly organized and slow, and he ripped them to shreds before they could even take aim. One of their lucky shots singed his mane of white hair, and he pounded that one to the deck with his disruptor. As he hit the being's face, sap exploded onto his hand and wrist, burning like the fires of *Gre'thor*. This only increased Maltz's rage, and he drew his knives and tore into the dumbstruck horde.

When he was done, Maltz stood panting over ten bodies lying in the scorched smoldering corridor. Bathed in ominous red light, the bloodied Klingon threw his head back and howled with victory, but he kept his celebration short. As long as this fake asteroid existed, the enemy had a base for their murderous ambition. He had to find its heart and destroy it.

With a grunt, the old Klingon jogged off down the corridor.

"Sorry, Number One, to disturb your rest period," Captain Picard said as he and Will Riker stepped into the turbolift.

"It's okay, I got almost two hours of sleep," the first officer answered, suppressing a yawn. "What's the emergency?"

"One of the asteroids in the Boneyard suddenly moved and started putting out unusual energy readings. We think it may be their hidden base. Through La Forge, we fed them misinformation to bring them out of hiding."

"Really?" Riker asked, impressed.

"Destination?" queried the computer.

"Bridge," answered Picard.

"Acknowledged."

The captain felt the slight sensation of movement, although he gave no thought to how fast they might be going. That is, until an explosion shook the conveyance, nearly throwing Picard and Riker off their feet. The turbolift stopped with a jerk and the lights dimmed, then turned blinking red. The computer intoned, "Red alert! Red alert!"

The captain slapped his combadge. "Picard to bridge! What is going on?"

"Data here," said a calm voice. "Captain, I regret to inform you that the bridge has been badly damaged by an explosion. Possibly a bomb, given the circumstances. No senior officers were present, but there are many casualties among the relief crew. In fact, I am the only one who is unharmed."

Picard breathed a sigh of relief at the news that Data was fine, but it was small consolation for the other casualties. "A bomb? Who had the opportunity to plant a bomb on our bridge?"

"The log shows that Romulan officers from the *D'Arvuk* were on the bridge to exchange information after the Genesis Wave hit Myrmidon," answered the android.

"Damn!" Picard cursed, slamming a fist into his palm. "Has the *D'Arvuk* returned?"

"Unknown," answered Data. "We are unable to use sensors at present, and they may be cloaked. Excuse me, Captain, but I must tend to the wounded until medical teams arrive."

"Of course," answered Picard. "Riker and I will go to the auxiliary bridge."

"I would not hurry, sir," said Data matter-of-factly. "The ship is badly damaged, and the hull may be compromised. We will not have mobility for several hours."

Picard's shoulders slumped. They were dead in space. "We'll still go to the auxiliary bridge. Picard out."

He turned to see Riker scowling as he inspected the access panel near the door. "I'm not so sure we'll be going anywhere. We were almost at the bridge when that explosion hit. We're at a lateral position maybe sixty meters to port. There's been damage this far out, and the safeties have kicked in."

"We're stuck," Picard agreed.

The first officer looked doubtfully at the strobing red light. "The ship is on red alert with major damage to the bridge. I figure everyone within five decks is stuck where they are . . . for now. What do the Romulans hope to gain from this?"

"Project Genesis," Picard said with realization.

The captain frowned as he looked around at the seamless interior of the turbolift. "Any chance we can get out?"

"I wouldn't try it, sir. If the turbolift came on suddenly, we could be beheaded, or cut in two."

The captain nodded grimly. "You talked me out of that notion. What about transporting out?"

"If we've lost hull integrity . . . ," muttered Riker, not finishing his dire thought. The big human rose slowly to his feet. "I think we'll be here until a repair crew reaches us, and they make sure this area is safe. As for the *Enterprise*, we could open the shuttlebay doors manually if we had to. We could muster a dozen shuttlecraft to investigate."

"To go up against a Romulan warbird?" the captain asked skeptically. "A warbird that is undoubtedly cloaked. No, I won't risk any more lives. If Jagron wants to play this hand alone, then let him."

Picard's eyes narrowed. "I just hope he knows what he's doing."

"I never gave you orders to detonate that bomb!" shouted Commander Jagron, shaking with rage as he stood before his subordinate and lover, intelligence officer Petroliv. He could speak his mind, because they were meeting in his private retreat near the bridge.

The lithe Romulan smiled seductively and touched Jagron's cleft chin. "I was just taking the initiative, darling. Isn't that what *you* were supposed to do? The enemy has shown themselves—opportunity is upon us." She pointed toward a small trapezoidal viewscreen, where an immense asteroid floated by itself in space. "We don't need the *Enterprise* getting in the way."

"They'll know it was *us*," he said, sensing that he was beginning to whine, a weakness that always delighted Petroliv. "This isn't a game—this is my *career*, perhaps the future of the empire."

"You know, you're quite attractive when you fret," the intelligence officer said, amusement dancing in her dark eyes. "Everything is a game of strategy. How are we going to get away from here with the Genesis Device unless we cripple the *Enterprise*? Now we can easily destroy her, if we have to."

Jagron shook his head, feeling his authority slip away, layer by layer. He loved this woman—or at least was obsessed with her—but he realized for the first time how dangerous it was to have this overloaded warp coil so close to him.

"Now we *will* have to destroy the *Enterprise*," said Jagron testily. "I was hoping we could get the Genesis data without the Federation knowing about it. The human scientist, Dr. Carol Marcus, is the key."

"Is she in there?" asked Petroliv, pointing to the asteroid on Jagron's viewscreen. "From our energy readings, we know something is happening."

"We could destroy them in a matter of seconds," said the commander. "Too bad that's not an option. Whatever we do, we have to take action before any more Starfleet ships arrive. Do they have shields?"

"Not that we've seen," she answered. "But they have weapons. They destroyed that *Defiant*-class ship without any problem. Many areas of the asteroid are hidden from our sensors, but they act as though they have nothing to fear."

"Since we're cloaked, they don't know we're here." The commander paced a few strides, then stopped abruptly, having made a decision. "We'll get so close to them that they can't fire weapons. I want you to lead an assault team. Board that fake asteroid and take it over."

"Me?" she asked with amusement. "Why me?"

"Because you're the only one I can trust to steal the Genesis secrets," Jagron answered with an encouraging smile. To himself, he added, *with any luck, you'll be killed in the process.*

•   •   •

Carol Marcus gaped in awe at the last thing she had expected to find on this ship, or whatever it was. Using a portable force-field generator taken from the storage room, she had broken through a locked door, hoping to find a central computer or some other crucial system. Instead she had entered a small greenhouse dominated by a single living tree.

Marcus set down the force-field generator, which stood on a tripod, and took out her tricorder. Although the tree stood a good fifteen meters tall, it was not an altogether healthy specimen, according to the readings. The grow lights and hydroponic system did not seem to be meeting all of its needs. Undoubtedly, the tree would be much happier outdoors, growing in real soil with sunlight and fresh air; its very presence in this bizarre place was something of a miracle.

Carol walked slowly around the tree, inspecting it with her tricorder. The plant was being housed with all the splendor of a visiting dignitary, yet it remained sick and frail—much like herself under the same kind of benign imprisonment. The old woman felt an instant kinship with the tree, and she wondered if it served the same purpose she did—a combination good-luck charm and crucial cog in their war machine.

"I wish I could set you free," she told the tree, picking a shriveled leaf off one of its lower branches.

This pathetic plant only reinforced her impression of her captors. They seemed to have everything going their way and were on the verge of remaking the galaxy to their own specifications, yet they were also desperate, missing some crucial part of their being. She didn't know why, but she knew that destroying this tree would wound them deeply, perhaps fatally.

It would also create the diversion she needed, and maybe it would reveal their weaknesses.

The old woman looked around for something that would burn, and she found it in the dried leaves scattered all over the greenhouse. She quickly assembled a pile of leaves around the spindly trunk, and she produced the small laboratory burner she had kept on her person. Marcus didn't have the sense that she was killing the tree—she was freeing it from this unnatural imprisonment. Feeling no sorrow, she lit the pile of leaves. Flames quickly rushed up the trunk and spread to the dried branches.

By the time Carol stepped back, the sick tree was ablaze. She barely had time to crouch behind a stubby bush when an unseen door at the back of the greenhouse whooshed open. At once, a dozen plantlike creatures shambled into the greenhouse, and she cleared her mind so as not to attract their attention.

She needn't have worried about that, because their attention was riveted upon the burning tree. The creatures milled around nervously; a few brave ones tried to put out the flames. For their efforts, they were set ablaze. Their panic screamed in Carol's senses.

Forgetting caution, she leaped to her feet, grabbing the force-field generator, and rushing out the door from which the creatures had entered. To her astonishment, she found herself inside a bustling control room, with row upon row of consoles facing a large viewscreen. The consoles were manned by humanoids afflicted with the moss, who scarcely noticed her as she entered their midst. Carol's attention was riveted upon the screen, where she saw a vast array of emitters and dishes.

She watched with alarm as immense space doors opened and the emitter array lifted toward the stars. A computer voice intoned, "Sixty . . . fifty-nine . . . fifty-eight . . . fifty-seven—"

They're getting ready to discharge the Genesis Wave!

The first thing she did was set up her force-field generator at the door she had just entered. This stymied the moss creatures who attempted to return to the control room, and she felt their frightened emotions screaming in her mind. Trying to block them out, the old woman staggered into the room, uncertain what she could do to stop the countdown.

"Stop! Stop it!" she yelled at the collected zombies. "You're *humans!* You're destroying the Federation!"

They paid her absolutely no attention, and she grabbed the closest human and shook him by the collar. He stared blankly at her, but the the moss extending from his neck, mouth, and ears twitched slightly.

"Thirty-eight . . . thirty-seven . . . thirty-six—" intoned the computer's voice.

Mustering all her strength, Carol Marcus grabbed the man and threw him out of his chair, then she sat at his seat and began to scan his readouts. There had to be a way to *stop* this countdown! Or maybe the entire vessel had a self-destruct sequence.

Kaboom! An explosion nearly knocked Carol out of her seat. Debris filtered down from the ceiling, and the giant viewscreen shimmered for a moment. But the countdown continued. Marcus looked toward the other side of the control room, where smoke and sparks billowed from a shattered door. Through the smoke strode a terrible apparition from the past—a heavily armed Klingon with a weapon in each hand, blasting anything and everything in his path.

Strafing the humanoids at their consoles, killing indiscriminately, the Klingon strode into the room like a messenger of death. He caught her eye and grinned fiendishly as he approached her.

"Carol Marcus!" he crowed with triumph, aiming his weapons at her. "Prepare to die!"

twenty-five

"Fifteen . . . fourteen . . . thirteen—" intoned the computer voice as hundreds of emitters on the viewscreen began to throb with pulsating energy.

"Go ahead! Kill me!" Carol Marcus shouted at the enraged Klingon. "But *stop* the countdown! Can't you see—they're going to discharge the Genesis Wave!"

The old Klingon's resolve faltered for a moment as he listened to the countdown. Then he looked around at dozens of mindless technicians he hadn't killed, all working their boards as if nothing were amiss. He whirled on the viewscreen with his disruptors and blasted it into silvery shards, then he turned on the rest of the workers and began methodically shooting up their consoles.

Marcus had never seen such a ruthless rampage in all her life, as the wild-eyed, wild-haired Klingon completely obliterated the control room. Sparks and flaming embers shot into the air, along with severed limbs and chunks of moss.

Finally the computer voice croaked a strangled, "Four . . . three . . . two—" then stopped.

Carol glanced at her board and breathed a sigh of relief—the discharge had been aborted. When she looked up, there was a disruptor aimed directly at her head.

"I can't let you live," said the old Klingon, who looked vaguely familiar.

"I know you can't." Marcus peered curiously at him. "You're . . . you're the one who survived all those years ago."

"Much to my shame," said the grizzled Klingon. "But I have redeemed myself, and the name of Maltz will no longer be spoken with contempt."

As he lifted his weapon to fire, the computer's voice broke in, "Intruder alert. Decks six and seven."

"Are there more in your party?" said Carol.

"No, I am alone."

No sooner had the words left his mouth than four figures materialized in the flash of a transporter beam. Maltz whirled around and fired before they even had a chance to get their bearings. A split-second later, four dead Romulans lay sprawled on the deck among the rest of the carnage.

"Romulans!" seethed the Klingon. "You know what *they* will do if they get their hands on the Genesis Wave?"

"No one will ever use Genesis again," vowed Marcus as she returned to the only console still working. "This vessel *has* to have a self-destruct sequence."

"How do I know that is truly what you're doing?" Maltz asked suspiciously.

"I was under their influence, but not now. Just watch both of those doors. I've got a force field on one of them." Carol Marcus began to work furiously, hoping that the enemy hadn't made self-destruction too difficult. They had been careful to base all of their systems on Starfleet technology, keeping it simple, knowing that humanoids with diminished capacity had to use the equipment.

Maltz dutifully checked both doors, the one from the green-house, and the one he had entered. He recoiled in horror from the moss creatures lined up pathetically at the greenhouse door, blocked by a simple force-field device. Many of the creatures were on fire, and the room was filled with rancid smoke.

As he approached the second door, a female voice called from the other side, "Hold your fire! We want to negotiate!"

He glanced back at the elder human, who replied, "I found it! Just give me a few more seconds."

Disruptors leveled for action, Maltz edged toward the door and said in a gruff voice, "We're in charge of this place now. Any more attacks, and I destroy the Genesis database. What are you offering?"

"A ship! A full pardon! Riches beyond your wildest dreams!" came the answer. "Just turn this facility over to us—intact. You can't resist us. At this moment, a Romulan warbird is docking with this fake asteroid, and hundreds of soldiers are boarding. They will join us in a minute."

That brought a smile to the old Klingon's blistered lips. "How fortunate for you. I must confer with my comrades. No false moves, do you understand?"

"You have five minutes," came the reply.

Maltz backed slowly toward the remaining console, where Carol Marcus was completing her preparations. The old woman looked at him and nodded, then she rose wearily to her feet.

In a voice too soft to carry more than a few meters, the computer said, "Self-destruct sequence initiated. Two minutes until detonation."

"You had better get away now," Marcus said urgently.

The old Klingon grinned. "I have no escape plan. Besides, I am going where I want to go."

"Me, too," replied the human, shivering.

"Come here, woman." The Klingon wrapped a strong arm around Carol Marcus and held her tightly as the countdown continued. "Death is not to be feared. It's an old friend who has waited patiently for us."

"Five . . . four . . . three . . . two . . . one. Self-destruct sequence activated."

Carol was very glad of the strong arm around her shoulders, holding her up as the deck began to tremble under her feet. At long last, the end was near.

"What are you doing?" screamed the female Romulan as she charged through the doorway.

"Dying in glory!" roared the old Klingon.

There were thousands of mammoth, misshapen asteroids in the Boneyard, but only one of them suddenly exploded like a balloon full of flaming hydrogen. Halos of fire soared outward, consuming the sleek Romulan warbird docked alongside. The emerald-green warship erupted with another momentous blast that tore the starscape asunder, causing a chain reaction among the closest asteroids. Twisted metal, scorched rocks, and flaming embers spread outward in a shimmering ripple of debris and gas.

On the bridge of the *Enterprise*, Data had just gotten an auxiliary viewscreen to work, and he cocked his head with interest at this extraordinary sight. Fortunately, their position was a hundred thousand kilometers away from the concussion wave, so they were in no danger.

The android tapped his combadge and said, "Bridge to Picard."

"Picard here," came a weary voice. "We're still stuck in this turbolift. Any sign of the Romulans?"

"Captain," said the android calmly, "the *D'Arvuk* has been destroyed, and so has the enemy's hidden base. I cannot tell you the cause of their destruction, but I can say with certainty that there are no survivors."

twenty-six

"I'm leaving now, Geordi," said a soft voice.

Geordi La Forge turned away from the railing on the gangplank that overlooked the bustling central mall of Starbase 302. He saw Dolores Linton and several more members of her geological team, dressed in traveling clothes and carrying their luggage. Forty-eight hours after the events that had ended the threat—events still not fully understood—the *Enterprise* had limped into Starbase 302 for repairs. Some members of the crew were being reassigned, including Dolores's team, which had never gotten to perform their survey on Itamish III.

Geordi looked apologetically at the party he was with, which included Captain Picard, Commander Riker, Counselor Troi, and Data. The captain smiled encouragingly and said, "Go ahead, Mr. La Forge, we still have a few minutes before the admiral arrives."

"Thank you." Geordi quickly shepherded Dolores out of earshot of the others, and they stopped in a secluded corner of the starbase, while travelers and Starfleet officers bustled past them.

"Um . . . so you're leaving?" asked Geordi. Even after all they had been through, he was still a bit tongue-tied in the presence of the attractive, young geologist.

Dolores smiled with fondness and brushed his cheek with her hand. "It's all right, Geordi. I heard that they found Leah Brahms on Lomar, and she's on her way here. But it was time for me to go, anyway. You know I'd rather be on solid ground, even if it's not so solid, than the classiest starship in the fleet. Besides, I know you don't love me."

"Dolores," he said, cupping her hand in his. "I . . . I really wish—"

"You've always been totally honest with me, Geordi," said Dolores, tears welling in her soft, brown eyes. "You're the most decent man I've ever met, and you're a great catch. But I didn't catch you."

"Dolores," he said helplessly, grasping for words. "Will you . . . will you stay in touch?"

"You bet!" Dolores answered bravely. "And you had better not make this sacrifice of mine go for nothing! You tell that lucky girl that you *love* her. And if she ever treats you badly . . . well, I've got an extra hammock in my duffel bag."

With that, Dolores grabbed him in a forceful bear hug, and he could hear her sobbing against his chest. When she let him go, she rushed away without even looking back.

La Forge stood on the busy gangplank for a moment, unable to move, or think. He was still staring into space when he felt a firm hand on his shoulder. He turned to see his best friend, Data.

"Your tear ducts are active," said the android.

That fractured observation brought a smile to Geordi's lips. "I'm still terrible with women, even when I'm not so terrible."

"That remains to be seen," said his friend.

"Now arriving at dock one, the U.S.S. *Sovereign*," announced a voice over the speaker system.

Geordi took a deep breath and composed himself before he and Data joined the others. Deanna Troi gave him a sympathetic smile, as did Captain Picard. Both of them knew that the course of love was seldom smooth. As the pipes sounded, announcing the arrival of a high-ranking officer, the entire company from the *Enterprise* came to attention.

Down the gangplank strode Admiral Nechayev, accompanied by Leah Brahms. La Forge gulped, somewhat shocked at their appearance. The admiral's burns had healed, but with unusual results— half of her face was as smooth and youthful as a teenager's, and the other half reflected her age. Leah looked drawn and haggard, as if she had been fighting a war at the front, which she had. He had never noticed gray in her hair before, but now he did. Still Leah was the most beautiful woman he had ever seen.

Despite her startling appearance, Admiral Nechayev seemed energized as she rubbed her hands together. "Thank you for meeting us. We only have a few minutes, but I felt that the crew of the *Enterprise* deserved to get a face-to-face briefing before I returned to Earth to address the Council. Do you mind talking here?"

"No," answered Captain Picard with a smile. "We have several questions."

"I'm not sure I'll be able to answer all of them," said the admiral. "If I can't answer, perhaps Dr. Brahms can. She uncovered their operations on Lomar. The planet appears to be deserted, but there are extensive underground facilities, where the moss creatures held thousands of humanoids in stasis. They apparently used them as slaves. In their moon base, they had a very impressive collection of hijacked starships, shuttlecraft, freighters—just about any kind of vessel you could imagine. It's safe to say that these creatures were preying on our shipping lanes for centuries before they launched their offensive with the Genesis Wave."

Geordi listened in amazement and horror as Admiral Nechayev described what they had found on Lomar. His eyes drifted toward Leah, and she gave him a wan smile. And he thought *he* had been through hell.

"We've turned over Lomar to a consortium of scientists from all the great powers of the quadrant," explained Admiral Nechayev. "However, the Romulans destroyed all of the creatures and a great deal of the complex before we got there. We're working to revive as many of the slaves as we can, but that has proven difficult. We found indications that Dr. Carol Marcus was there, but we didn't find her."

"Were there records of the Genesis Device?" asked Picard worriedly.

"No. There were fragments of data, but nothing anyone could use to re-create it. We can only surmise that all the records and equipment were destroyed in that explosion in the asteroid field."

"Why did they do it?" Riker asked bluntly. "If they were cruising along for centuries, without anyone knowing they existed, why did they feel the need to destroy so many planets?"

"Because they were dying," answered Leah Brahms. "They had lost the ability to reproduce. We found ancient records and physical evidence that Lomar had once been a garden planet, with many different species, including humanoids. It must have taken millions of years for the parasites to move from the trees to animal hosts, but that's when they developed their telepathic abilities. As they multiplied, they must have killed all the humanoid, animal, and plant life—they turned Lomar into a wasteland. That's when they went underground. Apparently, they needed the trees in order to reproduce."

"So they resorted to the Genesis Wave," said Picard. "Colonization and reproduction in one easy step."

"It may have been more complex than that," said Brahms thoughtfully. "I've been trying to figure out why there aren't any humanoids on the planets they created. Manipulating humanoids may have become something of an addiction to them. I believe they grew to resent it, and hate themselves for it—but they didn't know any other way of life. In those worlds they created, they were also trying to create a generation that wasn't dependent upon enslaving humanoids. In a strange way, they were trying to give up their bad habits . . . and get back to nature."

"At our expense," grumbled Riker. "Now instead of one home-world, they have dozens."

"Not for long," said Admiral Nechayev, "but we're not going to wipe them out either. It will require Council approval, but my plan is to leave them one planet—probably the planet formerly known as SY-911, which was a lifeless rock before the Genesis Wave. It seems to be the most stable of their planets, and nobody has any claims on it. Needless to say, it will be declared off-limits to every-one. On that planet, hopefully, they will never know what it's like to enslave a humanoid."

There was a moment of silence while everyone digested this knowledge, and Leah Brahms finally spoke up. "I have a question for you. Have you seen Maltz, the old Klingon who was on my shut-tlecraft?"

The *Enterprise* officers looked at one another, but no one could offer any information about the sole survivor from the original Genesis Planet. "No," answered Picard. "We haven't seen anything of Carol Marcus either."

"Maltz was determined to find her," Leah said softly. "Maybe he did."

Admiral Nechayev scowled. "The Romulans are demanding more information about how the *D'Arvuk* was lost. I don't suppose—"

"We don't know anything," answered Picard. "As I reported, a very suspicious explosion on our bridge put us out of commission. I would personally like to ask the Romulans more about *that.*"

"Perhaps some mysteries are best left unsolved," said Nechayev with a wry smile. "If there's nothing else, Dr. Brahms and I have to return to Earth. But I believe we have one passenger to return to you."

There was a sudden noise behind them, and they all turned to see a stout, blue-skinned Bolian hurrying down the gangplank, car-rying half-a-dozen large bags with difficulty.

"Mr. Mot!" exclaimed Picard with delight. "We had all but given up on seeing you back on board the *Enterprise.*"

"And you don't know how close I came to fulfilling that dire pre-diction," said the barber breathlessly. "If it hadn't been for Mr. Data here . . ."

While they exchanged harrowing war stories, Geordi tugged on Leah's sleeve and whispered, "Can I talk to you for a second?"

"Sure." She walked away from the others, and Geordi followed, screwing up his courage with every step.

When she turned to gaze at him with those beautiful hazel eyes, he blurted out, "Leah, I love you."

She smiled sweetly and touched his lips with her fingers. "Geordi . . . you mean so much to me, but I can't—"

"I don't want you to say or do anything right now," said La Forge quickly before he lost his courage. "I know you're not ready, and I know you've been through hell. Ten months from now, there's a conference in Paris on theoretical propulsion. I'm going to be there, and I'd like to see *you* there."

She nodded slowly, as if coming to a decision. "Ten months from now . . . Paris. I'll put it on my calendar. Until then, Geordi, don't ever change."

"Dr. Brahms," said Nechayev, stepping away from the *Enterprise* officers, "we have to be going. The *Sovereign* is on a tight schedule. Is there anything else you want to say?"

"No," answered Leah, smiling at Geordi. "I think we've said it all."

HTTP://
SO HOW WWW.
NASCOM.
NASA.GOV